DARK PEAK

Hellsborough Chronicles Book One

Van Hallam, with Pip Rippon

hellsborough.com

Copyright © 2023 Pip Rippon

All rights reserved

The characters and events portrayed in this book are fictitious. Any similarity to real persons, living or dead, is coincidental and not intended by the author.

No part of this book may be reproduced, or stored in a retrieval system, or transmitted in any form or by any means, electronic, mechanical, photocopying, recording, or otherwise, without express written permission of the publisher.

ISBN-13: 9798865470809

Cover design by: Pip Rippon

CONTENTS

Title Page
Copyright
Foreword
CHAPTER 1	1
CHAPTER 2	14
CHAPTER 3	29
CHAPTER 4	40
CHAPTER 5	50
CHAPTER 6	60
CHAPTER 7	68
CHAPTER 8	78
CHAPTER 9	87
CHAPTER 10	98
CHAPTER 11	112
CHAPTER 12	120
CHAPTER 13	129
CHAPTER 14	136
CHAPTER 15	146
CHAPTER 16	159
CHAPTER 17	169
CHAPTER 18	178

CHAPTER 19	185
CHAPTER 20	194
CHAPTER 21	207
CHAPTER 22	218
CHAPTER 23	229
CHAPTER 24	239
CHAPTER 25	257
CHAPTER 26	264
CHAPTER 27	271
CHAPTER 28	277
About The Author	283
FURTHER READING	285

FOREWORD

by Van Hallam

Is it normal to write a foreword for tha own book? I doant know, I doant read many books. Doant get me wrong, there is plenty here and hereabouts in Hellsborough, the nascenti likes the jellyheads to read -- it keeps 'em quiet and off the streets, doant it? That makes for a quieter place during the murkneet, makes it easier for the exacids to keep the peace. The library, it's stacked with books -- ones tha can read or them that tha can listen to, even them that tha can watch with tha's psycmask, but I doant want to read or listen to stories about the great achievements of nascenti building programs, or the life and times of Sophie Hinchcliffe, that first CEO of the DPDC, or nowt like that.

They is big on local history at the library, and geography, and folklore -- tha can find out all tha wants to know about Wadsley's bracken man, or the legend of the Loxley kraken, or the way that The Dark Peak is made up of ganister and gritstone. That stuff doant bother me so much. What I is interested in is tellin' me story, which tha won't find in no library. That's why I got Pip to write it, cos I reckon it's important. I's maybe selfish, I's maybe self-indulgent, but I reckon it's a story worth telling, and has some importance. I'll let thee be the judge of that.

Why I chose Pip to write me story is someat else I has to say. I first met Pip when I was out surfing the scerm, and the young'un had just arrived this side of thinge -- was taken out by t'murk reyt fast, it can do that to thee, the murk, can come over thee like a shroud, draining the life outa tha, as quick as that can say Jack Flash. Anyhow, I managed to drag the young'un back to me place, which were reyt close and get a psycmask on 'til things looked better. Tha didn't dee that day Pip, and tha's still gooin strong now, eh? But tha won't take that psycmask off again in an 'urry, that's for sure.

But I was saying about why I chose Pip to help me write me story. It ain't complicated -- I is no reader, and I ain't no writer neither -- but Pip is reyt educated in the ways and means of all that sort of thing and is reyt well read n'all -- was educated in some place in the off-world that's called Oxford before coming to Sheffield, so reyt clever tha knows, and was interested in what I had to say, so I thinked about it and reckoned it were worth a punt, and a few beers down t'pub and a few snorts of crust to get this thing done. Cos, tha never knows, maybe some good will come of it, and maybe them nascenti overlords will get what's comin' to 'em sooner or later.

Another Oxford alumni that I needs to thank is that bloke from down t'pub, Mike. He done a great job of picking out some of the stuff that I didn't get reyt and that sort of thing, anyway, he knows who he is.

I is gerrin old now, so I ain't so bothered about what them nascenti'll do to me -- they can't do much that ain't already 'appened, that's for sure. So I is just gooin to say me bit and be done with it -- I'll let Pip get into the meyt of me story proper...

CHAPTER 1

Crosslander, Barker, Ganister, Clown

```
        HMM::OUT('Who is Pip Rippon?')
`ask:: unknown // stat:: accept[ok]__ // src::
2001:0db8:85a3:0000:0000:8a2e:142j:i618 [loc::hellsborough//
unknown__location//000]__ // now:: 79.hail
ripperthroat.12.13.19.17.2`
`HMM::IN('..Pip Rippon is a PhD student at the university of
Hallamshire_')`
`:At where?`
`..The university of Hallamshire is a seat of further
education on the other side of the hinge_`
`:What is the hinge?  What is a seat of further education?`
`..The hinge is the gateway to a parallel universe...  A seat
of further education is a place where individual persons
improve their learning_`
`:More about 'parallel universe'.`
`..Classified_`
`:Classified by who?`
`..Classified_`
```

O ver there, across the other side of the bar near the door, there's a clown and a crosslander. Not normally close bedfellows, you'd have thought -- and these two, I know this -- they're plotting something.

We're in a bar, I said that already. We're almost always in one of them or another. We spend a lot of time in bars, me and Van, truth be told. It's where we do business, where we talk, where we socialise -- where we lose and maintain our mental health, for better or worse -- that's the excuse we tell ourselves anyway.

We're playing a card game called Cribbage -- I say we, he is, Van is. Van always plays alone these days. Well, alone against himself, that is. Me, I gave up a long time ago, I'm no match for him. He always beats me, always has -- seems to know what cards I'm going play before I play them. It makes me feel inadequate. So I gave up his game a while back. But no matter, I don't mind, it is what it is.

We're alone at our table, but there's other folk in the bar. There's talk going on, plenty of it -- some is animated, some just hushed whispers. The place is busy, noisy. A bluish oily haze unfurls like murk and a heady stench pervades the small room, no larger than a double garage in the off-world. The light is good enough to see Van by, but dank -- tiny creatures flip and flop about in the under-look and the corner-eye. Music plays -- a high-energy cacophony that I don't dislike; I reckon I'll memorise it and take it home with me -- who knows, could be the next big thing in the off-world.

The crosslander is gesticulating with one hand and the clown is nodding, understanding somehow -- it's news to me they share a common language, but I might not be right on that. The clowns and the rest of The Dark Peak's denizens share a common tongue, but crosslanders, they don't share that telepathic language. They must be communicating verbally, I guess -- in Ing -- unless that thing perched on his shoulder is some sort of translation device. I'm not sure what it is, it looks a bit like a toucan would look in the off-world, yet not if you know what I mean?

How do I know they're plotting something? Well I don't really, do I? You could say it's an educated guess. I've been about long enough and sat in enough bars with Van, and watched enough to know what plotting looks like and what it doesn't. While Van studies his cards, I study the folk, I people watch, that's what I do -- you've read my diaries, right?

Couldn't they just be a couple of young alternative types taking the first steps towards a future relationship? I mean, that's not really that unusual is it?

Yeh, they could be, of course they could. But I know what I have seen and I don't see this clown and that crosslander doing anything other than plotting something -- unscrupulous or otherwise. Clowns don't ordinarily get themselves involved in acts of rebellion or terrorism, they're performers and go-betweens, strictly neutral -- but crosslanders -- they're famous for it. Most ordinary humans, and when I say ordinary, I'm talking about your regular Hellsboroughite (I almost said jellyhead; a crosslander term of endearment for Hellsborough natives, and a turn of phrase which Van can sometimes use with careless abandon), regard crosslanders as being outside of the law -- rebels against society, trouble. And they are; but as you said -- I might be wrong, they're probably stoking the kindling of a fledgling relationship. Heh, I'm flexible, I'm open to suggestions.

We -- me and Van -- we've both consumed several measures of ale already, and the evening is still young. Van hasn't even started telling me his stories yet, which is -- of course -- why I'm here. Too much liquor could start making things dangerous -- you never really know what he'll come out with next, but hey ho, never mind, eh? Things are always prone to maybe get tasty at some point; not that I'm a fighter, like he was, but I guess I might be able to shout someone down if I need to. Anyway, with that thought, Van stirs and plays his cards to himself.

For the record, before we go any further, I'm Pip. I'm Van Hallam's occasional friend, and maybe something of a "lover", in that I do love him in certain ways. I don't know, and I doubt if

VAN HALLAM

he does -- or cares. We're close-ish I think, that's really all I can say, we share stuff, a lot of stuff, complicated stuff, you could say. Van's highly intelligent, but not greatly educated in the ways of grammar and the like, so I have fallen into this odd role -- confidante, drinking associate, sometime pusher, biographer -- at least I write down some of the things he says so maybe they can be turned into something useful. I record his stories so they can stand the test of time, that's all. How much truth do I transcribe? I dunno, only Van could tell you that.

I'm pondering the existence of an ash of rheum that has manifested itself on my boot; it is tucking into some muck that I must have picked up in the park. While I'm deliberating, Van seems to be playing the short game: He's dealt himself five cards, and his other self five cards, deals two into the box. He discards one card from each hand into the box, and makes the best hands he can out of the rest, then takes a long suck on his pipe -- I'd stuffed it earlier with one of his favourite off-world blends. I scrape the rheum off with my other boot, you wouldn't want to do it with an ungloved hand.

Van wears his minimalist DIY psycmask, a thing of his own design (honestly, I think it's just a disguise, so he fits in when he's here or hereabouts), that doesn't interfere with his drinking, or on the hefty pulls of the pipe to ingest those grasping fumes. I see that the mix of both is doing the do -- letting Van get wasted and slip into a state of forgive and forget -- since there is no forgiveness in this world, so it is better -- he says -- to forget. There is little point remaining sober, at all, ever, if you want to try and understand the world that you are in -- says Van.

They sound like wise words, whichever side of the hinge you live on.

This world, this Hellsborough, is not somewhere you can understand as a "normal" human being, unless you are well and truly muddled up in the head, and even then you only get to peek over the edge of the insanity pit. And Ha-ha, says Van, the insanity pit is a bottomless sewer of stench deeper than, well...

A fat house fly (musca domestica, I studied biology at Oxford in the off-world a couple of years back) coasts about the bar in squares. It's a warm evening for the time of year, and the murk isn't excessive -- but the ether is heavy enough to make it necessary to wear a psycmask; even the crosslander wears a nose piece. The clown, of course, being indigenous, is fine -- able to breath unaided anywhere in The Dark Peak. My psycmask is council issue. I've unclipped the feeding section, but it's uncomfortable. It means I don't stand out though, and that's how it has to be. Of course, I get to "benefit" from the council ads and all the rest of the hive chatter. Far from being a comfort, as it is to most of the pop, to me, it's a constant distraction -- but I guess that's the point, isn't it?

```
      HMM::IN('Phernoon Farantees!')
`hits:: 7419383 //
[this]2001:0db8:85a3:0000:0000:8a2e:037g:7334
[loc::hellsborough//middlewood_road//467]__ // now:: 79.hail ripperthroat.12.13.19.44.19`
```

`Phernoon, phernoon, phernoon, murktalk mentalists, make me big up you special Farantees, yousurf yo digginheads in this youw noze, youw get yezelf down to Farantees for special like deals and like, you know, proper sound like, yo diggin me ya fellas and ya lasses, time runnin out so youz get yersen downs that pronto likeio, megga bargains on ya booz and ya rock and ya snough an all that, no messin, nowt missin the cut bruvvas and sissers! Dancee, dancin, you be'll rockin areet murkers! Faranteeeeeees!!!`

See what I mean? I don't know anything about this Farantees, and I have no interest, but I'm sure they are more than a profitable enterprise in his world. If it's not some grifter selling something, it's DPDC propaganda -- and it's continuous. It doesn't stop, it's social media -- in your face, in your ears, in your head -- all of the time. If it wasn't for the murk, I could take the psycmask off, but Hellsboroughite's, with their nanotech and their implants, they're stuck with it, but I guess if you're born with it, it's normal.

Van plucks that fat house fly from the fetid air, smashing it into his ready maw. Deux for deuces he slurs, counting one of his cribbage hands. And one for his knob he says, jabbing his finger at the Jack of Strides.

That was what started it all, Pip. When I was a lad. Bit of a handful I was, says Van, having another suck on his pipe. I'd been dragged up, around here -- just round the corner over there, he says nodding his head upwards and outwards towards the Middlewood Road. Mother died giving birth to me, so I'm told. Taken in by a nice enough bunch of folk, my Mother's sister -- Mum -- don't know whether we were blood really. Some of the kids -- my cousins, I guess -- had grown up and I was the youngest of 'em left at home. Had to learn things quick and always needed to protect mesen from someone or something having a go. Was always a bit different to them though, could never quite put my finger on what it was. Just felt like I didn't always fit in, I had this independent streak: A need to stand on my own two feet, to forge my own way.

Van spits wings onto the quarry tile floor. Mum cried when she first saw me wearing make-up. But it never felt strange to me. The nethermen did, they're a strange bunch for sure, and hanging about with them, across the other side of the tracks got me into the make-up. They all use it, it's their religious beliefs. It became a part of me in those formative years, and never went away. Van briefly removed his trimmed down psycmask then, showing the heavily patterned skin around his eyes -- white stars with a green halo adorning that grey lined face.

My family, they weren't netherlanders. No, they were just jellies -- regular folk. They got up when their psycmasks told them to, they went to work and did their jobs, they ate what they were fed when they were fed it. They spent their earnings how they pleased. They were happy enough, I guess. We all grumble a bit doant we, but they weren't ever the types to go all weird and join any resistance or nowt like that. It wouldn't ever have crossed their minds that there were owt to resist against. They did what they did, and did what they were told and they got on with their lives, because that's what you do, init, when you're human? But as I said, I knew I was different. I tried the other side of the tracks, but you know, some things you know aren't you. The only thing that stuck was the make-up.

The nethermen -- the crosslanders -- of which Van speaks are the warring factions that exist beyond the murk of Hellsborough. The long displaced families of the Leys, the Woods, the Marshes and the Moors, they have been at war with each other for eons. Which tribe the crosslander in the bar tonight is from, your guess is as good as mine. I'm no expert, but looking at his markings, if you're putting me on the spot, I'd say Ley. Don't hold me to it. The differences between the tribes are subtle, and saying the wrong thing to the wrong one has been known to be a fatal mistake.

Anyway, so I'm told, these tribes of nethermen fight and squabble over nothing much, since there is little to fight and squabble over out there in the crosslands. Life -- at least so we are told, beyond Hellsborough -- is a miserable existence, and these crosslanders are no better than vermin. The hive chatter says so, so it must be true, eh?

It was a rite of passage, says Van, still pointing at the Jack card. I was that age. That age where fear doesn't come into the equation. Didn't know what an equation was back then anyway.

I wonder if he knows what an equation is now, but I let it go:

The Dark Peak, The Wisewood, The Barnsdale forest, they were just place names. I was brought up here, in Hellsbrough, those places held no fear for me, places to be explored and found out about. But now when I think back, I was lucky to ever come back. Of course, things were simpler then, they always are, aren't they, things are always simpler back in the day.

I don't ask Van for more details, just leave him to his rambling. I understand his way.

I'd followed the family tradition, of course I had, I didn't know any better did I really? Despite my dalliances with the netherfolk and the make-up. I kept the psycmask on, that's what my brothers and sisters did, what my mother and father did. I'd been working in the ganister mines, up on the common; toiling on me hands and knees for a dozen hours a day or more, pulling them carts full of the stuff down the pit lane and then bringing the empty cart back up again so it could be refilled.

It were gruelling work. The psycmask governed me daily life, provided me with everything I needed to survive: Food, breathing help, the entertainment I needed to get me through the working days and neets. After our shifts, we'd go down the pub, or go out and do some sort of activity, you know, picnics, walks, that sort of thing, on days when the murk wasn't so oppressive. I guess I was content, that's what they aim for I think, they aim to keep you content, and you don't notice owt is wrong, because nowt is wrong -- nobody says owt is wrong at home or down the pub or out on some social do. So nowt ever is wrong, is it? Everything is normal. So normal that tha never questions it. But is it? Is it normal?

I want to ask Van who *they* are, but he rolls on with his monologue.

I just knew there was someat better. The nethermen they made me question things, because of the way they attituded themselves. They didn't think us jellyheads were normal at all. They thought we was all soft in the head, that's where the phrase comes from you know -- jellyhead, pretty obvious, right?

I don't know what most of their upbringings was, some of them were like me. Some of them were poor, some of them were richer, I didn't really take them seriously. But they did make me look at things with a set of eyes other than me own, if you know what I mean? They gave me another perspective. I always had this yearning, this reason to strive for someat else, someat better, someat deeper. They -- me family -- would always try and tell me that the grass isn't always greener on the other side, but the thing is -- I knew it was. I wasn't just daydreaming as I pulled that ganister cart and listened to that drivel from the psycmask. I actually knew that the grass was greener on the other side. I just didn't know where it was, where that grass was greener -- where that other side that I was looking for, was. I just knew that someat was wrong in this place, and this place isn't the same as other places and maybe I could do someat about it, rather than just accept the humdrum as gospel -- like I had been brought up to do.

One day, after another twelve hour shift lugging another cart up and down that hill, instead of heading to the pub, I went straight home. I took off me psycmask and felt a wave of freedom come over me, free from the chattering of the hive and the constant ads and infotainment.

Back then, those psycmasks were full head affairs, not the slim fit models that we have today -- well mine is, obviously, yours is a bit chunkier Pip. But back then, they were real headbangers -- Anyway, I knew that I wouldn't survive long without one, I'd likely suffocate, since that was what we used to breath. But without that constant chatter and augmented view of the world, I could see and think freely for a change, and that, at that moment, was more of a prize than breathing. It was a first taste of freedom, a glimpse of a place where the grass is greener. But of course, I knew that I needed a supply of air, even if I didn't want the liquid feed. I wanted to eat solid food, wasn't sure if my body could handle it, but that's what I wanted to do, I wasn't exactly getting fat on that biofeed; none of us did, I think the design was to keep us in a state of emaciation, of constant hunger.

I decided that I needed to modify the helmet to me own needs, which was to keep the breathing apparatus and nowt else. I didn't want or need the infotainment or the hive chatter, so figuring that was delivered via the antenna at the back, I snapped it clean off. Placing the thing back onto my head, for the first time, I felt a blessed silence. My view of the world through the eye sockets was also clear -- no longer augmented at all. All that remained was the feeding pipe, which I pulled out and Bob's your uncle, a psycmask that did what I needed it to do, rather than it doing everything for me, like a mother does for an infant. I'd have to take it off to eat, but that was the least of my problems. Finding something to eat would likely be more of a challenge.

There was no scran in our kitchen; what with my parents and siblings varied comings and goings -- according to the needs of the world we worked in and governed and fed by the psycmasks, there was no need for actual food to be stored anywhere -- you simply collected your biofeed from one of the many community feed points: You collected your daily bread. There was nowt else to take, I would have to forage on my way and see how things went. I didn't bother washing, my face and hands were black with dirt.

Maybe these days you'd call it a break-down, or depression of some sort, but at the time I was liberating mesen -- I felt liberated. I had little else in the way of possessions -- a torn old map of The Dark Peak's closer villages, those not so far from the Damflask. I picked up a big old rust encrusted knife from the kitchen -- not sure why it was there, but it was; and I had the clothes I stood up in -- no more than rags. I bet you can envisage me, can't you Pip? A shoddy vagrant tike I was.

And that was that, I was on the road and on my way out of Hellsborough, fast as my legs would carry me. I can't say that

I didn't look back, because I did. I looked back at the place I was leaving with the kind of scorn I reserved for that hill that I pulled that cart up every day, and the kind of hatred that I usually reserved for... Well, I doant no what else, because since I said before, there was nothing I hated about the place, because what is there to hate when you're just someone who gets on and does tha job and spends time with tha family and friends? -- just grumbles, nothing serious, depression, distaste, malcontent -- minor dissatisfaction -- not hatred. It's not until tha have left somewhere and come back that tha can see it with renewed eyes and considered experience. Back then, as I said, I just knew there was someat more, and I was going to do my best to find it, or maybe dee trying; but who thinks about death like that?

That's when I met you, ain't it Shad? Says Van reaching down beneath the table and patting a big black barker with raggedy fur that shimmered an emerald hue in the bar's dull luminescence. The barker's fierce canines protruded from his smile and he nuzzled Van's hand -- a knowing gesture indicating the two had been in each other's company for quite some time.

Where was it we met eh Shad? In the Wisewood, wasn't it eh buddy, that's where it was. Tha was out there by thassen, ferrel as a monk tha were, chasing them damn scrufftails, weren't thee? And we saw each other, me stumbling about through them bind vines and briars and thorns. I think tha thought I was some sort of shabby scrufftail mesen. So tha came at me like a crazed sun, quick as a flash taking a piece of me, a chunk right out of my hand. Look, says Van, raising his fist. After all this time, tha can still see the scar where he had me. You'd probably have had more if I hadn't pulled that big old knife out on ya.

Took my own chunk right of thee and all, didn't I boy -- with that big old knife? And by the time we'd finished scrapping, I was so knackered-out that tha could have come and just ripped me throat out, but tha didn't, did tha boy, tha just came and laid down by me as I laid back against that big old yew. There in that

Wisewood we both fell asleep, didn't we eh boy? Both exhausted we were Pip. That was all it took to tame him, wasn't it, eh buddy boy?

Of course, that was before you passed, eh boy? Passing ain't so bad though is it, makes no difference at all now, you're probably even fitter now than tha was then, tha still keeps up with old Van. I think it's me that's the one who needs to be keeping up with thee more these days, eh boy? I still has the weight of this old carcass to carry around, tha were freed of that burden many a year passed.

That Wisewood, we didn't make it through before murkfall, it's a big old place that Wisewood. Didn't worry Shad of course, but for me, that was my first time away from home and I'd never experienced darkness for what it is. When tha wears a psycmask day in and day out, even the sleepy time isn't full on blackness like what I experienced then. I didn't know darkness until I was out there in that Wisewood. There is noises in there too that tha wouldn't ever expect to hear in a lifetime, no matter a single neet. And blackness. Blackness so dark, tha couldn't see your hand in front of tha face.

I guess that is what made me what I am, ey buddy? That first neet in that Wisewood forged me into this, the man I am today. Hah, whatever that means. Them demonspawn though, they came for us that neet, didn't they boy?

```
      HMM::OUT('Scrufftail')
`ask:: Rippon, Pip // stat:: accept[ok]__ // src::
2001:0db8:85a3:0000:0000:8a2e:037g:7334 [loc::hellsborough//
middlewood_road//467]__ // now:: 79.hail
ripperthroat.12.13.20.5.5`

`HMM::IN('..Colour:   Grey / mottled brown_`

`..Diet:   Seeds, nuts, eggs_`

`..Size:   10" (thumb)_`

`..Defining characteristics:   Bushy tail, clever_`
```

`..Class:   Vermin_`

`..Image:   Incoming_    ')`

CHAPTER 2

Demonspawn and Dirty Leaves

```
      HMM::OUT('Explain the hinge')
`ask:: unknown // stat:: accept[ok]__ // src::
2001:0db8:85a3:0000:0000:8a2e:142j:i618 [loc::hellsborough//
unknown__location//000]__ // now:: 79.hail
ripperthroat.12.13.19.26.54`

`HMM::IN('..The hinge is the gateway to a parallel
universe_')`

`:Where is the hinge?`

`..The hinge is located at 53.4023191236262,
1.501041553565726_`

`:Can I pass through the hinge?`

`..Unknown_`
`..Only person known to pass through the hinge is Pip Rippon_`

`:How does Pip Rippon pass through the hinge?`

`..Unknown_`
```

Van is on a roll and I'm keen to hear more, so I don't press too hard.

I've learned to get anything juicy out of Van -- there's no need to rush; his story will manifest itself sooner or later -- usually sooner, and played out in conjunction with a cribbage hand.

Run of four. Four in the box, thanks for the gift, meself... Yeh, they came for us good, them mardy bloody-minded demonspawn. No place being out there in the Wisewood, they should be in fields -- penned in. But we survived, didn't we eh buddy boy?

Has I said Pip? I don't think I has. When I'm out and about in The Dark Peak and I sees them demonspawn in the distance -- even now, knowing what I know -- they makes me blood boil. Scream in me head I do -- Demonspawn! Demonspawn! I don't let my face show it, but that's what me head is saying. I have so much hate for them things, I'm spittin' feathers, I'm seeing red, just because I see them on some distant pasture. I don't hate much, Pip, but them demonspawn I hates them with a vengeance. It's been a long time, but even now I'm barely in control of my distaste for them creatures.

Which means -- I say, in a moment of hubris -- you're not in control, are you?

I hate them things to their vile core, to my core. Demonspawn clovenfoot. Mindless creatures, the dullards of The Dark Peak. Cantankerous, messy, sinister. Evil. They're not, they can't help 'emselves, but they are.

Van takes another long suck on his pipe and downs a hefty mouthful of ale -- a gobfull, as he'd say. He's struggling to focus, I reckon, but still pretty coherent, it's almost like he's in some sort of hypnotic trance, but not quite:

It'd been dark for a while and we'd been in and outa sleep a bit, I remember. All those noises that are the Wisewood at night were going on and on. We ignored them though, me and Shad. Cuddling up we were, waiting for the murkrise, trying to get some kip. Floating in and out of consciousness, of dreamsleep. Nothing to fear here, nothing to fear here, that's what I kept telling mesen. Was probably saying it to Shad 'n' all, ain't that right you moochie old skriker?

Then they were there, them demonspawn. I couldn't see them, but I knew Shad could. And it were cold. So cold, that's why you could feel their breath, and the frigid heat coming off their flaccid bulk as they blindly ploughed their way through that impenetrable undergrowth. Couldn't see 'em, could sense 'em, and that's probably scarier than seeing the damn things. Knowing the repulsive things are there. But I couldn't see 'em. I felt 'em though. Smelt 'em. Heard 'em. Deep guttural lowing, cloven hoofs, duneweed and twig fall and fallen tree leaves crushed by their trampling.

It's the smell, Pip. If I sayed sulphur, you'd know, but that'd be easy, that's stinkegg. This weren't egg. This were death. The stench of a month dead track discarded grizzler. And that blood smell -- when meyt bleeds out and leaves the blood behind and that blood matures for a day or so, that smell; it's the stench of the dead: Of decay. That's your demonspawn. Mindless dullards, forever wandering murkwits; perennially lost. They mull about in bad dreams and terrorise waking thoughts.

That stench. That decay. I think that night in the Wisewood, I soiled mesen. I soaked my mesen at least. I puked n'all, or at least dry heaved, since me belly was empty. But apart from them involuntary functions of the self, I was frozen. Could barely move. Me mind whirred; I couldn't comprehend what was going on, and what, if anything, I could do. I was scared stiff Pip.

I remember this -- I don't know why I remember, but I do -- I remember pulling Shad close with one arm and biting down hard on the first thing that I grasped with t'other -- something to keep me quiet and stop me teeth chattering -- I was trembling like a smelting barker. Pip?

Van stopped talking and eyed me directly. It seems to me that you might have a question for me? He said, observing my expression. The question (and those eyes, those piercing eyes) made me jolt, spilling tiny sloops of ale onto the table. I hastily mopped them with my sleeve, for no other reason than to waste some time and gather my thoughts.

What did you bite on? I said as I recovered.

Could've been owt, but I reckon it was a sapling that had shot up from forest floor. Like I said, it was blacker than black out there. After that, I remember nowt of what you would say was tangible.

A bit like now, I thought to myself. But Van had already moved on. His search was now for something of more interest than me -- his part time temporary biographer. He had renewed interest in things other than his life story.

His left eye gurned with something like recognition. Hah! That clown over there, I know her, he said. She's Pandora: Pandora of Hathersage! He wasn't discrete with the volume of his exclamation, the whole bar -- it seemed -- turning in his direction; but the thud thud of the music soon drowned out whatever chatter Van's shouting had prompted.

I know this too; I'd already recognised this clown as one of the Hathersage performing troupe. They're a seemingly informal bunch, and will perform anywhere and pretty much do any sort of clowning that you'd expect -- magic tricks, busking, joke telling, general clowning around, miming, you name it. There's a reason for that, I know. Whilst they're performing, whilst they're entertaining you and yours, they're also observing, taking notes, recording: People they see, interactions they witness, movement of goods they chance upon, that sort of thing. These clowns you see, this Hathersage troupe, are spies.

Yes, spies.

They survive in Hellsborough performing for scraps. Scraps of anything - food, drugs, drink, information. Information is the most valuable, obviously. Why? Why do you think? Because information is tradable. Little snickets of information, things noticed here, interactions observed there. Information can be traded for better bits of information -- Better secrets. Bigger secrets. More information yields deeper and more important knowledge. More little gems that further the cause.

What cause? You ask. Any cause that betters the clowns. For The clowns only exist for their own kind, their own tribe, their clan -- not for the crosslanders, not the jellyheads, and certainly not the nascenti. No, clowns is clowns, and clowns act in the interest of clowns and clowns alone.

It's not just information though. They move things -- physical goods. Drugs, parts, weapons -- between different cells of the resistance, or the different empires -- whatever side to wherever you need. Clowns have no favourites, they have no fear, and they have no compunction to take sides. To be clown is to be mercenary -- You pay what they ask, and they don't ask questions.

Put simply, clowns are the courier service of Hellsborough and The Dark Peak, and as if reading my thoughts, the hivemind chimes in with an ad of its own:

```
    HMM::IN('Call 333 555 333555 333 555, ask for Penny,
Pandora...')
`hits:: 9624155 //
[this]2001:0db8:85a3:0000:0000:8a2e:037g:7334
[loc::hellsborough//middlewood_road//467]__ // now:: 79.hail
ripperthroat.12.13.21.7.0`

`..Pietr, Piers, Ptol or Pal: Any package, any place, any
time.  No questions asked, no package too small (or too
large), nothing turned down.  We see you right, tell us what
you need, we deliver.  We always deliver.`
```

I've seen that number on a sticker on a rubbish bin somewhere too.

My knowledge of Pandora and the clowns seems to be vaguely in tune with those of Van. He now casually discards observations from his past experiences:

Pandora of Hathersage, hah. She's all skin and bones, ain't she? All skins and bones, says Van. Why does tha study her so intently Pip? A couple of generations ago, they were a proud species, rulers of The Dark Peak. Look at them now: Debased, a poor reflection of their former glory. Hathersage. It was the centre of the universe. Them clowns now, they're just parodies of what they were -- if her mother saw her now, she'd turn in her egg.

Hah! Hah-thersage! They've returned to type, no more caring about the wellbeing of The Dark Peak, like they did. Now just caring about their own selfs. They was saviours, now they is parasites -- like the nascenti prey upon the jellyhead. Makes me sad, it does. Make's me angry. What's the youth come to, ay? Van huffs up a gob of phlegm, depositing it on the quarry tiles. A blackworm, crawling out from the grout and grime, feeds soundlessly on the green. Shad makes short work of both, settling down with a grin.

But they are mercenaries, right?

They wasn't Pip, says Van. Back when I knew them, they were the opposite of mercenaries. The clowns were the rulers and the gods of The Dark Peak, huge in number, they kept the nascenti and the xin in check. Then I brought the Hatherans and the xin together, but that was a while back now. They've suffered as a species, I don't doubt. Now, they cling to life -- like Pandora over there, forever playing catchup with the might have been and the once before -- look at her, all skin and bones she is, all skin and bones.

What Van is saying is news to me. My only experience of the clowns, has been -- if not bad, then not good either. Yet Van talks of a time not so long ago when the clowns were rulers of a land not so far away from where we sit now. And that makes me wonder what happened in this couple of generations since

Van worked whatever magic he did in these tales he is telling me now, but it's early days yet and so I'm sure we'll find out soon enough.

Pandora's having an animated conversation with a xaexs on that table over there now. She -- the xaexs -- is an unusual sight in Hellsborough, she walked in a few moments ago. She hasn't even gone to the bar yet, going straight over to the clown and the crosslander. To my reckoning, something is seriously afoot. I'm keeping my eyes on these three, could be that there's trouble brewing hereabouts.

Van, relaxed as ever, is dealing himself a couple more crib hands; yet, I know his eyes are watching -- he monitors things closely, even if you don't think he is. He takes another long slug on his pipe, his pupils following the vapour as it trails upwards in spirals.

Hey, hey, you got some of that pretty green? Shouts Van, suddenly twisting around and looking directly at Pandora. I need a hit love, someat to speed me up a bit. Getting slow in me old age, you got some fruit, murker?

Pandora ignores him.

I'm sure I detect a flaring of her nostrils and a sneer, which I didn't expect. I'd have thought a clown would be all over a request like that like a rash, but she knows who Van is -- I get that now -- and for whatever reason, that means disdain.

A line, just need a sliver, continues Van. The xaexs seeing Pandora's sideways looks, breaks away from their conversation, and pivots towards Van. It's a pivot that scares me, like you'd expect from some sort of automaton in the off-world. Alien. Somehow. And I'm thinking: This is not a good sign.

I feel uneasy. I'm not someone who starts fights, and no-one in this bar is going to ever defend themselves against a xaexs. This one stands 8 feet tall and has two sets of fully developed and very muscular arms -- she is nothing if not intimidating. I don't tend to swear, but there's only one word that is front and centre of my mind -- it begins with C and ends in L! (which might not make sense if you're not from around these parts, but what I mean is: Chuffin'ell!)

I'll tell you more about the xaexs, it might provide some context. Just think Samurai cockroach. Independent, disciplined, well trained, hard to kill and -- utterly, utterly -- ruthless. That's a xaexs. And this one, as I said, is with a clown and a crosslander, and they're talking in shallow clicks and whispers. What they're discussing, I can only guess.

The xaexs are, like the clowns, by my approximation at least, mercenaries.

From what I know, they're fairly small in number, but since they are such effective combatants, you don't need many of them to do a lot of damage.

Van would be able to tell you more, and he will if I ask -- assuming he's coherent -- but I'm pretty sure the xaexs are related in someway to the dyapnids. They're both insectoid at any rate. But then so are the clowns, not that you'd ever guess, since they resemble humanity so closely. But whilst the dyapnids are more likely to be found in huge groups -- swarms, I suppose -- the xaexs are rarely ever seen together. They operate alone. Silent killers. If you need a job doing, so the saying goes, hire a xaexs.

I once heard a story -- for a change, it didn't come from Van -- about a xaexs contracted to destroy a nascenti communications cluster -- an organic network hub for all of the incoming communications from the various plants and fungi that the nascenti use to monitor and control their jellyhead underlings. The communications cluster was staffed by forty three exacids. Exacids are the nascenti's muscle, their security guards. Their bouncers and enforcers. There was another four nascenti who ran the cluster during murklight. Maybe the numbers are wrong, who knows, it's a story after all, it's probably embellished to make it sound better, but then, when I think about it, maybe it isn't...

Anyway, let's say the numbers are correct. This xaexs, the story doesn't mention her name, breaks into this communications cluster -- evading all of the security systems -- and they're pretty sophisticated, if you know what I mean? I mean, this bit baffles me, exacids and nascenti have all of the benefits of a hivemind and the organic network, and still this happens -- incredible. But then, the xaexs is also plugged into the hivemind through her breeding as well, so I guess being an off-worlder, I just can't fathom it so well. Anyway, the xaexs gets into the perimeter and the main building of the hub undetected by the exacids, kills the four nascenti officers who are maintaining the facility -- injecting them all with a poison straight through that heavy carapace of theirs, killing them instantly.

The data in the network hub is then scrambled by the xaexs, so that it's of no use to the nascenti without a time based quantum code dependent on the temperature of the murk at the point it was compromised. Of course, this code is believed to be simple and easy to remember, but whoever tries to enter the code to unscramble the data, gets just a single chance, or the data is wiped -- forever. It doesn't matter that the nascenti have the data backed up, because by chaining the data by its relatedness to the organic world, once the source data is scrambled, so are all of the replicated versions. Using a backdoor only known to this xaexs, she then uploads the data from the cluster to an encrypted server held by the crosslander resistance.

Apparently, that was that. If you wanted more technical details, then I am definitely not the one to ask, but I'm not sure who you would ask either, or rather who I would ask, since the technology here is so different to that in the off-world. Organic technology is so dissimilar to that silicon stuff that you find at home.

Then the xaexs, she's gone. Out of the communications cluster, over (or under, maybe through, who knows?) the perimeter, and away. An alarm wasn't raised for another six hours until a change of shift was due and the outgoing nascenti failed to leave. And that's pretty funny, because if exacids had a sense of smell, they'd have noticed much sooner. Maybe they should also get a jellyhead guard or two on staff, since the stench of four dead nascenti after six hours -- in this mumid (that is, this humid, murky) climate -- is apparently nothing short of putrid.

At this point the xaexs has already been paid half by the crosslanders for the initial sabotage, and as per their agreement, they owe her the other half because they now have the data. But the xaexs has the passcode for the scambled data, so she can blackmail the nascenti should she wish to, which will effectively render the copy the crosslanders have redundant, since the nascenti will know what it is they have. Of course, the data could be useless intelligence, who knows, but are the crosslanders prepared to take that risk, or do they just pay the other half? The xaexs in the meantime, has decided that it's in her best interests if she just sells the information she holds to the highest bidder.

Ey up pal, didn't see you there, says Van as the xaexs swivels on her pivot, how's it going you sun?

I've never seen a xaexs smile, they don't tend to have what you'd a call smiley face. At least not one that a human like I can discern. But the xaexs seems to be content: She hasn't automatically removed Van's head, and that's a good sign. With her right second arm (leg?) the xaexs reaches beneath her -- carapace, her epidermis, like she's reaching into her own gut -- and retrieves a small baggy of shimmering yellow-green goo with those delicate pincers of hers. Standing to her full height, she takes a single stride, handing the baggy to Van.

Much obliged, Dirty Leaves, says Van with a toothy smile, the xaexs chirps something back in her own strange tongue.

What she said, I have no way of deciphering, there was no violence -- quite the opposite. The xaexs does something of a half bow, and then turns back to the clown and returns to her seat where they continue their chitter-chatter.

What did she say to you? I asked Van.

She just said, there you go pal, enjoy.

And what did you call her, it sounded like 'dirty leaves'.

Yeah, that's her name.

Dirty Leaves?

Yeah, well that's as near as a translation as tha's ever gonna get.

Van carefully pours the shimmerating gook onto the table. With no ceremony, he snorts the squirming mass directly up his left nostril. Lolling back in his chair, his eyes roll back into their sockets. Twin full moons, if such a thing existed in this world, or the off.

When you have experienced the things that Van has, I don't think that's unreasonable behaviour. To have developed a massive capacity for drugs and drink in the way that he has, that's normal isn't it? A normal way for the human mind and body to accept trauma? A coping mechanism. I do wonder if it's within the human capability to be able to do what he does though. I can't even come close.

That *is* the finest crust in all of The Dark Peak, hah, in all the world, says Van with vigour. Then he regains some semblance of normality and realises where he is: Oh, sorry Pip, I didn't save tha none. Did tha want to slip a bit?

I really have no idea what he is talking about -- crust? Slip? Nah no, I'm good.

Rockcrust, Pip. Everything is possible, it's subliminal, I fell in love with it many a time past. It only grows here, try it, tha can't get it nowhere else. I can get some more, it's fine.

I'll pass for now -- but what is it, this rockcrust?

Moral worth, Pip. Existence. The cause and the course. The will of Dunlockslyn: Scerm. Listen. Does tha hear that? Does tha hear the silence?

I have no idea what Van is waffling about.

The fragility Pip, tha grok? It's murk immersion. Not just the thick oily ether that tha thinks about when tha looks out of that window there, it's the consciousness of it. The livingness, the deathness -- the being. It's Scerm: The afterlife, the out of body floaty-time; it's everything tha expects the murk to be, it is, what it is.

Wahaha..huh! Studdered Van, it's visceral Pip. You sense it, its being, its essence, its dirty stink, the crashing of its noiseless gongs as they reverberate through your soul. This is us, he stabs the bottom left of the table with his index finger. This is the murk he says, stabbing the top right. This is the murk where the Dun flows through the Ripperthroats: There is nirvana -- where life returns to the sand.

That is crust. *That* is what tha gets when tha slurps the slime Pip.

Later, I researched it a little more. Slime, crust -- rockcrust -- is a type of lichen found only in The Dark Peak.

The denizens -- the clowns, the xin, xaexs, the nascenti, maybe the fungal network, synthesise it into this faster moving organism, this embodiment, as Van put it, of the murk. This is nothing like any drug you can get in the off-world; this is not like heroin or cannabis or crack. Rockcrust seems more like a "smart drug" -- an integral experience, it takes your further than any powder or pot can ever take you. My own frame of reference might be psilocybin, which would make sense here as well, with the fungal network being what it is.

A crickerjack lands on the table. Van blats it with the heel of his palm, sending its backside through its brain; he picks off the legs and wings and feeds them to Shad. What's left of the cadaver he pops into his mouth, biting down hard and crunching loudly.

Reading my thoughts, Van posits his own analysis: Tha'll never get crust in the off-world. Can't happen. Tha ingests a living creature whose only purpose is to take tha to places that only exist in the nether. Crust transverses dimensions. Time is a useless construct of the off-world. The murk is quantum. Tha see forwards in time, tha see backwards, tha see what has happened, and what will happen, maybe what will never happen. How can tha ever know?

That was the last coherent sentence Van uttered tonight, not that I fully understood it. Then he howled. I say howled. It wasn't a sound I've ever heard come from a human before -- but howl is the closest verb I can think of.

I fly, slurred Van. I am flutterby. I am mentiloth of xin: Death winger; venomtooth of hail and mist. I am mystic stinger of legends past, I am prophesy.

Van Shhh! I implore, but he's too far gone and, he's going to start talking about the prophesy. No Van, not the prophesy, it's not safe. There's little point in me saying anything, since he's so far out of it, he can't hear me.

Speaking about the prophesy is banned in Hellsborough, luckily the organic network isn't going to pick this up from in here. But we're in a public place, and this is a really bad idea. Anyone -- any of the jellyhead bar staff -- or the other customers, could shop Van for talking like this -- and everyone knows Van Hallam.

First the xaexs, the crosslander and the clown, and now this; it's not a risk that I'm comfortable with. I'm flusteredly calculating how I am going to get out of this bar and then out of Hellsborough before the authorities are alerted.

Maybe I worry too much, maybe I don't. I'm just trying to cover myself. Friend, Van may be, but I am not prepared to risk my liberty because he is shouting his mouth off in a bar about some crackpot prophesy. And when I say risk my liberty, I of course, mean my life. I know what the prophesy is, and so does everyone else, that's why its mention is forbidden -- the overlords loathe it more than anything else.

Van is on his feet. Raise your chalice, he shouts, sloshing his ale about: Drink the blood of Dunlockslyn -- the great curator, the bringer of life and the harbinger of death. I taste me mother's milk, I feel the space, I feel the reality, the air, the vibrations, the rotation of the Earth, me every memory. Oh D'divi! I am ready for thee -- I am primitive again! I walk tha muddy banks; I sail tha brackish waters to the Ripperthroats, to the end of the infinite, to the finality -- my deserving after all this service, hail thee -- the most noble creature in all The Dark Peak!

And now I have even less idea what he is going on about, but no matter, at least he's gone back to talking about Dunlockslyn, which is accepted by everyone. No more of that prophesy talk Van, please.

Yet, sorry state that he is in now, the man is an iconoclast. A true lone ripperthroat in this strange and barely comprehensible world.

Pandora gets up from her seat, nodding at the xaexs and crosslander, who also start to rise. The toucan looking thing on the crosslander's shoulder -- it's called a symbiot -- eyes Van and clicks its bill. Its hands are not feathered and it displays a gesture to Van with its fingers. No-one else in the party pays any attention, but Van sees it and rabidly howls and gnashes his teeth.

The din of the bar and the heady infecting atmosphere say closure is close, but Van has more story to regurgitate, so we stay, rooted to our table as last orders are called by a klaxon.

```
      HMM::OUT('jellyhead')
`ask:: Rippon, Pip // stat:: accept[ok]__ // src::
2001:0db8:85a3:0000:0000:8a2e:037g:7334 [loc::hellsborough//
middlewood_road//467]__ // now:: 79.hail
ripperthroat.12.13.22.59.33`

`HMM::IN('..Colour:   Variable_   Pale through dark_`

`..Diet:   Prepared food solution, fermented beverage_`

`..Size:   5    6'6" (feet, thumb)_`

`..Defining characteristics:   Humanoid_`

`..Class:   Worker_')`
```

"Worker", yeah. Slave more like.

```
      HMM::OUT('Symbiot')
`ask:: Rippon, Pip // stat:: accept[ok]__ // src::
2001:0db8:85a3:0000:0000:8a2e:037g:7334 [loc::hellsborough//
middlewood_road//467]__ // now:: 79.hail
ripperthroat.12.13.22.59.45`

`HMM::IN('..Colour:   Variable_`

`..Diet:   Variable_`

`..Size:   3    7" (thumb)_`

`..Defining characteristics:   Variable_`

`..Class:   Familiar_')`
```

CHAPTER 3

To t'otherside o' t'Wisewood

`HMM::OUT('Tell me about dark matter')
\`ask:: unknown // stat:: accept[ok]__ // src:: 2001:0db8:85a3:0000:0000:8a2e:142j:i618 [loc::hellsborough// unknown__location//000]__ // now:: 79.hail ripperthroat.12.13.19.44.3\`

\`HMM::IN('..Dark matter is a form of matter that is believed to exist in the universe but does not emit, absorb, or reflect light, making it invisible to instruments that detect electromagnetic radiation. It is called "dark" because it does not interact with light or other forms of electromagnetic radiation_')\`

\`HMM::IN('..It is estimated that dark matter makes up about 27 of the total matter in the universe, with the remaining 68 being dark energy and only about 5 being normal matter that can be seen and interacted with. Although dark matter has not been directly detected, its presence is inferred from the gravitational effects it has on visible matter, such as stars and galaxies_')\`

\`HMM::IN('..There are several theories about what dark matter is made of. The most widely accepted theory is that it consists of particles that interact only weakly with normal matter. These particles are thought to have been created in the early universe and have been slowly moving through space ever since_')\`

\`:I've heard things about this movement of dark matter, that it's somehow leaving here, is that true?\`

\`.._ .._ ..Analysing_ .._ .._\`

\`:Explain more\`

VAN HALLAM

```
`.._ .._ ..Analysing_ .._ .._`
`..Refer to previous conversation, the hinge_`
```

Van is now tripping like -- in his words -- a monk.

In his reverie, we're starting to get to the nits and details, and as a professional, it's my duty to stay and have one more for the road, as that final (and I'm really hoping it is the last one, I really am ready for my bed) drink is known.

(And after all the excitement of the crosslander, the clown and especially the xaexs, I'm really hoping that Van doesn't invoke some sort of pally after hours drinking arrangement, which I'm pretty sure he has the ability to do around these parts.)

I'd bitten down on this sapling to stop me screaming. I'm sure I did stop, since I had the fear of Dunlockslyn in me, I doant think I'd ever been more scared in me life before then, than I was that neet. But I was paralysed, I couldn't move. Whether it was fear, or what, I doant know. Tha knows, when tha's a youngen, tha hears stories. All sort of tales about bogey men and trolls and that sort of thing. And then, when tha's there, when tha has to face tha fears, all them sorts of stories start flooding back into tha 'ead. Tha knows they were just made-up nonsense. Tha knows that they ain't true, that these ogres doant really exist. Don't thee? Tha tells yourself that it's all just make-believe. But I tells thee Pip, tha try being somewhere like the Wisewood, in murknight with tha body frozen to the spot, and tha mind full of monsters, and tha tells me, that tha wouldn't be scared, because tha would. I'm pretty sure tha'd be cacking yersen, like I was.

I nodded stiltingly, since it was true, I would be messing my pants sure enough.

That demonspawn horde approached then, lowing in their

murderous tones, mindless dumb demonspawn, crushing the undergrowth under their heavy cloven feet; their eyes burning dark red through the greyness of the murk. They were all around us, I could smell their odorous stench and hear their grotesque snoughing as they cleared their snouts and throats. The clattering and clanging as they sharpened their horns against one another in readiness for spearing mine and Shad's soft flesh. Shad started to make a low growling sound, but this did nowt to stop them circling us. I could hear their throaty breathing and see the burning of them deep crimson eyes that showed no mercy, just coldness.

My mind wandered -- if demonspawn are such mindless and abhorrent creatures, how do they act with such calculated cruelty...

Pip, pay attention! Says Van.

A low moaning come from the forest behind us then. And this may sound funny in some ways, but this ain't Shad, this is someat else. This is someat far more heinous than Shad could ever be. And so I'm being circled by demonspawn about to skewer me on those horns and now I have a growl scaring the d'divi out of me as well.

But that moan -- subsonic it was, I reckon -- it reached the ears of them demonspawn, and all of a sudden, they was routed; they were fleeing in terror. Panic-stricken. Their lowing replaced by a strangulated screaming -- nothing like their normal dimwitted bass tones. So frantic they were to escape from the unseen thing behind me and Shad that one of them ran headlong into a great unyielding beech tree, breaking its neck. It smashed into the undergrowth, where I could hear its laboured breathing, as the damn thing drew its final breath.

The sound which had frightened them demonspawn didn't happen again, but it had been enough to start me thinking about what it was back there in the shadows. I still couldn't move --

held stiff as a board with my back toward whatever this was -- the sound that had made them demonspawn stampede. Shad too was rooted to the spot, must 'ave been as tangled up as me; but tha's a loyal boy eh Shad, tha always was weren't thee, tha old pad? Says Van ruffing Shad around his scruff.

Van stops and stares up into a corner of the bar now. I'm not sure what he is looking for -- if anything. Probably nothing.

Backflit he says distractedly, running his tongue over his lips -- but it's leaving, I can tell, it's away to that dark.

He moves on leaving me none the wiser.

I reckon we was in someat of a predicament, he says, draining his glass, and inexplicably managing to get table service. Our tankards quickly being recharged with ale -- not something I was hoping for.

A few times that night, I heard sounds behind me -- movement, twig snap and the like, like we was being hunted -- like a flatface hunts a gnawmard. Shad is bristling and on constant alert, but it all comes to nowt. In the end all the rustling and the leaf chop and the crackling, it all stops. Then the dew it's rising, and it's the still of them early hours. I don't think I got no sleep -- I was just left thinking about this place we was in, and still couldn't move a muscle.

I has no idea what is causing me to not be able to move -- I has a better idea now of course -- and I was ruminating on it all night. Maybe them thorns has cut through an important nerve, I thinks, or maybe that sapling I had chomped upon -- it could have drugged me with its sap, I reckon that's what it was Pip. Course, it could be someat else, who knows what you can contract in that murk. All I knew was I couldn't move, I was frozen to the spot. That night though, I hoped that whatever it was that kept me numb might fade away, or when murklight broke I'd be able to better see what t'problem was, and be able to sort it out.

I'll tell you Pip, right then in that Wisewood, I feared for mesen. I don't think I'd ever been more scared than I was then, bound to that forest floor. Surrounded by the murk and them tangled branches, with this unseen beast stalking me. Many a time in Hellsborough I've fought mesen out of some dark corner -- out back of some lane or some shadowy ginnel that I shouldn't have been in -- or ran as fast as my legs would carry me when some feral animal had been in the streets in gloaming or after murkfall; but then I always knew how to escape, because I knew every road, every lane, every ten foot, every path, I knew well the lie of the land. Here, in this wooded prison, I had no way out, and only the coming of murkrise would give me some hope. All I could do was wait, with fear in me 'eart and buzzing in me 'ead.

And me mind that night, it played the worstest of tricks on me. Many a time I thought I'd be eaten alive by that beast in the shadows. I was awake and could hear everything, yet my body could do nowt to escape, or even move. I'm sure I might have died of fright only to be resurrected as some revenant, to forever stalk the Wisewood. I imagined mesen with me arms of twisted sharp briars, with legs of bandy ash and a scream in me throat.

And this monster - this me of me murknightmare - carried a big old knife in its bloodied and broken hand of thorns.

I'm listening to Van telling me this, and my first thought is of an ancient poem: "Brackenman of Wadsley Common". The common is not so far distant from the Wisewood as the corvid flies, and Van's description certainly bears a distinct resemblance to the creature of the poem -- a cryptid from here or hereabouts:

"Bracken Man of Wadsley Common". I researched it in Hellsborough library. Decide for yourself, but to me, it sounds very similar to what Van is talking about:

The Common at Wadsley was ever dark, ancient and sinister.

Its man of bramble, thorn, bracken and briar;

And no one scrambles over the sliding ganister

Bowed legs of ash, four arms of yew and perishing juniper

Down the precipices of its sides, with tangled roots

Swirling fronds of green and purple heather shoots.

So the old poem goes. "Witnesses" of the creature, according to the ancient legends, at least had the Brackenman of Wadsley Common with his half dozen arms and legs made from twisted and bendy tree stalks with his body as a tangle of bramble and briar.

In an account that I read doing my research, a middle aged chap -- he'd been quite wealthy and of high standing, something of an engineer by all accounts, so a trustworthy type; not some fly-by-night who was likely to profit from some sort of supernatural tale. This engineer had been out for a few beers (and, if he's like me and Van, likely several more after that) at the Star Inn on Fox lane and had taken the Coal Pit lane back across the common, heading for his home somewhere off the Stubbing.

It is extremely dark up there on the common, and this was a late Windstrom evening, so it had been dark for some time that night. The murk hung low and heavy, making it hard for this chap to keep to the path and avoid the rocky outcrops, of which there are many. He had fallen several times, bruising shins and other limbs, but had still managed to get as far as the standing stone circle, at which he paused for a while to catch his breath; he'd ascended to quite some height by that time.

The legend has it that whilst resting against one of the great stones of the circle, he was attacked by a beast that came forth from the centre of the circle.

The beast had a body of thistles and thorns, legs of bandy ash and arms formed from twisted briars. Its head was a gorse bush. Its eyes were the orange of burning coals.

The bracken man beast enveloped the exhausted engineer where he stood and encased him in those spiky arms of briar.

The engineer's skin was punctured many times, causing him to almost bleed to death.

He was found sometime after dawn by a passing knife grinder. The engineer lay in the undergrowth in a sorry state, barely alive. His body -- but not yet his corpse -- had been picked over by scavenging slyfluffs and grizzlers through the night, and corvids during murkrise.

But that's just a legend. The poor bloke probably just lost his way on a murkfull night and fell into a briar patch, succumbing to the thorns and passing out. I'm sure this is just me, thinking out loud, putting two and two together, and making 19.

Anyway, Van is still in full flow, but at least he is over the worst part, it would seem...

From then until midmurk, or the wee small hours at least, all was silence. Then, suddenly, the awful chatter of...

```
     HMM::IN('Sleepytime story..')
`hits:: 94542 // [this]2001:0db8:85a3:0000:0000:8a2e:037g:7334
[loc::hellsborough//middlewood_road//467]__ // now:: 79.hail
ripperthroat.12.13.23.30.0`
```

`Once upon a time, in a peaceful forest filled with tall trees and chirping birds, there lived a little bunny named Benjamin. Benjamin loved to hop and play, but he also knew how important it was to get a good night's sleep.`

`Every night, Benjamin would curl up in his cozy burrow and close his eyes, listening to the gentle rustling of the leaves outside. He would take a deep breath and imagine himself floating on a soft, fluffy cloud, drifting away into a deep sleep.`

`As he closed his eyes, Benjamin could feel his body getting heavier and heavier, sinking into the soft earth beneath him. The sounds of the forest began to fade away as he fell into a peaceful slumber.`

I wave my hand about in front of Van's face to try and get him to stop, and he does with a puzzled look on his face.

This psycmask is telling me a sleepytime story, I can't hear what you're saying, how do I make it stop?

Well, just tell it you don't want to hear it.

How do I do that?

What's your psycmask's handle?

Handle? I don't know, I was just issued it by the council, they didn't tell me about any handle.

OK, don't panic. Oy, Shales-o shouts Van to the barman, what's the default psycmask handle these days?

Shalesmoor looks up from polishing glasses, pushing his thick rimmed specs onto his nose. He likely wears them as a fashion accessory, there's unlikely to be anything wrong with his eyesight in this place. There is a pause, and he seems to be asking himself a question, but what he is actually doing, I reckon is communicating with the hivemind -- unencumbered by a physical psycmask, like I am forced to wear -- his nanotech version is implanted. I see him looking over, checking the type of my mask.

There isn't one, he says, even that one of yours uses the same version as me. Just say "skip sleepytime".

Thanks. Why didn't I think of that?

```
      HMM::OUT('skip sleepytime')
`ask:: Rippon, Pip // stat:: accept[ok]__ // src::
2001:0db8:85a3:0000:0000:8a2e:037g:7334 [loc::hellsborough//
middlewood_road//467]__ // now:: 79.hail
```

ripperthroat.12.13.23.32.9`

`HMM::IN('In his dreams, Benjamin visited.._)`

It's stopped. Sorry Van, please carry on. He does:

From then until midmurk, or the wee small hours at least, all was silence. Then, suddenly, the awful chatter of the murkrise come into me ears, and then there came again from the dark shadows the sound of that moving thing, and a rustling of the leaves. The shock caused me convulsions it did. It was then that I broke off them bonds that had tied me to the forest floor. It was me mind, me will, that did it; not me muscles, because I couldn't move even so much as me little finger. And I didn't have much in the way of muscle neither. Then something gave, I felt as sick as a rooter, then there was a sharp click as if steel wire had snapped, and I stood with me back against the tree facing that unknown creature of the murk. Shad too, seemed to have more life in him.

Me heart was pounding in me chest, me rib cage heaving from exerting mesen so much. Me breath was coming in quick, short gasps, cold sweat running down me forehead. I pinched mesen and figured I wasn't no revenant yet -- I was still in the land of the living, even if I didn't much feel like I was.

That weird moaning from the depths of the wood brought me back to my senses -- quicker than you'd say Jack Flash I reckon. Tha knows I didn't have much of a weapon, I've said that already, and I didn't want to face this unseen thing, whatever it was. Even with Shad at my side, I didn't fancy a face off with whatever this thing might be. I decided I should run off -- and then the rustling sound happened again, so in the dark of the wood, with my imagination running riot -- I was being hunted -- that denizen of the murk was creeping up on me, stealthy like.

I needed to escape this horrible place Pip. And then, as the murklight began to seep through the blackness, I ran as quick as me legs would carry me through the trees and into an opening -- a ley, a clearing in the forest. Not sure why, but courage flooded into me body and me veins. I felt strong, emboldened somehow. On the far side of the clearing, I stopped. Told mesen off for what now seemed to be stupid and unneeded mithering. I reasoned in me head that I had lain helpless for many hours within the wood, yet nowt had come at me. If only I was to think a bit clearer and apply a bit of normalness, then I would convince meself that the noises I had heard would have resulted from natural and harmless stuff. Probably just the wind in the trees. At that point, I felt kind of daft, it was just the breeze through the trees all the time, how could I be so silly -- what a daft berk I was, Pip.

I had me psycmask on, but right then, the murk lifted and thinned out a bit, so I tipped it back and took a gobfull of air -- the purest air I had ever drank, I reckon. I lifted my head and filled my lungs with it. Then, I saw stretching in front of me, the most phenomenal landscape. The best landscape in all of the world I reckon. We're so lucky to live around here, Pip -- yet few ever venture out as far as I did, very few.

Rocky gorges, jutted hills, heather-studded moorland, and I'm just starting out. The Dark Peak landscape -- silvered mountains in the distance, strange lights and shadows upon hillocks and streams, and the spiky details of those stiff, beautiful gorse bushes echoing their vibrant yellow back against the murk. Tha ain't lived until tha's immersed thasen in The Dark Peak, Pip. It's the glory of Dunlockslyn. No Hellsboroughite jellyhead can ever experience its splendour without surrounding thasen in its being, in experiencing the scerm of it. Pip, this is the most wonderful place in all of Dunlockslyn's universe.

And then Pip -- as I stood there with me eyes wide open, it was like I had caught a glimpse of some forgotten world. It can be extreme cold and utter darkness can The Dark Peak, but it can also be such a stunning place -- so different to owt here in Hellsborough. So different to anywhere else.

DARK PEAK

Hah, Pip, so me and Shad finally passed through them remnants of the Wisewood, and into that vast and dangerous place that is The Dark Peak.

```
      HMM::OUT('Jack Flash')
`ask:: Rippon, Pip // stat:: accept[ok]__ // src::
2001:0db8:85a3:0000:0000:8a2e:037g:7334 [loc::hellsborough//
middlewood_road//467]__ // now:: 79.hail
ripperthroat.12.13.23.39.3`
```

`HMM::IN('..Colour:   Pale`

`..Diet:    .._  .._  ..Analysing_  .._  ..Blood_  ..Carrion_`

`..Size:   7'6" (feet, thumb)_`

`..Defining characteristics:  Humanoid, capable of huge leaps, breathes blue flame, glowing red eyes, metallic claws_`

`..Class:   ..Analysing_ Revenant_`

`..Nicks:   Spring heeled Jack_)`

CHAPTER 4

Murklight

    HMM::IN('Ladies, you tired of those bad hair days? Say no more! We got you covered with the perfect haircut that matches your face shape.')
`hits:: 81961 // [this]2001:0db8:85a3:0000:0000:8a2e:037g:7334 [loc::hellsborough//middlewood_road//467]__ // now:: 79.hail ripperthroat.12.13.23.44.27`

`Yo, listen up! If you got a round face, we suggest a cut that adds some height and length to your face, like a layered bob or a long, side swept fringe. If you got a square face, we got some dope styles that'll work for you too. Soft layers and textured ends will add some movement and soften up your angles. For all my oval face peeps out there, you're in luck! You can rock almost any cut, but we recommend showing off your bone structure with a long, blunt cut or a textured pixie. And last but not least, if you got a heart shaped face, we got you! A layered bob or a side swept fringe will balance out your features and give you a fly frame for your face. So, come through to our salon and let us hook you up with a fresh cut that's perfect for you!`

`Book Now, we don't sleep, cos you don't: 333 777 333777 333 777   Faranteeeeeees!!!`

Van had dropped off at this point, eyes closed, arms outstretched, palms upturned, like some meditating divinity.

His beer glass seemingly like his mind, was an empty void; as empty as the vastness of The Dark Peak. I alighted to the bar to recharge his glass, and mine, since I too had drained my vessel. Despite the lateness of the hour and our apparent intoxication, the re-fills weren't questioned; if anything, they were welcomed, and apparently, free of charge. When I returned to the table, Van is playing out his crib hands against himself, and getting engrossed in a run culminating in a four and a jubilant fifteen-two. He accepts his recharged glass with thanks and slurps noisily at the foamy head. He pauses slightly to admire the played out cards laying on the table and then continues his oration.

The landscape was familiar and alien at the same time, purple heather and yellow gorse covering them moors. It was murkrise, and outcrops of gritty rock glistened in the drismal half-light. Down from where I stood was a low walled pen, much like tha might keep wooltards in. I was parched from nowt to sup and with no water in sight, not even a syke, I thought it best to make me top priority to do some exploring. This pen was the only sign of life hereabouts, so keeping low to the ground, since I didn't know who -- or what -- was likely to be about, I made me way over to it. Me shabby clothes blended in well with the grey of the rock and the green of the moss and bracken, but I was pretty much out in the open, so I felt vulnerable I did.

I couldn't see no doors, but the wall was only about four foot high, so I peeped over the top. What I saw was the strangest of things: It had a roof made of some solid material, but opaque and four or five thumb thick, but not of any material I had ever seen -- it reminded me of webbing, perhaps from some giant spider; or maybe ice. Beneath it I could see several dozen big eggs, all round and pinkish-grey -- like the colour of the sky at murkrise.

Five of the eggs had hatched and their contents sat blinking in the dull light. That may sound odd Pip, and maybe it's a bit rude to say it like that, but had my stomach had anything in it, the sight of them things would have emptied it. They was all 'ead, with scrawny little bodies, short fat necks and six legs; greenish-yellow and warty, sweaty things they were, all covered in slimy mucus, which they licked at with their long curly tongues. There's a word for how those tongues looked, some animals have a tail like it.

Prehensile? I said.

Yeh, that. They had what you said -- pre-ensile tongues. I later learned they had two legs and two arms, with ones in the middle that could be used as either. Their eyes were like them you see on a fly, but on the sides of their 'eads, sticking out so they could be moved forward or backards: These toady fly things could look in any direction, or in two at once, without having to turn their 'eads. It was all a bit weird Pip, I'll tell ya that for nowt.

    HMM::IN('Yo, fellas! Are you tired of having a wack hairstyle that's not doing you justice? Say no more!') `hits:: 43987 // [this]2001:0db8:85a3:0000:0000:8a2e:037g:7334 [loc::hellsborough//middlewood_road//467]__ // now:: 79.hail ripperthroat.12.13.23.56.58`

'Our crew of skilled barbers knows what's up. They're gonna assess your face shape and recommend the perfect cut that's gonna make you look sharp and on point. Whether you got a round, square, oval, or heart shaped face, we got the skills to make you look like a proper gent.`

`For all my round faced dudes out there, we recommend a cut that adds some height and length to your face, like a textured crop or a side parted pompadour. If you got a square face, don't sweat it, we got you too. A taper fade or a slick back undercut is gonna give you that masculine edge.`

`And for all my oval faced fellas out there, you're lucky as hell! Almost any cut is gonna work for you, but we recommend a classic side part or a short back and sides. And last but not least, if you got a heart shaped face, we gonna help you balance out them features with a low fade or a textured quiff.`

`Book Now, we don't sleep, cos you don't: 333 777 333777 333 777 Faranteeeeeees!!!`

Have I got bad hair or something? I must have. But then judging by the hit count and the content, most of the ladies must have retired for the night.

```
     HMM::IN('Yo, fellas!  Are you tired of having a wack
hairstyle that's not doing you justice?   Say no more!')
`hits::  43987 // [this]2001:0db8:85a3:0000:0000:8a2e:037g:7334
[loc::hellsborough//middlewood_road//467]__ // now::  79.hail
ripperthroat.12.13.23.57.24`
`So,  come  through  to  our  barber  shop  and  let  us  show  you  some
love.  We  gonna  hook  you  up  with  the  perfect  cut  that's  gonna
make  you  feel  like  a  boss.  Say  goodbye  to  them  bad  hair  days
and  hello  to  a  fresh,  clean  look  that's  gonna  turn  heads`
```

Have you finished?! I meant to say it to myself, but I must have blurted it out, because Van interjected:

Why is I not interesting enough? He said, clearly disgruntled.

No, sorry Van, not you -- it's this damn psycmask and these infernal infomercials.

Ah yeah youngun', they're a pest ain't they, tha needs to rid yourself of that stuff, it'll make you blind. Tha needs to find a way to stop them targeting thee, tha can distract it tha knows, put it off the scent.

I wanted to ask Van what he meant -- how am I supposed to rid myself of this mask, or as he said, put it off the scent, but content that my outburst wasn't meant for him, he's already carrying on; I hastily try and concentrate on what he's saying now:

Shad was 'ungry, he wanted to eat the little things and was whining and scratching at that enclosure. I held him back, afraid of what they might be, and young as they clearly were, what instincts they might have which could do one of us harm. More of the eggs were hatching as we watched, and we was both fascinated -- which meant that neither of us noticed a dozen full-grown adults coming at us from behind.

They came on their mounts, soundlessly skimming across the heather. If it hadn't been for the clanking of metal from the one out front, we'd have been skewered and that would have been me gone, but that dull clank made me turn me head, and there not ten foot from me chest was this 'uge spear.

Them hatchlings in the enclosure, they looked harmless now. This one now full in me face was ferocious, with tusks curving up to sharp points, ending near where its eyes would be, if it were human. I reckon this thing was about six foot in height and it sat on its mount like I'd sit on a onetoe, grasping the animal's belly with its lower limbs. The hands of his two right arms held its spear low at its side; its two left arms were hanging out to keep its balance.

The mount itself was probably eight foot long and its head was all big compound eyes and long antennae. It's six spindly legs were tucked under its belly, and it glided over the terrain like a syncarid, slowly beating them broad wings.

Behind the first, were eleven others, all looked the same, but as I later found out, they is all different -- much like we are, eh, Pip?

With that spear aimed at me 'ead, I took the only route I could and scrambled across that webbed dome, my featherweight making it possible -- D'divi thank the nascenti for their feeding -- or lack of it! Once up and over it, I could see why I wasn't followed. If my pursuers had tried, they'd likely have crashed down on their own young and crushed 'em. Lean as the build of the xin -- as they are known -- they is still massive compared to them feeble babies, and when you add to that the weight of their armour, they'd be too heavy for that delicate looking roof, whatever it is was made of.

Just like sliding on them icy ponds in the Rivelin, I made it to the far side without mishap, but turning saw Shad impaled on the shaft of that spear -- such was his lust for them hatchlings, he hadn't sensed that incoming danger. Part of me crumbled as I watched his lifeless body thrown to the floor, discarded like some soiled rag, but I had no time for tears, I had me own life to think of, and I wasn't out of the line of fire yet.

The horde landed their mounts and lined up against the wall, looking at me with expressions I couldn't work out -- later, I realised that they were astounded by me fancy footwork.

They were talking in low tones I couldn't understand, pointing at me and checking that their hatchlings hadn't been touched. Seeing that I was, compared to them, unarmed, that must have made them look at me in a different light. After all, they had already despatched Shad whose teeth were far better weapons that anything I had.

Each of them was armed with half a dozen other weapons, as well as them big old spears. The one weapon which stopped me thinking about trying to escape was a rifle which some of 'em held, and I kinda knew, for some reason they were gonna be good at shooting with.

The xin, after talking for a short time, turned and flew away the way they had come from, leaving just one of them with me by that enclosure. The rest of 'em went about two hundred paces then stopped, turning back to watch.

The one who stayed was the one whose spear had so nearly had me, and did skewer poor Shad, who now lay lifeless in front of him. He was clearly the leader, and they had gone to where they were now at his command.

He dismounted, threw down his spear and arms, and came around the end of that incubator -- that's what that enclosure was, an incubator -- towards me; unarmed and naked, except for the ornaments strapped to his body.

Naked? I asked.

Yeah, them xin have tough warty hides, and no real need for the clothing that we are used to -- and you have to remember that that murk, because of the humidity plants pumping warmth into it is how they evolved to live; so they don't need anything more than their armour, their weapons and the badges of honour that they wear that proves their rank.

Sounds similar to the military in the off-world.

Does it? Yeah well, if you say so, then I guess it is. Your soldiers are naked then?

No, they wear uniforms, I meant that the badges of honour that you talk about to show rank, sound like the insignia that the military in the off-world wear to show their rank: Major, Captain, Sergeant, Lieutenant and all that.

Yeah, sounds similar, anyway, when this xin was about fifty paces from me he took off one of the metal bits that he had had around his arm and held it out to me.

He said something in a clear and strong voice, but I didn't have a clue what he was saying -- the language was all over the place, and I didn't understand a single word. Then he stopped and seemed to be waiting for me reply, cocking his head over to one side and pointing both of them swivelly eyes at me.

He'd killed me dog he had Pip, and that's how I thought about Shad, even though I'd only known him for a few hours, me and Shad had a bond like I'd never felt with any other living thing in my whole short life back then. Yet this scary looking bloke seemed to be giving me some peace offering; not only was he 'olding out that bit of metal off of his arm, but he had also thrown down all his weapons and sent his mates -- his patrol, I guess -- way back so that they wouldn't get involved. It was just me and him.

So I kinda did the only thing that felt right at the time, I puts me hand over my 'eart and says to him -- in Ing -- that I ain't a clue what he was going on about, but the way he acted seemed like he was up for peace, and despite him murdering me dog -- I pointed at poor old Shad -- I was up for a bit of peace. I don't think there was much else I could do anyway Pip, if I hadn't been smiling, and instead had pulled out that big old knife, I'd have been toast, wouldn't I?

When I pointed at Shad the fella looked over, and I thought I might have seen a little remorse in them odd eyes of his, but as for what I said, I might have been babbling like the Storrs brook for all I knew. I reckon it got the message across alright though. Because when I stretched my hand out towards his, and took his metal thing, he seemed sound enough.

I clamped it about my arm around me bicep -- is that right, this bit.

Van correctly indicated his bicep muscle.

He'd had it around 'ere, he said, indicating his forearm, but he were quite a bit more muscular than I was. Then his wide mouth spread into a smile, and he locked one of his middle arms in mine, and we walked back toward his mount. At the same time he motioned his patrol to come towards us.

They started towards us at a wild run, but he told 'em to slow down with a wave of one of his hands. He presumably -- and correctly -- feared that their charge might be enough to make me run off, which I might well have done, taking my chances with them rifles of theirs.

He said a few words to his men, indicated that I would ride behind one of them, and then mounted his own beast. The one designated as my ride reached down two or three hands and lifted me up behind him, I hung on as best I could to his belts and straps.

I said to the one who I was now riding with to pick up Shad's body -- it was just a few feet a way -- but the fella just grunted and kicked his heels into his mount, sending us forward and leaving Shad's broken remnants exposed to the elements, in the heather and bracken at the base of that incubator that housed them hatchlings. I have to admit Pip, a tear welled in me eye then.

Where in The Dark Peak is this Van? I asked, as he came to a natural pause in this part of the story, counting his crib box and moving one of the pegs along the board by nine holes.

At the time of course, he said in answer, I didn't really know, having never visited before, but later on my return to Hellsborough, I studied any map fragments that I could find that showed the area. There wasn't much to go on, a scrap here, a ripped section there, but I decided that, as it was xin warriors that I found, and not nascenti, then I must have been in the uplands somewhere; which is, of course, pretty obvious when you think about it. The xin, being composed how they are, are creatures of the uplands, and their natural environment is the swamps, marshes and wetlands that are the sources of the rivers in the area as they drain away from The Dark Peak and head down towards civilisation. Well, our human civilisation at least, if you can call it that. If you asked me to put money of it, I'd say we were somewhere beyond the Lodge moor, but it was a long time ago and my knowledge sparse, so tha forgets and as time goes on those memories turn into false memories, rewritten with newer stuff -- tha knows how it is.

But one thing I does know is that those mounts of the xin -- they're called mentiloth -- they move with the swiftness of anything that I've ever experienced before or since. That made them powerful and fearsome allies, and I'd have many a battle against them in the years to come.

```
      HMM::OUT('Xin')
`ask:: Rippon, Pip // stat:: accept[ok]__ // src::
2001:0db8:85a3:0000:0000:8a2e:037g:7334 [loc::hellsborough//
```

```
middlewood_road//467]__  // now:: 79.hail
ripperthroat.12.14.0.19.8`
```

`HMM::IN('..Colour:  Light yellow green (immature) through dark olive`

`..Diet:  Mentiloth milk and derivative products, carrion, omnivorous_`

`..Size:  4   7' (feet)_`

`..Defining characteristics: .._
Amphibian_ .._ ..Analysing_ .._ ../|\/|\/_ Insectoid_`

CHAPTER 5

Siltibog, Fenimoss, the dyapnid and the barghest

`HMM::OUT('The hinge has been breached by this Pip Rippon and dark matter is leaking out of Hellsborough, is that right?')`
`ask:: unknown // stat:: accept[ok]__ // src:: 2001:0db8:85a3:0000:0000:8a2e:142j:i618 [loc::hellsborough// unknown__location//000]__ // now:: 79.hail ripperthroat.12.13.20.17.14`

`HMM::IN('..Not enough data to give a formative answer_')`

`:assume statement true`
`:What will happen because of dark matter leaving Hellsborough?`

`.._ .._ ..Analysing_`

`:Explain`

`..Matter attracts anti matter, on contact, annihilation`

Looking at him, Van bears a striking resemblance to Nosferatu, the vampire from old films in the off-world -- albeit, without the fangs. He is lithe and svelte, completely devoid of hair -- on his head or anywhere else judging by his arms, and incredibly ancient. Of course, Van sees this as a sign of advancement, the hairless ape and all that, being better developed evolutionary and cognitively superior, but that's just Van's view, of course. Yet despite his advanced years, he is every bit the formidable opponent, especially when it comes to cribbage.

I've got qualifications coming out of my ears, but there's something about that game -- cribbage -- that I just don't get, something that Van understands that I don't, and I'll be damned if I can get it. He just always beats me at the final post, which is why I gave up playing against him and he gave up playing against me. One day, I'll try again. I keep watching and learning. One day I'll pluck up the courage to chance him again, and I *will* better him. But that day is not going to be this evening.

That beer that I went and fetched a while back, that's gone. And another one after that. This one that we have now is finely crafted, and generously hopped, with peppery undertones -- and again it's hitting the spot. Van has been absorbed in his game throughout those last drinks, and I have been biding my time, just enjoying the quiet of the place and soaking up what's left of the atmosphere -- Shalesmoor, the bar guy, appears to be in no rush to close after all.

This evening is a drismal one, typical in Hellsborough, a place seemingly with its own ecosystem; so these last few drinks maybe weren't such a bad thing. The wind is fair howling outside and Shalesmoor has taken to watching the flotsam and detritus blowing along the street and against the outside of the building. Occasionally, the leaves and litter and other assorted earth manure thrown up by the stormy weather stick to the window in clods. The two of them: Van and Shalesmoor, are used to this weather, as is Shad, and they bid it no notice, but for me it's fearsome and I would rather be inside this bar than outside it, but then I am something of a fair weather tourist.

```
      HMM::IN('Hexikid!   Hexikid!   Hexikid!')
`hits::  42  //  [this]2001:0db8:85a3:0000:0000:8a2e:037g:7334
[loc::hellsborough//middlewood_road//467]__  //  now::  79.hail
ripperthroat.12.14.0.23.54`
```

VAN HALLAM

`Hexikid! Hexikid! Hexikid! Hexikid!`

A hexikid street cleaner is slithering down the road consuming the muck and polishing the street in its slimey wake, its immense bulk pulsating amber, reflecting off the glass of the window; a brace of barker nip its chitinous shell -- one was natural, a small breed, probably escaped from its owner's house to run amok. Its furless companion was made, with a yap like a gabblerachet.

Van, noticing my mind wandering, draws me back in by continuing his story:

We had gone perhaps ten thousand paces when the ground began to rise up fast. We were near to the edge of one of The Dark Peak's vast reservoirs, where my encounter with the xin had taken place. In a short time we gained the foot of the hills, and after going through a narrow gorge we came to an open valley. At the far side was a hidden xin village, which we glided towards on the mentiloth, entering the village by a bare and tatty track.

When I say village, it was no more than a camp really. Huts constructed from the stems of ash trees and tents covered in raggedy canvas. In the buildings of the camp were some nine or ten hundred creatures of the same breed as my captors, which I now thought I was, a captive, I mean -- in my naivety I'd allowed myself to be trapped, Pip.

The women didn't vary much to the men -- their tusks were larger in proportion to their smaller stature, and they were lighter in colour, ranging in height from four to five foot. The children were light in colour, even lighter than the women, and all looked the same to me, except that some were taller than others; older, I reckoned. But then all kids look alike to me Pip, they always have, I guess that's just my lack of interest in youngen's.

There were no one about who tha'd say was old, and there ain't any difference in their appearance from their age of maturity, about forty, until around two hundred, when they go on their last pilgrimage to the Ripperthroats. It's like I say about us humans -- that indeterminate age of a bloke between 18 and 65 -- except that them xin live a darn sight longer than us humans do.

You excluded, I had to say (it's the drink talking), but Van either didn't hear me or ignored my comment.

Do you know the old poem? Said Van, looking at me quizzically (he had heard my comment, I saw, and he'd chosen to ignore it), picking up his pint and quaffing enthusiastically.

Old poem? I rifled through my mind for which one he might mean, there are several. The story of the Dun?

That's the one.

Yes, back in the way back then, it was known as the dark river and there's a rhyme about human sacrifices being offered to it:

The shelving, slimy river Dun,
Each year a daughter or a son.

Yep, said Van, but not just human sacrifice. Tha'd think that we humans and the xin had little in common, but that dark river, that's a shared experience. They think of it the way that we do. But tha knows, only about one xin in a thousand dies of sickness or disease, and maybe about twenty take the voluntary pilgrimage. The other 979 die in duels, or hunting, or fighting wars -- but the biggest loss is in childhood, when many of them youngsters become victims of the murk -- and whatever exists in there.

Tha knows Pip, them xin have remarkable skill in caring and surgery and are reyt good at healing 'emselves -- and that's a reason they consider life so lightly -- that's why they carry on the way that they do -- their dangerous sport and fighting and whatnot.

Anyway, we neared what seemed to be the village centre, and we were surrounded by hundreds of the creatures who seemed anxious to pluck me from my where I sat. A word from the leader of the party shut 'em up, and we proceeded at a trot to what seemed to be some sort of community meeting space. The building was low but covered a large area. The main entrance was several paces in width and projected from the building proper to form a straw thatched canopy. There was no stairway, but a gentle incline to the first floor of the building opened into a large space with a gallery above for those who wanted a gander.

On the floor of the chamber sat around fifty of them in front of a platform. On the platform sat one who wore bright feathers on 'is 'ead, lots of jewels in his trappings, and a cape of dull white silk lined with some greyish fur around the edge.

Ooh pretty, I said, without really thinking what I was saying.

Yes, pretty majestic, I reckon, said Van, this was the chieftain of the whole clan, it seemed to me. That cape was a similar sort of material to that dome that I had skidded over earlier, and I later found out it was woven from the silk of a cryptobite. The fur was from a grizzler.

My captor had stopped and locking his arm in mine, he marched me into the chamber. The chieftain got to his feet and spoke the name of my escort, which I now knew was Siltibog. He chattered away to the chieftain and must have explained the results of his mission, including my capture. Some question that I didn't understand was asked at me and I replied in Ing, even though I knew we couldn't understand each other; but I noticed that when I smiled slightly, Siltibog did as well. This made me think that we at least had something in common -- the ability to smile -- possibly the xin had a sense of humour after all.

Haha, get this Pip -- I was to learn very quickly!

The xin smile is a rather indifferent thing, and their laugh is not at all like ours -- those green men's ideas of humour is nowt like ours. They get their biggest kicks out of watching their fellow men die, find it wildly hilarious they do -- but then, I have often said myself, there is nothing funnier that someone else's pain.

Then Siltibog came toward me. I didn't know what he was going to do, but I wasn't long in finding out. The chieftain clearly wanted to see what I looked like behind my mask. Siltibog like a conjuror, his arms dodging left and right, distracting me, swiftly removed my psycmask, before I even had time to object or raise my own hands to stop it happening.

At this point, I gasped, and emboldened by the amount of ale consumed, I interrupted Van with a question. He paused his monologue and looked at me strangely, but directly in the eyes.

In answer to your question, he continued after a lengthy pause, nothing happened, at least not at first. They examined me closely, feeling my scrawny body and the texture of my smooth skin -- a complete contrast to their warty hide.

It was only after several moments of being subjected to this manhandling, that I then began to wheeze heavily, and fear must have shown in my eyes, so that Siltibog returned the mask to me and with some trouble due to my now extremely laboured breathing, I was able to refit the thing onto my face. That restored some energy to my legs, I were trembling like a smelting barker -- and then I did hit the ground, as my legs collapsed from under me.

I was roughly jerked to my feet again by a big fella who had laughed the most at my --

What's the word Pip?

Predicament?

Yeah, that. He banged me down on me feet and bent his face close to mine, laughing at me. He didn't scare me though, he made me blood boil and someat surged through me veins it did.

I would have to say that I'm a little embarrassed about it Pip, but I did the only thing tha might do -- I steadied myself and swung my fist squarely at his jaw. He weren't expecting that, I can tell yer -- and if truth be known, neither was I, having almost been out for the count moments earlier, but as I said, someat was triggered in me, and after that first time of the murk almost taking me, I thinks that maybe I was getting used to it.

Acclimatised? I offered.

Bless you, said Van. Hah! And this one, he went down like a sack of spuds. I wheeled around with my back toward the nearest wall, expecting to be attacked by the rest of 'em -- and I was going to give them a good feight, I was, even though I knew the odds weren't in my favour and I knew I'd get a reyt pummelling.

It never happened though, the other xin, they was struck dumb with amazement, and they all started laughing raucous like and clapping they were. I didn't recognise it at the time, but later, when I had become acquainted with the xin's customs, I learned that I had won a minor victory, and a little bit of their approval.

Siltibog and the chief exchanged a few words, and the former, calling to a young lass, gave her some instructions and motioned me to go with her. I grasped her arm for support, since my legs were still a bit wobbly, and together we crossed toward a shack on the far side of the village square.

This lass was around three and a half foot tall, not yet her full height. She was of a light olive-green color, with a warty, dull hide. Her name, I learned later, was Fenimoss, and she was part of Siltibog's extended family. She took me to a small room in the shack looking out onto the village green. There was sackcloth and fur all over the floor, and it looked like a few of 'em slept there.

Fenimoss indicated that I should sit upon a pile of sacks near the centre of the room, and then made an odd hissing sound, calling something from another room. The thing come in on its six short legs, and squatted down before her, just like a barker. It was about the size of a wooltard, but its head bore a huge pair of sharp mandibles -- jaws as sharp as razors. Fenimoss stared into its wicked looking eyes, muttered a word or two, pointed to me, and left the shack.

I expect, said Van, you can imagine what my friend Shad here, to whom he pointed with a wizened index finger, thought about that thing!

I nodded trying to understand. But, Shad's dead, I said.

At this point, that is very true, said Van. But you see, such it is that when we was out in that Wisewood and we was bound to its floor by them briars and the thorns, trussed up like animals, you could say, we became mighty close. Closer than just the physical closeness we already 'ad from bonding over our fight. This was more, this was a connection, some sort of meeting of minds, of souls maybe, if tha believes that they exist. Something happened out there, maybe it was that unknown creature in the woods, maybe it wasn't. Maybe it was something altogether more supernatural than that. I don't rightly know to be perfectly honest. All I does know, is that when Shad was killed by that spear, part of me was crushed, like part of my own soul had been ripped out.

Now Shad here, said Van, is a good and kind hearted creature, but he probably has the brains of a two year old child, human child, I might add. But deep down, or not that deep actually, he is a wild beast. Tha has to remember, it is not all that long ago in the scale of things that he was a ripperthroat, and it is only through training by us humans that barkers have become the kind hearted, obedient and loyal companions that we know them as today.

I nodded again, understanding where Van was coming from with this, but not entirely sure where he might be going, but urging him on all the same, to find out the next stage in the story.

So Shad here, just being a loyal and faithful guard to mesen he arrives in that room that night. I didn't have a clue how he'd got into that room, nor even how he'd managed to follow me back to where I'd been taken, but then barkers are renowned for their sense of smell, so back then I put it down to that. And Shad, well he goes for the throat of this wooltard size thing which the girl Fenimoss has brought into the room. Shad presumably sees it either as a threat to me, or maybe he was just hungry, I thinks at the time. Or maybe, regardless of either of those things, he is just a barker and saw something that he thought in his two year old human brain might be prey and decided that his instinct was simply too much and he had to go and take a chunk out of it. I doant know. If barkers could talk, we'd know the answer to these things, but they don't talk do they, so we're none the wiser why Shad tried to take the head off this thing.

Caught by surprise, the creature -- I later found out it is called a dyapnid -- did not put up much of a fight -- at first. It went down as if to Shad's command. But its leathery hide must have been able to withstand Shad's teeth, for after it had feigned death long enough for Shad to release his grip, the creature reared from the floor, and in a reversal of Shad's attack, clamped its mandibles onto Shad's neck and clean ripped out his throat.

It all happened so quick that all I could do was grasp poor Shad as he fell away from those razor sharp mandibles and cower in the corner over his body, as the last gasps left him -- again, as it were. The dyapnid paid no heed to my sobs, simply staring into my soul with its listless eyes. But then the murk seemed to volumise in the shack, and Shad was up again and growing larger and more shaggy, his eyes the size of saucers, the colour of the moon. He howled madly at the dyapnid, and launched himself at it, his teeth ripping into its head. The dyapnid reared up to defend itself, but then under the pressure of Shad's onrushing force, toppled onto its back, exposing its belly. Shad's rabid teeth cut fresh wounds that squirted turquoise blood.

That was when I knew Shad was a barghest -- an undead hound sent to protect me -- and when he's not doing that, get himself up to some serious haunting. I now knows we got this bond that was capable of crossing the void that lies between the planes of life and death, and Shad was just attracted back to me by this bond forged in the darkness of the Wisewood.

After that, Pip, said Van, draining what was left of another pint, my soul seemed to be restored for the better.

```
      HMM::OUT('Dyapnid')
`ask:: Rippon, Pip // stat:: accept[ok]__ // src::
2001:0db8:85a3:0000:0000:8a2e:037g:7334 [loc::hellsborough//
middlewood_road//467]__ // now:: 79.hail
ripperthroat.12.14.0.33.49`
`HMM::IN('..Colour:  Black_`

`..Diet:  Insects, vegetable matter, detritus, carrion_`

`..Size:  4"' (hand, at shoulder), 5' long_`

`..Defining characteristics:  Large mandibles, fast, denizens
of a third kind_`

`..Class:  Denizen_`

`..Image:  Incoming_    ')`
```

CHAPTER 6

Snap, sup, sleep and slips

```
    HMM::OUT('Why is this Pip Rippon character breaching the
hinge, and why so often?')
`ask:: unknown // stat:: accept[ok]__ // src::
2001:0db8:85a3:0000:0000:8a2e:142j:i618 [loc::hellsborough//
unknown__location//000]__ // now:: 79.hail
ripperthroat.12.13.20.19.27`

`HMM::IN('..Thermal imprints suggest the movement of amorphous
substance_')`

`..Frequency sporadic no linear pattern_`

`:Tell me more about this amorphous substance`

`..No data_`
```

The dyapnid lay dead on the floor, and Shad huffed at its carcass making these guttural noises. He was making me nervous 'nall, he was Pip. He stalked about impatiently. I called him over to where I was sat and put my arm around his neck, trying to calm him, but he was proper agitated an' there was no soothing him.

I never feared for my own safety with what was now a huge beast, but knew that this tremorousness --

Is that a word, Pip? Tha's the educated one, tha sort it out.

No, I don't think it is.

Anyway, his excitement, needed to be shushed, otherwise he might be minded to rampage through the camp and cause all sorts of damage, which wouldn't bode well for our future safety, I were sure of that.

Shad's anxiety quietened after a while, and I was able to have a good look about me. The floor was covered with sackcloth, silks and furs, but there was no furniture or owt like that. A picture hung skewly on the wall opposite me, it felt completely out of place, as if it had been taken from somewhere else -- maybe it were a spoil of war; this was the only example of any art I had seen since I'd been brought to -- what I now realised, was my prison.

I know what tha's thinking, Pip -- I've only been here a few hours, how could I make such a rash statement. But I tells thee why, Pip -- if tha was in the presence of this warlike race, tha'd have thought the same. Tha just knows when someat ain't reyt, and this piece of art, slung casually from the wall of a ramshackle shed, were out of place.

I'm not saying that there is no xin with an artistic bent, because maybe there may have been one of them in all those fierce warriors -- later, I thought that maybe Fenimoss could have had the sensitivity to paint something so beautiful, but she was still young, so that thought never entered me 'ead then. No, this piece of art, was definitely not xin, it was alien.

I continued to look at that picture for clues as to my whereabouts -- mountain and hill, river and lake, moor and marsh, the deep foreboding sky of The Dark Peak.

Fenimoss come back with what I assumed was snap and summat to sup. She put 'em on t'floor, and sitting down a little way off, looked on as I took a gander at what she'd brought. I was hungry and thirsty, but not being used to solid food, and unsure how to eat it -- I had always taken my food via the psycmask's feeding pipes -- I took a little while to figure out what was what, despite the hunger crawling about me stomach.

There was an hefty lump of some solid substance -- that I'd now know as cheese. It were almost tasteless. The liquid was apparently milk from some animal, which was more familiar to me, it being a liquid. It was not unpleasant to the taste, slightly salty, and I learnt to prize it, it filled me and took away them pains of 'unger. Both products come, I later found out, from the females of those winged xin steeds, the mentiloths.

At this point, I felt I needed to stop and ask a question, something from Van's story was playing on my mind and I just couldn't let him continue without asking:

Was Fenimoss not concerned by the dead dyapnid?

Van answered quickly.

It's the strangest thing, that, he said. The xin have this ability to ignore and not even notice death. It's just not something that ever comes onto their radar. They're a focused race -- and as I've said already: Warlike and bent on destruction, and to them, death is cheap -- or at least the price of life for the xin is very little. So she entered that room, looked at the dead creature -- she didn't see Shad at all -- and saying nothing, nothing at all, just accepted the fact that the dyapnid was no longer on guard and was, well, dead, and offered me the food. Not once did she ask me what had happened or why, she just carried on as if nothing had happened at all.

Can I carry on? Asked Van. I indicated for him to continue.

After I had eaten I felt a darn sight better, but I needed to rest, I were shattered. I stretched out on the sacks and fell asleep.

I must have slept for ages, but when I woke up, I was freezing -- them nights in The Dark Peak are reyt cold and I was proper nesh. I noticed that someone had thrown a fur over me, but it had fallen off and in the darkness I couldn't see to put it back. A hand reached out and pulled the fur over me, then stuck another on me.

I presumed that my watchful guardian was Fenimoss, and I weren't wrong. This girl alone, among all the green xin who I'd come in contact with, showed sympathy, kindliness, and affection unlike any of her race; her care for me was reyt proper, and she saved me from much hardship.

The xin are a nomadic race and doant go in much for schooling or owt like that, a bit like me really -- they tend to live off their wits most of the time. Because of that, they only have crude lighting; relying on torches and candles -- they can render them from the fat of their animals -- but they doant use 'em that much as they're not easy to make, so they hardly ever bother. Them xin, their only thought is for today, and they'd rather go to war for what they need, rather than do any manual labour. That's what's kept them in their semi-barbaric state -- they're not lazy as such, they just doant want to do nowt but fight.

After Fenimoss had covered me up again, I slept, not waking until the weak morning light began to melt into the room. I could now see other shapes in there -- five female xin, all still sleeping, piled high with sackcloth and furs.

I'm an adventurer, you know that, I can't help mesen, and I has to investigate and experiment where wiser folk would do well to leave alone. I just can't seem to help myself exploring an alley or ginnel and taking the pathway less trod to see where it goes. In the same way that I pour over maps, I has a need to picture where I am, so I know what leads to where and what connects with elsewhere.

```
      HMM::IN('Background music: Uplifting and adventurous
tune.  Aerial video, moorlands, rolling hills of The Dark
Peak')
`hits:: 49 // [this]2001:0db8:85a3:0000:0000:8a2e:037g:7334
[loc::hellsborough//middlewood_road//467]__ // now:: 79.hail
```

VAN HALLAM

ripperthroat.12.14.0.54.11`

`Escape to a land shrouded in mystery, where rugged beauty and untamed wilderness collide.`

`Image: Hikers on scenic trail.. waterfall.. wildlife..`

`Welcome to The Dark Peak, for nature lovers and adventure seekers.`

`Image: Climber on rocky peak.. cyclists..`

`Unwind and indulge   where comfort meets nature.`

`Image: Sunrise over The Dark Peak..`

`The Dark Peak. Discover the magic. Experience the adventure.`

`This was a public utility broadcast by The Dark Peak District Council.`

I decided I needed to learn about my surroundings and it would be good to get out this prison room while I had a chance, so that's just what I did -- got mesen out to see where I was and what was about. I got out to the edge of the village and scrambled up into the branches of a tall fir tree to try and get me bearings.

I hardly got above the murk when a xin warrior sitting high on his mentiloth jabbed his spear at me. Shad, launched himself into the air and took a chunk out of the mentiloth's undercarriage. That frightened the thing and it bucked wildly, not unseating its rider, but unsettling him enough so that his spear was no longer on target.

But that mentiloth's wing hit the branch where I stood, and that was enough of a jolt to knock me off. As luck would have it, I didn't fall into briars and thistles, but a deep pile of leaf fall, and that spared me from any broken bones. I was still battered and bruised though Pip.

It turns out that when Fenimoss had woke and found me missing, she had gone straight to Siltibog. He had raised a search party and easily found me, not that I was trying very hard to remain hidden. Fenimoss had tagged along and so now come to me, examining me body for injury. Satisfying herself that I'd survived unscathed, I saw her smile quietly to herself, and taking me hand, she led me back toward our shack.

Shad trailed behind at a distance; I'm pretty sure he'd be keeping a wary eye on them xin warriors, but I think he sensed I were ok with Fenimoss, so let me be. I found this to be the way with Shad -- he would stay away, but should I ever need him, all I would do is whisper "cam-ere" and he'd be there. That's not to say that I didn't hear of the odd story of him up to some haunting here or thereabouts in The Dark Peak, and my suspicion is that he frequently returned to the Wisewood as well as to grimy streets of Hellsborough for his own ghostly and demonic entertainment.

It was with the last story that Van drained his glass, and yawning widely, started to make his excuses for leaving. The bar was empty, save for myself, Van and Shalesmoor the bar man, and had been for quite some time, not that Shalesmoor, who was paid by the moment, minded -- he would keep the place open for as long as you wanted him to.

Van was looking decidedly grey, and knowing that we could continue his story telling tomorrow, I did not try to continue this evening -- although I hoped that we would get some more good meat for his biography then.

And so it was that we bade each other farewell, promising to return tomorrow afternoon after lunch to continue our discourse. Van headed towards his house on the corner of the crossroads, and I sleeping in digs out the back of Owlerton headed in the other direction up Middlewood road, needing to cross over Hellsborough park. A sign at the entrance to the park reminded me that wearing a psycmask was a good idea -- not that I'd dare take it off:

PSYCMASK FOR SANITY
(and this is the thing, the psycmask feeds your brain with

advertising and hivemind chatter, but is promoted as being for your sanity, since not using one might make you insane)

-- and I automatically went to adjust the way that the thing sat on my face; finding that it was sitting as snuggly as it is intended. It was dark in the park and the place surrounded by the thick suffocating murk, which made for a quiet and lonely walk, but the chance of encountering any unpleasantries was slim due to the inability to see more than a few feet ahead and the lateness of the hour. Yet I could still determine isolated pockets of chatter and the occasional laughter, which made me quicken my steps, just to be on the safe side.

I was pretty sure that I had a guardian though, because Van would have seen to it that I had. Every now and then I would hear a subtle sniff or some shuffling of leaves, but the noises never came any closer -- Shad wouldn't want to distress me unnecessarily.

```
        HMM::OUT('Barghest')
`ask:: Rippon, Pip // stat:: accept[ok]__ // src::
2001:0db8:85a3:0000:0000:8a2e:037g:7334 [loc::hellsborough//
park//467]__ // now:: 79.hail ripperthroat.12.14.1.7.23`

`HMM::IN('..Colour:   Black_`

`..Diet:   anything, but inconsequential_`

`..Size:   5"'' (hand, at shoulder), 8' long_`

`..Defining characteristics:  Barker, shapeshifter, shaggy
fur, eyes the size of saucers_`

`..Class:   Undead_ Revenant_`

`..Image:   Incoming_    ')`

        HMM::OUT('Nesh')
`ask:: Rippon, Pip // stat:: accept[ok]__ // src::
2001:0db8:85a3:0000:0000:8a2e:037g:7334 [loc::hellsborough//
park//467]__ // now:: 79.hail ripperthroat.12.14.1.7.47`

`HMM::IN('..Someone susceptible to feeling cold
temperatures_')`
```

```
      HMM::OUT('Mesen')
`ask:: Rippon, Pip // stat:: accept[ok]__ // src::
2001:0db8:85a3:0000:0000:8a2e:037g:7334 [loc::hellsborough//
park//467]__ // now:: 79.hail ripperthroat.12.14.1.7.51`

`HMM::IN('..My self_')`
```

CHAPTER 7

Enter hive

```
      HMM::OUT('Where is Pip Rippon now?')
`ask:: unknown // stat:: accept[ok]__ // src::
2001:0db8:85a3:0000:0000:8a2e:142j:i618 [loc::hellsborough//
unknown__location//000]__ // now:: 79.hail
ripperthroat.12.13.20.33.32`
```

`HMM::IN('..hellsborough//middlewood_road//467_')`

`:Describe Pip Rippon`

`..Signatures indicate average height / weight, indeterminate age, no other defining characteristics_`

`:Oh come on, that's not much to go on    boy / girl / man / woman?`

`..Signatures indicate maturity, but not excessive age_ Heart pattern has similarity with Ripperthroat, but no exact match possible_`

`:Ripperthroat? You're kidding me, hallucinating right?`

`..I apologise if my assessment did not meet your expectations_`

I made it back to the guest house without incident, and the snuffles behind me faded into the distance, as Shad clearly realised that his job was done and presumably returned home to Van -- or to do a little bit of haunting on the streets of Hellsborough; probably both.

Back at the guest house my way was blocked by the clowns who had clearly decided to do an impromptu performance for some of the other guests. Pandora was amongst their number, and it did cross my mind that she might be waiting for me to return home, possibly to keep an eye on my movements, because, as I said, the currency of the clowns is information, and anyone spotted with Van might be of interest, regardless of whether what I was doing was of any importance at the time.

That got me to wondering about how she knew I would be staying at the guest house. I could quite as easily have stayed with Van for the evening, he lives alone and has plenty of rooms in that old house of his. Which led my thinking onto the clowns and how they fit into The Dark Peak demographic.

Clowns are not entirely human, in fact they are not human at all: They just appear to be human. The clowns share as many similarities with the xin, the nascenti and xaexs, being denizens of The Dark Peak and hatched from eggs, rather than born in utero, as we humans are.

Similar to the rest of the denizens they are able to breathe unaided in the murk, as well as being linked into the hivemind, as all those in The Deak Peak are, which led me to thinking about the psycmask. Of course, that would be how Pandora knew that I was at the guest house, rather than at Van's, since, the psycmask linked me into the infotainment systems of the vast organic network and by necessity the hivemind. She would simply have picked up the information on my whereabouts from there.

This power of telepathy, this hivemind, is well developed in all of the denizens, and accounts largely for the simplicity of their language and the relatively few spoken words exchanged even in long conversations. It is the universal language of The Dark Peak, through the medium of which the higher and lower animals of this world are able to communicate to a greater or less extent, depending upon the intellectual sphere of the species and the development of the individual.

And that is the dichotomy of the psycmask; the council issue one has the infotainment services built into it, which means that your brain waves are connected to the hivemind, and you are constantly bombarded -- with images, ads, news -- propaganda, chatter -- and augmented data, or rather a view of the world that you are allowed to see -- according to your rank within the world -- your social standing. Yet, without a psycmask, breathing in Hellsborough is difficult -- and almost impossible in The Dark Peak, were you to venture out there.

Add to that, if you have the feeding attachment, the automatic delivery of nutrients designed for your health and wellbeing, and there you have the perfect way for the overlords to control the human population.

It isn't illegal not to wear one, of course, that would be far too dystopian. Which is how Van is able to wear his modified version that does nothing but aid his breathing.

Van has no need for an augmented view of the world, nor the propaganda -- the news, the infotainment, the constant chatter -- and the powers that be are fine with that. They can still monitor his whereabouts, should they want to, using the organic network. Or the clowns. Or just other inhabitants who are wearing psycmasks -- which is the majority, and why I wear one when I'm here to blend in as much as I can -- although these days, because most folk wear nanotechnology versions, which are essentially invisible, I look odd wearing a mask -- but it's not that different to the off-world after the pandemic.

The crosslanders, if you see them at all, since they tend to keep to their own areas: The ghettos and the estates on the other side of the great causeway, they'll probably forego all but the most minimal of psycmask for breathing purposes, or maybe use an alternative type of purification mask altogether, or maybe nothing at all -- in Hellsborough the griminess of the air -- the murk -- is bad, but if your lungs can cope then it's not the end of the world -- unlike in The Dark Peak proper.

Anyway, I slipped past the clown troupe and into the guest house, making straight for my room and letting myself in. By the time I got there, the slight noise from the clowns had subsided and they had gone, so maybe they were waiting for me to show myself after all. Whatever, I bade it no mind and got my head down for the night, I'd had a skin full of ale, and tomorrow was an altogether new day.

```
      HMM::OUT('Clown')
`ask:: Rippon, Pip // stat:: accept[ok]__ //
src:: 2001:0db8:85a3:0000:0000:8a2e:037g:7334
[loc::hellsborough//great_causeway//467]__ // now:: 79.hail
ripperthroat.12.14.1.29.49`

`HMM::IN('..Colour:   Patterned_ Highly colourful_`

`..Diet:   Omnivorous_`

`..Size:   3'6"    6' (feet, thumb)_`

`..Defining characteristics:  Humanoid_  Insectoid_`

`..Class:   Denizen_`

`..Image:   Incoming_    ')`
```

◆ ◆ ◆

I got to thinking, said Van when I met him the next day in the bar, last night, after we had parted, about the type of people that the xin are. In fact, said Van, I have been ruminating on it all night and throughout the contents of a bottle of my favourite brand of dark rhum, and well into this morning.

So you've not really slept then, I hazarded.

In and out, he said, in and out; I never sleep much anyway, so not really all that unusual.

VAN HALLAM

So tell me, what sort of people are they, the xin?

Tha never knows where your next meal is coming from and tha doant know what's going to happen tomorrow, this may be tha last day in The Dark Peak, so tha better make t'most of it.

Is that how they think then?

It is, and so do I, said Van, quickly closing his hand round a fly which had landed on his palm. Care to join me?

No, I'll pass.

The xin are hardy and warlike, and there's a reason for that, chewed Van. Last night I mentioned an enclosure that I were able to clamber on to avoid me death when I first arrived in The Dark Peak.

When Shad got killed the first time, yes I remember, I said.

Yes, when Shad got killed...

Where is Shad by the way?

I doant know, probably asleep in the pantry, said Van, I haven't seen him today, I suspect he got in late last night, later than us I imagine.

Anyway, that incubator contained the young hatching xin. But those eggs in the incubator, they were no part of any brood like you would get with cluckers or quackers, no, that incubator was filled with the eggs of the whole community -- think of it as like all the frog spawn from a small pond; all mingled together and then when the frogspawn emerge together, all around the same time, they're all brothers and sisters, regardless of their parents -- no-one even knows who their parents are -- and from then on, it's simply survival of the fittest.

```
    HMM::IN(' BackflitPirate: incoming')
`ask:: unknown // stat:: accept[ok]__ // src::
2001:0db8:85a3:0000:0000:ff32:8877:7b45 [loc::hellsborough//
```

```
unknown__location//000]__  //  now::  79.hail
ripperthroat.12.14.13.9.45`

   Interference and static

`Ey up, I got what you're after, it's never too early for a
slurp of slime, paste me back  BFP121413.  Sound.  Gotta go,
call me, you know it's reyt.`

   Interference and static
```

What was that?

What was what?

Some gravelly voice going on about Backflit Pirate and slurping the slime.

Aye, that'd be Delf, said Van, he's always getting in on the hivemind and pushing his wares -- did he give you a tag?

By tag, if you mean "#BFP121413", then yes.

Ok, nice one.

Van tapped his psycmask without actually doing much else -- I had no idea his psycmask was capable of anything other than acting as a breathing device, but he could clearly use it for communication as well.

That's done then, he said, with a small grin on his face. Anyway, what was I saying? Ar, that's reyt:

Each adult xin female lays around a dozen eggs each year, and those which meet the size, weight, and other tests are hidden in an underground vault, where the temperature is too low for them eggs to hatch. These eggs are then carefully examined by senior community midwives, and all but the most perfect are destroyed out of each year's supply.

Destroyed? I said, incredulous, that's barbaric.

Yeah Pip, destroyed. Eggs is protein, ain't they; like I said, survival of the fittest. And yeah, it is barbaric, and the xin are.

VAN HALLAM

At the end of five years about five hundred almost perfect eggs have been chosen from thousands of 'em. These are then placed in them almost air-tight incubators to be hatched by t'warmth of that teeny sun.

But Van -- you know what you're saying, don't you? I had to say it, I couldn't stop myself. You're saying the xin destroy their eggs, but because they're protein, they consume them?

There just ain't no love with them xin, Pip, not like it's common with us humans anyway. They've carried on for eons with this 'orrible system of theirs, and I reckon it's the reason for the loss of any higher instincts, like what we might still have -- if we really still has 'em.

```
      HMM::IN('Alert! Anti social: Youths. Fire. Refuse bin.')
`hits:: 8766749 //
[this]2001:0db8:85a3:0000:0000:8a2e:037g:7334
[loc::hellsborough//middlewood_road//467]__ // now:: 79.hail
ripperthroat.12.14.13.39.1`
```

`Hellsborough park. Exacids on route. Avoid area until further notice.`

`This was a public utility broadcast by The Dark Peak District Council.`

Remember last night when I said about that dead dyapnid that Shad dispatched, and then Fenimoss just didn't say nowt about it when she came back into the room, I'm sure you do. That's because from when they're born, they know no father or mother love, they doant know the meaning of the word home; they are taught that they are only suffered to live until they can show that they are fit to live -- by their physical strength and their ferocity. If they're deformed or defective or cack handed, they're deed meyt, crozzled -- and you know what, none of 'em sheds a tear. They are born for cruel hardship from when they's weeny, and for the rest of their lives they suffers.

I doant mean the adults are intentionally cruel to their young, but it's a struggle for existence in a cruel world, and each additional life means an added tax on the community. I mean, that's not unlike here or hereabouts in Hellsborough, but it's not as savage here as it is out there -- the nascenti value what humankind is, and knows it's an important resource to be cultured and supported, but out there in The Dark Peak, the xin, they doant have no benefactors, and that makes me sound like I'm a fan of the nascenti, but believe me Pip, I ain't, but life here is almost cushy compared to life out there.

Van is describing some fascinating stuff, which I hadn't expected. Let me get this right, I said: Basically then, the xin are, by careful selecting their hardiest specimens, practicing genetic engineering -- and -- and I'm impressing myself with my own insight -- they're regulating the birth rate to offset the loss by death.

I'm not sure what genetic engineering is, but if you say so, then you do. From the moment they is born they is heavily armed and their only education is in fighting and how to survive in The Dark Peak.

I was new to this place and needed them skills too, so I began to learn the ways of the xin and follow their teachings so that I might survive in that place. The xin language, as I have said, is reyt simple, and in a week I could make all my wants known, and understand nearly everything that was said to me. With Fenimoss as my tutor, I developed my telepathic powers so that I could sense pretty much everything that went on around me.

What surprised Fenimoss was that I could catch telepathic messages from others, when they weren't meant for me, but no one could read a jot from my head. At first this annoyed me, until, said Van with a wink, I realised it was an advantage.

OK, that's interesting, I said, jotting down a few words in my notepad as Van came to a poignant pause in this story.

What is?

The hivemind, and you being able to read the thoughts if the xin, but not visa-versa. And of course, your recently found ability to communicate with the dead, via Shad.

```
    HMM::IN('Farantees Riiide up!')
`hits:: 9978154 //
[this]2001:0db8:85a3:0000:0000:8a2e:037g:7334
[loc::hellsborough//middlewood_road//467]__ // now:: 79.hail
ripperthroat.12.14.14.1.2`
```

`Yo, listen up, I got something to say, about a ride that's gonna blow you away, introducing the freshest whip in town, our car gonna turn youz around`

`Get ready to roll, in style and grace, with this ride, you're gonna own the place, traveling in style, like youz never seen`

`Farantees Riiide up!!!!`

Ah! Well, the xin, that was a gift, and a definite advantage over them -- and, by association all the denizen races of The Dark Peak; they have their organic network and their hivemind, but if I got close enough, I could literally hear their thoughts, which come in very handy.

But our Shad 'ere, that's different. Our souls were conjoined before his demise, I won't say that the bond hasn't strengthened since though. As a kid, my "mother" had said that I possessed this gift for talking to people who weren't there. I didn't realise at the time cos I was too young, but it was the same, it was talking to dead people. That incident after Shad become a barghest, that was just this thing that had always been there, I guess.

Sometimes Pip, I wondered why this might be, but it gave me a complete advantage. I have always thought that my space lies between the living and the dead, as you maybe witness here in Hellsborough. You have surely noted that whilst I am not invisible, I am largely ignored by everyone, yet I am not insignificant.

Tell me more about some of your childhood experiences, I said, but I could tell that Van had little interest in telling those stories the way that he picked up his pint and just quaffed, as if snubbing my question. I guess he was just too young to understand such things and took them for granted, it's just the same old story about talking to imaginary friends, and didn't we all have one of them, eh?

```
      HMM::OUT('Deed meyt, crozzled')
`ask:: Rippon, Pip // stat:: accept[ok]__ // src::
2001:0db8:85a3:0000:0000:8a2e:037g:7334 [loc::hellsborough//
middlewood_road//467]__ // now:: 79.hail
ripperthroat.12.14.14.7.9`

`HMM::IN('..Dead Meat, Cooked.. Toasted_')`
```

CHAPTER 8

Long, low, and gray-green

`HMM::OUT('What pronoun is appropriate for Pip Rippon?')
`ask:: unknown // stat:: accept[ok]__ // src::
2001:0db8:85a3:0000:0000:8a2e:142j:i618 [loc::hellsborough//
unknown__location//000]__ // now:: 79.hail
ripperthroat.12.13.20.53.3`

`HMM::IN('..No data_')`

`:Symbiot pronoun?`

`..No symbiot identified for Pip Rippon_`

`:No symbiot, what none at all   we all have a familiar of
some sort here or hereabouts. That's a defining feature, or I
doant know what is.`

`.._ .._ ..Refer to previous conversation on the hinge_`

The next day I was scuffing about in the fields where the mentiloth grazed. The sun were trying to meek its way through the murk, without success, when I heard this noise that nearly melted me brain in me 'ead.

Any xin that were about were suddenly nowhere to be seen, and the animals gone without a trace.

I strained my eyes looking out over the valley, and there, edging through the murk, came this huge thing -- long, low, and gray-green -- it swung slowly over a mid-distant hill. Following it come another, and then more, until there were seven of them, all sailing towards the xin camp.

      `HMM::OUT('Long low gray green sailing thing')`
`` `ask:: Rippon, Pip // stat:: accept[ok]__ // src:: 2001:0db8:85a3:0000:0000:8a2e:037g:7334 [loc::hellsborough// middlewood_road//467]__ // now:: 79.hail ripperthroat.12.14.14.34.19` ``

`` `HMM::IN('..Based on the description you provided, it is difficult to determine exactly what you are referring to_` ``

`` `..However, based on the keywords "long", "low", and "gray green", it is possible that you are describing a submarine. Submarines are watercraft that are designed to operate underwater, and they often have a long, streamlined shape. Their coloration can vary, but some submarines may be painted in shades of gray or green to blend in with the ocean environment_` ``

`` `..If you are referring to something else or need more specific information, please provide additional details, and I'll be happy to assist you further_` ``

`` `:yeah, we're talking supermarine, not submarine.` ``

Each craft had a banner strung from one end to t'other, but I couldn't make out the writing, and if I could I wouldn't know what it meant -- could have been owt, but it weren't Ing, that's all I can tell yer.

How can I describe it better, Pip -- it was like some great gruizer up there in the air, but like maybe ten gruizers together with a big flat roof on top of 'em. There was folk crowding on the decks of this floating thing -- who they might be, I had no idea. Whether they had discovered us or were just looking at a deserted village, I didn't know, but whatever they wanted, they got a rude reception.

Without warning the xin warriors fired from the windows of the shacks facing the valley, across which these big old gruizers were now moving -- but they had been moving peacefully from what I could see.

As soon as that first sky gruizer received incoming fire, it swung toward us and brought its own guns out, the others doing the same. Each one shot on us like the first, but their incoming fire weren't good -- as the xin had first targeted the sighting equipment of their guns, making these bloats sitting quackers.

Yeah, it may have been callous Pip, but doant interrupt me until I get to the end (I hadn't said a thing!).

The xin didn't stop their shooting, and I doant reckon that a quarter of their shots went wild. I'd never seen such accuracy, and each xin shot took someone out from them enemy craft. Those banners, they dissolved in flame as them xin bullets cut through 'em.

A sluggish black worm slimed across the table. I noticed it, it made me feel queasy, I have to be honest. Van -- with some difficulty -- scraped the thing off the table and then sucked it off his fingers. And if I was feeling queasy before, I now felt doubly so.

He smiled at me with teeth covered in the creature's black slime and swallowed with difficulty, turning my stomach to the edge of vomit; I retched, dryly, luckily. Van cackled wildly and pulled a full grin.

You're heinous, I said (with a smile), feeling greener than xin skin. Van didn't answer. He didn't need to.

I learnt that day, he said, that every xin warrior has a purpose: A specific task to do, and each of 'em will do it until they can do it no more. Some of 'em, the best marksmen, direct their fire on the sighting apparatus of the big guns; others target the smaller guns; others pick off the gunners; some the officers; and others concentrate on other members of the crew -- their aim is simple, to bring the craft to a complete standstill.

Twenty long moments after it had started, the fleet departed, heading back off where it had come from. A lot of them craft were limping and hardly under control. They had stopped shooting and all their energy was on escaping. It was then that the xin warriors went up top of the shacks and just kept shooting to see 'em off.

```
      HMM::IN('Background music: Uplifting and adventurous
tune.  Aerial video, moorlands, rolling hills of The Dark
Peak')
`hits:: 7896649 //
[this]2001:0db8:85a3:0000:0000:8a2e:037g:7334
[loc::hellsborough//middlewood_road//467]__ // now:: 79.hail
ripperthroat.12.14.15.17.16`

`Escape to a land shrouded in mystery, where rugged beauty and
untamed wilderness collide.`

`Image: Hikers on scenic trail.. waterfall.. wildlife..`
      HMM::OUT('skip ad')
`ask:: Rippon, Pip // stat:: accept[ok]__ // src::
2001:0db8:85a3:0000:0000:8a2e:037g:7334 [loc::hellsborough//
middlewood_road//467]__ // now:: 79.hail
ripperthroat.12.14.15.17.18`

`HMM::IN('Welcome to the Dark Peak, for nature.._)`
```

One by one, them gruizers escaped, ducking below the crests of those nearby hills, until only one was left. It was barely moving. This craft had received the brunt of xin fire and looked like no one aboard was left alive. Slowly it swung from its course, and circled back towards the village. It was only now that the xin warriors stopped firing, realising it was on course to plough into a number of the sheds.

As the ship neared the village's edge the xin warriors rushed out, mounting their mentiloths and headed towards the sheds that the vessel seemed destined to destroy.

As the craft neared the buildings, the xin warriors swarmed on it, with their spears raised to steady it. In a few moments they had thrown out grappling hooks and it was hauled down to the ground.

Secured, the ship was searched from one end to t'other. All on board were dead, and it seemed like there was no sign of life -- until a slim figure was dragged from below deck. The creature was weak from the fighting, and from where I stood, I could see that whatever it was walked like me, on two legs instead of the two-four of the xin.

The prisoner was removed from the gruizer and then the vessel was raped of anything of use. Several carts were used to transport the booty that the piratical xin now considered theirs: Arms, ammunition, silks, furs, jewels, and a lot of stuff that I didn't recognise at all.

After the last load had been taken, the warriors fixed ropes to the craft and towed her far out into the valley. A few of them boarded the ship and doused the decks and dead bodies with some sort of fuel, then set it alight. That done, the ropes were released, and light now after the removal of the loot, the gruizer soared into the air, a blazing flapper.

The gruizer drifted off, rising high into the murkfull sky as the flames ate away the wood and lessened the craft's weight. I watched for hours, until I lost it in the distance. I still didn't know who these beings were, but I felt a sense of loss at the wanton destruction of this fine vehicle at the hands of these violent green men, and felt a strange yearning toward these unknown folk.

Later, I was with Fenimoss and Shad. We walked about the village. We neared a throng of xin, and I caught a glimpse of the prisoner from the craft, who was being roughly dragged into a nearby shack by a couple of xin females.

Now that I was closer, I saw a girl. She was about my own age, and just like the girls back home in Hellsborough. She didn't see me -- not at first. but as she was about to disappear into the building which was to be her prison she turned, and our eyes met.

I tell you Pip, I think I might have whined like a pup, uncultured boggart that I am. She were beautiful. I was close enough to see into her big brown eyes. Her head was covered in a mass of hair so blue, it was electric, and her skin was painted or tattoo'd with many curious and pretty patterns.

Like the naked xin, her clothes were skant, which I put down to the humidity of The Dark Peak. It might not be right to say so, Pip, but I was -- what's the word -- entranced. I loved her from the moment that I saw her. Van is now looking wistfully at -- well, me -- caught like a flufftail in the lamps of a gruizer.

I have been hogging his pipe whilst he's been dishing out these details, and have had a good time listening to his tales and imagining -- originally the carnage -- and now this love story unfold. Damn fascinating and fine stuff. Caught in his rapture, I pass him his pipe back. He downs the remainder of his pint and, banging his glass onto the table with his right hand, takes the pipe back, simultaneously swiping a sizeable passing moth in his left, squishing its bodice between his thumb and index finger nails, killing it instantly, and popping it perfectly into his mouth.

If the whole thing wasn't so effortless, you'd wonder how it was even possible at all.

```
      HMM::IN('Have you had a fall?  No win, no fee.')
`hits:: 1385454 //
[this]2001:0db8:85a3:0000:0000:8a2e:037g:7334
[loc::hellsborough//middlewood_road//467]__ // now:: 79.hail
ripperthroat.12.14.15.53.2`

`Are you a victim of a recent fall? Don't suffer in silence!
We're here to help you get the compensation you deserve.`

`Introducing our expert legal team that specialises in
personal injury claims for falls. With our "No Win, No Fee"
guarantee, you have nothing to lose and everything to gain.`

`Contact us now for a free, no obligation consultation. Our
```

dedicated team is ready to listen, evaluate your situation, and guide you towards the compensation you deserve. Remember, with our "No Win, No Fee" guarantee, you have nothing to lose!

I remember this vividly, he said. Her gaze rested on me and her eyes were wide open in astonishment.

She made a little sign with her free hand -- but I didn't understand it. Just a moment we gazed at each other -- then the look of hope in her face as she discovered me, faded into one of utter dejection. Even hatred I reckon. I realised I had not done the right thing straight way. I had not answered her signal. I was ignorant of The Dark Peak's customs and somehow Pip, I'd mucked up like a murkmoon gnawtard.

She'd appealed to me for protection, but in my ignorance I'd failed to answer.

She was dragged off then, out of my sight. Something inside of me felt crushed and deflated.

But you'd seen a clown before, right Van? I said. I mean, she was a clown, right?

She was, and back then, not so much, said Van. I grew up in Hellsborough and clowns were occasionally about, but they weren't as desperate as they are now. Tha didn't converse with them, they were mainly merchants back in the day, not the entertainers that they are now. I know now how I should have responded though, but at the time her hand signal meant nothing to me, and completely caught me out.

What should you have done? I said, since, like Van I've seen many a clown, but am not familiar with the ways of them.

What I should have done is responded to her hand signal with the same hand signal. I should have given her the finger. The giving of the finger is the common clown greeting of friendship, and much used as a tool of love.

Had I known this I would have given her the finger instantly, but I didn't know clownish ways and so I did nothing, and she took that -- at the time -- as me being unfriendly. I wish now that I had given her the finger back then. It would have given her hope. Shown her that a friend -- and fellow captive -- was with her, and I was not what I appeared -- to be in with the xin, which back then, I wasn't at all.

But that is all history. Needless to say, it took me a long time to overcome it.

```
      HMM::IN('Call 333 555 333555 333 555, ask for Penny,
Pandora...')
`hits:: 155432 //
[this]2001:0db8:85a3:0000:0000:8a2e:037g:7334
[loc::hellsborough//middlewood_road//467]__ // now:: 79.hail
ripperthroat.12.14.16.0.3`

`..Pietr, Piers, Ptol or Pal..`

      HMM::OUT('skip ad')
`ask:: Rippon, Pip // stat:: accept[ok]__ // src::
2001:0db8:85a3:0000:0000:8a2e:037g:7334 [loc::hellsborough//
middlewood_road//467]__ // now:: 79.hail
ripperthroat.12.14.16.0.5`

`HMM::IN('Any package, any place.._)`
```

Lolling back in this chair, Van sighed and picked up his pint, which had been recharged in the meantime. He took a great heave -- as if trying to expunge his memory of the event. He readily snapped up a large passing bluebottle from the ether.

Blood hungry, said Van, hardly eaten a morsel since I saw you last night, but then I'm not in eating mode right now anyway.

Food is interesting in Hellsborough; you have a few options. You've got the pscymask for a start, which, if you use the feeding attachment -- because it's part of your work, or that's just the way you want to live, then that'll keep you fed and nourished no problem at all, and no need for anything else, unless you want it. Of course, your selection is always going to be determined by your social score as governed by the organic network, but to most, there is the usual mix of food vendors -- sandwiches, Indian food, Italian, Chinese, Mexican, Thai, French, Spanish, Turkish -- you name it, everything you'd expect to find in a city -- some bars serve a selection of the same. Why would you think anything differently?

Or, of course, if credits are shorter in supply, you can buy your food from a market and take it home and prepare and cook it yourself. All you need is a recipe, time and a source of heat. How hard can that be? And then there's the Van option, fresh as it comes, but that's not something that appeals to me right now.

Van cups one hand around a cockroach that is scuttling across our table, and with the other pounds it with his fist. The critter barely stops in its tracks, only slightly dazed, until Van stabs a long index fingernail into the gap between its abdomen and thorax, cutting it in half and separating its brain from its legs.

Starving, he said, through a mouthful of squirming legs.

```
      HMM::IN('Indulge in Exquisite Tapas Delights at
Hellsborough's Finest Restaurant!')
`hits:: 731243 //
[this]2001:0db8:85a3:0000:0000:8a2e:037g:7334
[loc::hellsborough//middlewood_road//467]__ // now:: 79.hail
ripperthroat.12.14.16.13.2`
```

`Looking for an unforgettable culinary experience? Look no further! Discover the best tapas restaurant in town, where flavours come alive and every bite is a delight.`

`Welcome to Farantees Espanyol, where we invite you on a tantalising journey through the vibrant world of tapas cuisine.`

`Taste the Magic of Tapas at Farantees Espanyol  Where Every Dish is a Work of Art!`

CHAPTER 9

Why not visit The Dark Peak?

```
    HMM::OUT('Tell Pip Rippon I'd like to meet')
`ask:: unknown // stat:: accept[ok]__ // src::
2001:0db8:85a3:0000:0000:8a2e:142j:i618 [loc::hellsborough//
unknown__location//000]__ // now:: 79.hail
ripperthroat.12.14.16.13.3`

`HMM::IN('..Request made_')`
```

D'divi! That is rooter-smelt Pip! It stinks like a dead grizzler you sun!

Van had just in and exhaled on his pipe with a fresh blend I had brought in from the off-world.

He belched with satisfaction after both ingesting the heady infusion and finishing off the second half of the cockroach.

Again we weren't the only folk in this bar on the Middlewood Road. Shalesmoor wasn't working yet, too early for him, he'd be back in later, I'd guess. But strewn here and about were numerous tables of people chatting and socialising, despite it only being mid-afternoon; I had no doubt that the place would only increase in capacity as the time drudged on towards the evening, but for now, the hum of the place was satisfying and Van had so far resisted the temptation to get out his cribbage kit and was more than happy to talk about his experiences in The

Dark Peak, which is all fodder for my research.

As I came back to mesen I glanced over at Fenimoss, said Van, catching me by surprise as he went back into his memoirs from the previous night. She had witnessed my failure to give the finger to the clown and I noted a strange expression upon her face.

```
    HMM::IN('DM')
`hits:: 1 // [this]2001:0db8:85a3:0000:0000:8a2e:037g:7334
[loc::hellsborough//middlewood_road//467]__ // now:: 79.hail
ripperthroat.12.14.16.13.8`

`From unknown, hellsborough//unknown__location//000`

`Hi Pip Rippon, this is unknown//unknown__location, I'd like
to meet`

    HMM::OUT('delete, flag as scum')
`ask:: Rippon, Pip // stat:: accept[decline]__ //
src:: 2001:0db8:85a3:0000:0000:8a2e:037g:7334
[loc::hellsborough//middlewood_road//467]__ // now:: 79.hail
ripperthroat.12.14.16.13.9`
```

She knew, I reckon, that I had made a mistake in not returning that clownish gesture.

As we reached the doorway of our shack, a warrior approached bearing arms, ornaments, and other xin stuff. He presented them to me with a few words -- garbled and unintelligible they were -- but he was somehow respectful and menacing at the same time. But from now on I realised, I'd be dressed in the garb of the xin.

Only trouble was, you could see my you know, woo-hoo, says van with a whistle. Dangling about in the breeze I was.

Don't the xin dangle about then, I said; because I haven't ever met one, and I only know what they look like from Van's descriptions.

No, their genitals are internal most of the time, he explained, unlike us humans. Which when you think about it, is pretty sensible. I mean they're a warlike race, and the two most vulnerable places on the body when you're fighting are the brain and the genitals. The brain is encased in a skull for both of us races. But the genitals, us humans have them waggling about, whilst the xin tuck 'em up inside -- makes sense to me. Why evolution didn't do the same for us primates, I ain't no clue.

Anyway, continued Van, after scanning the room with what might have been an embarrassed hue -- yet I doubted Van could ever be embarrassed of anything or ever regret a single moment of his long life -- from then on Fenimoss taught me the ways of the xin -- the mysterious operation of their many weapons, and with the younger xin, I spent several hours a day practicing in the village square.

It took me a while to get proficient with all of them tools of warfare, but a life feighting on the streets of Hellsborough had made me an apt pupil, so I progressed well.

Me training and that of the young xin was done only by the women, and we only learned about the arts of war: Defence and offence.

And they were thorough in their training, because they are the artisans who make everything used by the xin when they need to feight. They make the powder, the cartridges, the firearms; everything of value is produced by the xin women. In time of actual warfare, they are the reserves, and when needed, they feight with more intelligence and ferocity than the men do.

The men are trained more in strategy, in the art of war; of manoeuvring large numbers of troops and that sort of thing -- methods of attack and what to do with resources and what-not.

Outside of feighting, there ain't much for the xin. They make up laws as they're needed; a new law for each new emergency. They're not bothered about what happened earlier when dishing out justice. Customs have been handed down over the ages, but punishment for ignoring some custom or rite is for individual treatment by a jury of the culprit's peers, and justice is usually severe.

As Van had previously exclaimed, the bar did now stink like a dead grizzler, as he took another long slug on his pipe and exhaled fully, passing it over to me. I thought about declining, but didn't out of politeness, and realising that we were now onto something of a roll, and who knew when this ride was going to end, inhaled fully myself, letting the hazy feel infect my mind and limbs. Both of our tankards were dry, so I dopily signalled to the bar for re-fills, and Shalesmoor, now on duty, duly obliged.

I didn't see her again for several days after that, continued Van. And then it was only a fleeting glimpse: She was being moved to the central audience chamber, probably to see the xin chieftain. The xin treated her harshly, brutally, it angered me. And it was so different to the way Fenimoss treated me; I had realised for some time that Fenimoss was different to the others, but seeing the clown pushed and pulled about made it sink in all the more.

I'd noticed on the two occasions when I had seen the prisoner that she talked with her guards, and this convinced me that they spoke, or at least could make themselves understood by a common language. With this added incentive I grizzled away at Fenimoss to make my education happen faster, and within a few more days I had mastered the xin tongue well enough so I could carry on a passable conversation and understand most of what I heard.

```
      HMM::IN('DPDC Alert: Report of bin fire on Hellsborough
Park')
`hits:: 347836 //
[this]2001:0db8:85a3:0000:0000:8a2e:037g:7334
[loc::hellsborough//middlewood_road//467]__ // now:: 79.hail
ripperthroat.12.14.16.15.42`
```

`Bin fire reported adjacent to duck pond.  Avoid area.`

In our sleeping quarters there were usually three or four females and a couple of the recently hatched young, as well as Fenimoss, myself, and Shad. After turning in for the night it was usual for the adults to chat for a bit before going to sleep -- and now that I understood their language a bit, I was keen on listening in, although I never spoke up mesen.

Did that not seem a bit odd to you? I stopped Van with a question; I was feeling quite heady and journalistic.

Odd, what? Said Van.

The sleeping arrangements.

Nah, doant be daft. You're thinking about me having me wicked way with them or someat. That were never gonna 'appen, you ain't seen one of them, have you?

Before we started talking yesterday, I hadn't even heard of them, I confirmed.

Van now opened his cribbage kit and slipping the cards from their packet into his hand searched through them until he came to the one he wanted, the queen of hearts. Here, he said, passing it to me, imagine that is green, that's a xin.

I took the card and studied it. As Van had previously described the xin were not pretty, at least not to us humans, I took his point, nodding with a grimace.

Besides, Van added, if I had ever touched one of them -- sexually or otherwise, and accidentally or with some perverted purpose -- they're all, as I said, accomplished feighters in their own reyt, and they would have killed me there and then. I have no doubt about that.

Are you finished with your little fantasy? Said Van, you're as daft as a brush for thinking that. Are you paying attention now, can I go on -- this is why this is taking so long, you and you're little diversions and fantasies.

I have to say, I was a little hurt by that, I didn't think I was holding up this process of documenting Van's stories, but then I realised I was dealing with a diva, and let it go. Always best to stay professional and move on, even when mildly stoned.

So on he went: On the night following the clown's visit to the xin chief, the chat finally came to that -- and I was all lugs. I hadn't raised any questions to Fenimoss, as I remembered her odd face from when I first saw the prisoner, when I failed to give her the finger.

I dunno, maybe now I thought it might have been Fentimoss being jealous, but more likely it was just her indifference, or then again she might have been concerned about my welfare, I doant know, could have been owt really.

Gorsithorn, the eldest women -- I guessed -- who shared our shed, had been in the audience as one of the captive clown's guards, and it was toward her that the questions were asked.

When will we enjoy the death throes of the clown? or does our chieftain, intend holding her for ransom? Asked one of the women.

They have decided to keep her with us in Stanningxin, and exhibit her at the games in the swamp, said Gorsithorn.

What will be the manner of her going out? inquired Fenimoss. She is very small; I had hoped that they would hold her for ransom.

Gorsithorn and the others grunted, angry like.

You are weak, grow up, said Gorsithorn. You want to be careful that Siltibog doesn't learn that you have such degenerate sentiments, as I doubt that he would care to entrust such as you with the responsibilities of motherhood.

Van took another long suck on this pipe, priming himself, or so it seemed. A june bug -- or at least that's what it would be called in the off-world -- scuttled past his peg board. Strangely, he let it go on its way, just curling his top lip lavishly, a want in his eyes, but obviously no hunger to satiate.

```
     HMM::IN('DPDC Alert: Report of murker running amok,
Hellsborough park')
`hits:: 1226354 //
[this]2001:0db8:85a3:0000:0000:8a2e:037g:7334
[loc::hellsborough//middlewood_road//467]__ // now:: 79.hail
ripperthroat.12.14.17.42.3`

`Exacid alerted.  Two people stabbed, stable.  Report of
gunshots.  Avoid area until further notice.`
```

Van exhaled, pouring voluminous clouds of smoke into the room and readying himself for something clearly important. The look on his face and his intense gaze made me realise that what he was about to say was pivotal somehow. He paused and took another great heave of clammy air, inflating his chest before continuing:

This is reyt important I reckon, Pip. Because after that, Fenimoss was quiet for a few short moments, but then she spewed a load of abuse at them other women in the room. I was shocked, I was. I thought someat bad was going to happen reyt then, such was the look on them other women's faces.

What did she say?

I can't remember it word for word, said Van, it were a long time ago now and me mind is fuzzy on the details, but I reckon I can still summarise it ok. She said stuff like she didn't see owt wrong with having an interest in the clown woman, and that she had never harmed the xin, or would she were they t'fall into her hands. She said that the only reason that the xin hated her was because of the men clowns who fought against the xin, and the only reason that they did feight against the xin was because the xin were a warlike race who are interested in nowt but feighting for feighting's sake.

She ended up on something quite poignant, and so I still remember what she said to this day, since it got to my core in that moment, she said: Life is awful -- it is bloodshed from when they break the shell until they take their trip to the ripperthroats.

Yes, poignant, you're right.

Aye, but she weren't done yet: Those of us who meet an early death are spared, she said, so, Gorsithorn, say what you want to Siltibog, he can do no worse for me than this horrible existence.

Her outburst surprised the other women so much that after a few grumbles, they all went silent and were soon asleep.

Van was now pensive and shuffled his cards, dealing them in front of himself onto the table, but with no real intent or focus. His glass was empty again, so I went to the bar myself to order re-fills, but I was lagging behind already, so stacked it against the first. When I returned to our table, with freshly charged glasses, Van was engrossed in a game of crib with himself, and so I just sat and watched him play, and took in the atmosphere of the place.

Over by the door, the clown Pandora was sat, today by herself. I wasn't sure when she'd come in, presumably during Van's last monologue. She was looking directly at me, but I couldn't decide whether she was actually looking at me or just looking in my direction, since she was just staring. Maybe she wasn't looking at me at all. Maybe she was just staring into space and in her own clownish dreamworld. Today, she was wearing a wide brimmed black hat, with her blue hair tied up into a bun beneath it, and almost entirely covered. Her leggings were pink with wide black stripes, and a dark grey baggy jumper mostly covered a bright orange blouse. She retained the same black military style boots that she had been wearing yesterday, with the same vibrant fluorescent green socks poking out of the top. I wondered whether they were a clean pair. She doesn't look like she's eaten since I last saw her, she's still all skin and bones.

The bar serve brings a drink over to her table, even though she hasn't been to the bar, so I am assuming that she ordered it via the hivemind. I can't really see what it is, some sort of cocktail by the looks of it.

```
     HMM::IN('Background music: Uplifting and adventurous
tune.  Aerial video, moorlands, rolling hills of The Dark
Peak')
`hits:: 7896649 //
[this]2001:0db8:85a3:0000:0000:8a2e:037g:7334
[loc::hellsborough//middlewood_road//467]__ // now:: 79.hail
ripperthroat.12.14.18.13.19`

`Escape to a land shrouded in mystery, where rugged beauty and
untamed wilderness collide.`

     HMM::OUT('skip ad')
`ask:: Rippon, Pip // stat:: accept[ok]__ // src::
2001:0db8:85a3:0000:0000:8a2e:037g:7334 [loc::hellsborough//
middlewood_road//467]__ // now:: 79.hail
ripperthroat.12.14.18.13.20`
```

Forget that advertisement, The Dark Peak is a dangerous place, at least so I am led to believe. But the nascenti overlords are obviously keen to share the impression that it is something of a leisure space for their unsuspecting human slaves to enjoy, despite the risks. Maybe they're correct, I suspect they have it pretty well segregated so that if you were to visit the Winnats Pass or the Ladybower lake, or you were to hike up Kinder Scout or run along Stanage Edge, you would not see a single xin or dyapnid, or any other of the warlike denizens that live out there. They will have had some fenced off reserves constructed, I'm sure, just to provide some semblance of normality -- but rest assured, should you cross the fence, or wander off the track well trod, you would be taking your life into your hands. Should you not return to Hellsborough, would you be missed? Likely not.

The Dark Peak isn't just the preserve of the various insectoid hybrid races that live there, you also have several cryptids of renown -- monsters that have, at certain times been reported and their existence suspected: The Don Bog Beast, the Loxley Kraken, and more. And I'll not even detail the revenants that haunt the moors: The murk wraith, as they are known.

I wonder again that if you didn't return to Hellsborough, whether you'd be missed? Your existence, even to members of your family would simply be erased. You would have memories of a person, there's no doubt about that. A psycmask cannot remove your memory, yet you'll not be able to talk to them on the hivemind, all memory or evidence that they ever existed would be removed, and you'll eventually forget about them. Out of sight, out of mind, as easy as that.

This hivemind I keep talking about. You might be wondering why clowns -- who, as I have said appear human in every way -- have access to the hivemind. It's more than that. You'll never see a clown wearing a psycmask neither, they don't need them. The clowns are human-insectoid hybrids. Hatched from eggs in deep caverns beneath The Dark Peak, the clowns look as human as you or I yet they are able to breath in The Dark Peak unaided, and they can tap into the hivemind naturally. Their make-up -- what appears to be face and body paint, is part of their genetics -- it is their skin, patterning from their insect heritage, not a painted veneer.

One can only hazard a guess as to why they lost their additional appendages, which the xin and the xaexs and all of the other denizens of The Dark Peak retain, but presumably, back in the dim and distant past, they were things that just evolved out of existence, like you and I lost our prehensile tails.

Van played out his cribbage hand and slurped his ale, then continued his story:

One thing about all that before sleep talk, was to assure me of Fenimoss's friendliness toward the clown girl. It convinced me as well that I'd been reyt lucky to fall into her hands -- rather than them other female xin. She weren't like the rest of 'em -- cruel and barbaric -- I reckoned then I could depend upon her, and that me and the clown could escape.

I didn't even know that there were any better conditions to escape to, but I was willing to take my chances among people shaped like me, than to stay with this lot of bloodthirsty toad-folk.

CHAPTER 10

Rockcrust

      HMM::OUT('Pip Rippon hasn't replied, say I'd like to meet again')
`ask:: unknown // stat:: accept[ok]__ // src:: 2001:0db8:85a3:0000:0000:8a2e:142j:i618 [loc::hellsborough// unknown__location//000]__ // now:: 79.hail ripperthroat.12.14.18.22.2`

`HMM::IN('..Request made_')`

`..Direct Message rejected_`

`:Why rejected?`

`..Flagged as scum_`

You with me, Pip? Said Van.

I think that the early drinking and smoking had sent me into some sort of reverie. Yeah, yeah, I'm here, I said, recovering my mind from its current trajectory -- I was somewhere out there, adventuring in my own thoughts; I'm not sure whether I was in The Dark Peak or back in the off-world -- maybe I was lost in The Hinge, I dunno, anyway, I'm back now in the land of the living, in reality, or at least I can focus.

Time for a little crust, ain't it? Said Van.

I paused slightly, deciphering what he had said. Crust. Van

wants us to take rockcrust at -- what is it -- three in the afternoon. The man is insane, surely. No, I faltered, Van, it's too early, I have my job to do.

Jobs, snobs, said Van. Come on Pip, it's time for you to slurp the slime, time for you to be one with Dunlockslyn -- tha's traversed The Hinge, what, how many times?

Maybe twenty now, I said.

Yeah, twenty, maybe thirty, tha's met the murk and the scerm and tha knows what tha's doing -- so come on, there's no time like the present -- and get this, it'll help thee do tha job better, I promise!

I wasn't sure. From what Van had said previously, I wasn't sure whether my frail mind could take it -- maybe it would send me mad. Maybe I'd never recover, maybe I'd never wake up from a comatose state that it put me into, and I'd be forever trapped in Hellsborough, forever condemned within the maze of my own mind, going around and around and around: A proper jellyhead.

It won't be like that, said Van, interpreting my frown, presumably -- he doesn't have any other way of reading my thoughts, does he?

I'm not paranoid. It'll be fine. What am I saying?! This decision is the product of a diseased mind, I'm sure, I've been in this place for too long, I've been in Van's company for too long, the man has infected me with his talk and the access to some of his innermost thoughts.

Yeah! And I haven't even started yet, Pip.

He's done it again. It must have been the furrow on my brow.

It was, said Van, it was that deep furrow, right above them pretty eyes.

His tongue is a bit too sticky-outy and wiggly-waggly.

Now I don't know where I am or what I'm doing. I'm in a state of panic. My brain is telling me: No! My mind is telling me that it will all be fine.

Van has hydrated some rockcrust on the table in front of me. It squirms and undulates in front of my eyes.

Where did you get it from, I managed to stammer.

Last night, from Dirty Leaves of course, said Van, I bumped into her again after thee and me had parted. In fact, she is one of the reasons I didn't sleep much, or at all, thinking about it, last night; she came around to my place and we chewed the fat and other stuff about the old times. Got her right messed up, I did, she wasn't fit for anything after that -- mind you, neither was I, we both crashed in my living room all night. That's what you get for burning the candle at both ends. Dirty old Dirty Leaves, eh? D'divi bless her! Hah! She's lovely ain't she?! Yer ain't jealous is tha Pip?!

Van has already slurped half of the slime straight up his right nostril and is holding the same straw outstretched towards me, beckoning me forwards to do the same, which ever so slightly disgusts me.

Sensing that disgust, Van rotates the straw 180 degrees, so that the slimy rockcrust end is now the bit that I feel myself inserting into my nostril. I'm not sure I want to do this.

It's fine Pip, don't worry about it. Once tha's there, thee'll thank me.

I'm not sure about that I think to myself -- but as Van seems to be able to read my thoughts, then maybe I said it to both of us, but on this occasion, he doesn't say anything in response.

I aimed the straw towards the slime, but I didn't inhale, just hovered over it, still unsure of my intention. But that is the thing with rockcrust -- *it* is sure of your intention, whether you are or not -- and without any inward breath, the slime slid smoothly up the centre of the straw, into my nose, and up my olfactory canal.

I wanted to gag, or maybe to sneeze, but I did neither and in fact, despite my initial reservations, it was painless and beautiful. I slumped back in my chair, my arms outstretched palms upwards on the table.

See, said Van, without moving his lips. I told thee tha'd enjoy it. Now, pay attention, I'm gonna start rattling through this, and don't worry about taking notes, you ain't gonna forget a thing, trust me -- it's gonna go straight into your 'ead, it's like tha'll be there as I tell me tale, like tha's watching the 'ole thing. Oh, and that clown over there...

Pandora, I said, feeling myself slur a little, but without moving my lips.

Aye, her, Pandora. She's not who she seems, or maybe she is, but we'll get to that soon enough I think, anyway thee, listen up, I'm getting to the good bits:

Fenimoss had told me that as long as I didn't try and leave t'village, I could come and go as I pleased. She warned me to be armed, but other than that, I had a long leash, I was trusted to do what I wanted, as long as I didn't leave Stanningxin.

On this morning I had chosen a new lane to explore when I found myself at the gates of the village. Before me were low hills and narrow ravines. I desperately wanted to explore the landscape before me and the summits beyond that. My walk to the hills was just a few minutes, and I found nothing of particular interest. The wild flowers were brilliantly coloured and dotted the ravines and from the summit of the first hill I saw still more hills stretching off toward the north and west, and rising, one range above another, until me eyes were lost in t'mountains.

I now knew why I were free, and a prisoner n'all. I decided it would be sensible to not leave the village again until I was ready to leave for good, as any attempt at that, if I weren't prepared, would lead to no good.

When I come back to the village I saw the captive clown again. She were standing with her guards in front of the entrance to the audience chamber, and as I got near she turned her back on me; she were reyt haughty she was. That stung my pride, it did Pip.

Pip? You ok, you still with me?

That back turning though, it was good to know that someone else in this xin village beside myself had some civilised instincts. Had a xin woman wanted to show contempt, she'd just have stabbed me or shot me.

Fenimoss, would be the exception of course; I never saw her perform a cruel act, she was always of good nature. One day, Pip, I'd find out why that was, but I'll come to that in a bit.

I hung around to watch what was going on, and didn't have to wait long. The chieftain and his crowd approached the building and the guards followed with their prisoner into the audience chamber. As I had the freedom of the village and my knowledge of the xin language was now pretty decent -- as well as practical use of understanding them without any words at all -- I chanced at following them in, so I could listen to what might be going off.

The council squatted -- as they do -- on the steps of the --

What do you call it Pip? It's like a stage, but it's more official than that, what do you call it?

My mind was whirling as I grasped for a few words that might help Van continue with his oration -- a dais, I said -- a pulpit -- a rostrum?

That's it -- a rostrum. Anyway, them xin squatted there on that rostrum, and their prisoner stood there in front of them with her guards. There were two of them, one of 'em was Gorsithorn. I now understood how she knew what she knew -- the details of what she had told the folk in our shack last neet.

Her attitude toward the captive were harsh, she were reyt brutal. When she held her, she sunk her nails into her flesh or twisted her arm. When she needed to move her from one place to another, she jerked her about or pushed her headlong before her. The other woman was less cruel, but totally indifferent; if the prisoner had been left to her alone, and luckily she was at night, she received no harsh treatment, but no attention at all, she were totally ignored and abandoned.

```
      HMM::IN('Farantees Riiide up!')
`hits:: 9978154 //
[this]2001:0db8:85a3:0000:0000:8a2e:037g:7334
[loc::hellsborough//middlewood_road//467]__ // now:: 79.hail
ripperthroat.12.14.19.14.7`

`Yo..`
```

Hah what happened there then? It stopped. Thing is, I didn't say anything, I did that with my mind... I willed it to stop, and it did -- maybe I'm somehow tuning into this hivemind thing. How is that possible? Is it the rockcrust maybe? Ah-ha, maybe this is what Van meant when he said I needed to find a way to stop them targeting me, a way to put it off the scent.

Job done then Van, no more distractions. He nodded knowingly and winked. Told you fella, he said without moving his lips, like he'd filled my consciousness with his other-worldly-worldliness: Told yer it'd make yer go blind otherwise young'en.

I'm not blind -- I grok Van! I howled like a ripperthoat, like a murker.

Van smiled. It was a coy smile, he knew; even if the rest of the folk in the bar staring in dis-comprehension had no idea.

I knew then what he meant by blind; it was a metaphor for

the jellyhead state of continuous distraction. With crust, I saw through the noise of the hivemind, I understood -- I perceived this world, like I had never perceived or appreciated any of it before, before now. I got it's beauty, I understood the power of Dunlockslyn, the primeval draw of The Dark Peak, I wanted to rush out onto the Middlewood road and exclaim my love of the place; I was ecstatic, I was in ecstasy. I got up and pulled Van towards me, kissing him on the forehead. Letting him go:

```
     HMM::IN('DPDC Alert: Update on murker in Hellsborough
park')
`hits:: 1226354 //
[this]2001:0db8:85a3:0000:0000:8a2e:037g:7334
[loc::hellsborough//middlewood_road//467]__ // now:: 79.hail
ripperthroat.12.15.19.17.13`
```

`Reports of gunshot fatalities. Continue to avoid area until further notice.`

You can't stop the DPDC alerts -- they get through whatever, so the murker in the park alerts still come through, and I guess I'm pretty glad of that -- after all, we are sat just along the road from where all this violence is happening. No one in the bar seems particularly tense though, which to me is strange. But I think this is quite commonplace here or hereabouts, so that's why I don't think there is much panic -- everyone is happy to sit and chat and enjoy their food and drinks.

It makes me think a little of something Van said last night about the xin -- that life is cheap, and so folk just get on with their lives and don't worry so much about death -- maybe deep down, beneath all the in your face consumerism and capitalistic fervour, the jellyheads of Hellsborough are the same?

I was off and away with my own thoughts there for a while, but meanwhile Van, resettling himself after my emotional outburst, had started talking again. I had been watching his mouth move, but my mind was elsewhere, but he did say, that I wouldn't forget or miss anything and he was right. I felt myself rewind the conversation in my own head, and rewatch the discourse:

As the chieftain raised his eyes to the prisoner, they fell on me and he turned to Siltibog with a word -- a sign of impatience. Siltibog made some reply which I didn't catch, but it caused the chieftain to smile; after that, they paid no attention to me.

Now, Pip, this was a while back, so I'm not a hundred percent that I am getting the words right, but they will be there or there abouts, so don't give me any grief about it, but make sure you pay attention, because these are some of the most important words ever spoken in The Dark Peak.

I nodded my understanding, I think. I was in another world, but I understood, I followed everything.

Areyt youth, who's thou then? said the chieftain.

Pandora Heatherington, daughter of Ptolemy of Hathersage.

And why was you out this way lass, what was tha doin'?

It was scientific research, sent out by my father, clown lord of Hathersage, to rechart the air currents, and to take atmospheric density tests, Pandora said.

We weren't prepared for battle, she carried on, we was on a peaceful mission, as our banners showed we were. The work we were doing was as much in your interests as in ours, you know that were it not for our scientific work there wouldn't be enough humidity in The Dark Peak to support a single denizen. For ages we have maintained the air and water supply at practically the same point without an appreciable loss, and we have done this in the face of your ignorant interference.

The chieftain grunted, Huh! Nascenti, but gestured for her to continue.

Why won't you lot learn, she started, but the chief butted in, shouting over her -- you think we are dumb: we doant write, we lives with no art, no homes, no love... Tha thinks we should pull our weight in The Dark Peak! Tha thinks we are freeloaders! But we sees you clowns as meddlers in a world that doant need to be meddled about with! The murk is the murk, always has been, and always will be, we trust the power of Dunlockslyn. Dunlockslyn will keep us safe -- not you mithering clowns.

The two now stared at each other, before the clown began to speak again, be that as it may, you are the victims of eons of a horrible socialist idea. Owning everything in common has resulted in your owning nothing in common. You hate each other as you hate everyone else. Come back to the light of kindliness and fellowship. The hands of the clowns will stretch out to aid you. Together we can do so much more to regenerate our shared environment. The daughter of the greatest and mightiest of the clowns asks you: What do you say?

The chieftain and the warriors sat looking at each other, none of 'em even raising a snough. They glowered at the young clown for ages after she'd stopped talking. What was passing in their minds I had no clue, but they were moved I reckon, and if one of 'em had been strong enough to rise above custom, that moment might well have marked a new era for The Dark Peak.

Siltibog got up, I could see that he was preparing himself to say someat, but he was struggling to know what to say, I reckon -- his mind was in turmoil, like he was battling with his own self against ancient customs. He almost seemed to be smiling as he started to speak, but he didn't get as far as saying owt.

Whatever he was about to say never got said, because a young upstart who must have sensed the thoughts of the elder men leapt down from that rostrum and thumped Pandora clean across the face, flooring her, where he put his foot upon her and turned to the rest of the assembly and laughed in that 'orrible way that only xin can do.

For moment, I thought Siltibog might strike him deed, and the chieftain looked at him in a way that didn't bode well for this idiot's future, but the mood seemed to pass, and moments later they all smiled -- yet none of them laughed -- even though according to xin custom, this would have been a reyt funny moment.

Of course, I was there, Pip. How could tha think I wouldn't be? Soon as that blow landed on Pandora -- in fact, before it landed -- I was halfway across that hall, and moments after he had laughed at his little victory, I was on him.

This brute was six foot tall and armed to the teeth, but I'd have taken on the whole room of 'em, I was that angry. I smacked him full in the face as he turned at me scream, and then as we drew our whipo'wil's, I was on him, hooking one leg over the butt of his fungun and grasping one of his tusks, and delivering blow after blow to his thick skull.

I was too close to him for him to use his whipo'wil properly, and he couldn't take out his fungun -- even though he tried to, which weren't xin custom -- tha has to fight with the weapon with what tha is attacked with. That's very important, Pip, the xin are all about custom, and he would have been extra-- what's the word, Pip? I'm stumped with that one.

Extradited. Or maybe Expelled?

Yeah, he'd have been that, had he pulled his fungun on me, it's just not proper and not the way that the xin do stuff. For a warlike load of toads, they do have standards.

Anyway, so I was on 'im, and despite all his efforts and his flailing about, he couldn't get me off. He were a big lad, but me pounding his noggin with me fist was enough to put 'im to the floor -- and that's where he stayed.

You killed him? I said.

I bettered him, which made his life worthless and as good as dead. He would be an outcast, forever doomed to wander alone and without his belongings in The Dark Peak -- that's the way it is with them xin.

Pandora had raised herself upon her elbows and watched the fight with wide eyes. When I had got back to my feet I picked her up and took her over to a bench.

None of the xin interfered as I ripped silk from my cape to try and stop the flow of blood from her nose. She weren't looking her best right then. Her injuries were no more than a nosebleed, and when she could speak she placed her hand on my arm.

Why did you do it? You who refused me in my first hour! And now you risk your life and condemn one of your companions to the wilderness for my sake. I don't understand you. What sort of man are you, that you consort with the green men, though your form is that of my race? Tell me, are you clown?

I ain't clown, love, I said, I come from a place not so far away from 'ere, but I has to wear this mask to breath, I is an human -- but like you I am a prisoner, and you need to believe me that I am your friend.

It were then that I took off me mask Pip, to show Pandora me face. And that were the last time that I wore me mask, as I realised that I could breath without it in The Dark Peak.

You had become acclimatised.

I Had. But Pandora had a load of questions: Why do you wear the arms of a xin chieftain? What is your name? Where are you from?

My name is Van Hallam, and I claim Hellsborough, in Hallamshire, the West Riding of Yorkshire, as my home; why I'm allowed to wear these arms I doant know, and I weren't aware that this is the garb of a chieftain.

Siltibog approached then, bearing arms and ornaments, and that answered one of Pandora's questions: The body of the young warrior had been stripped, and now I knew that by defeating him in a feight, his belongings were now mine; which of course, is why I had become dressed like this to begin with -- after my first feight in the chamber.

The reason for the xin's attitude toward me now made sense; I had become a conqueror -- so I took the armour and the position of the man I expelled from society. In truth, I was a xin chieftain, and this I learned later was the cause of my great freedom and their toleration of me.

Tha speaks the tongue of The Dark Peak well for one who was deaf and dumb a few short days ago. Where did you learn it, Van Hallam? Said Siltibog.

You're responsible pal, I thank Fenimoss for my learning. I said.

She's done well then, Siltibog answered, but tha needs a bit more polish in other stuff -- does tha know what would've 'appened if thou hadn't bettered them two chieftains whose metal you now wear?

Had I failed, I'd have been deed, I said with a smile.

Tha's wrong there -- only as a last resort of self defence would a xin warrior kill a prisoner. We like to save you for other purposes.

So is I a prisoner or a chieftain? I said -- If I is a chieftain then it is a fair fight, if I'm a prisoner, then not, that doant make much sense to me Siltibog.

You following Pip, yeah, course you are, you're all crusted up now. Here's what Siltibog said in answer to me:

Basically pal, only one thing can save you, and that's the will of his holiness, the imperial xin commander, who we'll go and see in the swamp in a bit. Until we get there, our Stanningxin chief has said that we should treat you as if you were a xin, and so that's why you're a chieftain here or hereabouts -- but doant forget that every chief who outranks you is responsible for your safe delivery to the swamp.

I 'ears you, I answered, even if I have no idea where the swamp is. Tha knows I'm not from 'round 'ere; your ways ain't the same as mine, and I can only do things in the future as I've done in the past, in the way I was brought up. If you leave me alone I will go in peace, but if not, let the xin who I must deal with respect me rights as a stranger, or take whatever consequences I might have to dish out.

Of one thing let us be sure, whatever your intentions toward this unfortunate young lass, whoever tries to injure her or insult her in the future, will have to deal with me. I understand that you don't really give a stuff about being kind or caring or owt like that, but I do, and I'll take on any one of thee that thinks they're man enough, if tha comes near this woman again.

I am not normally given to long speeches, I is a man of very few words usually, but I reckon that those few words went down the right ginnel.

I now turned my attention to Pandora, and getting her to her feet I turned with her toward the way out, ignoring her hovering guardians. I'm now a chieftain n'all I thought, so I'll be one, leave me be. They did not try and stop us, and so Pandora Heatherington, clown princess of Hathersage, and Van Hallam, man of Hellsborough, walked in silence out of the Stanninxin's audience chamber.

You need to tell me more about this chieftain of the Stanninxin, I said.

Why? Said Van

Because he seems important.

No, not really, he is a minor character in this story, Siltibog and the imperial xin commander are far more significant characters.

Actually, I can't even remember the fellas name, I must have known it though. Gimme a minute, said Van, pondering over my request. I could see the cogs whirring in his mind, the concentration in his eyes.

The imperial xin commander, his holiness, before you ask, goes by the name of Hagibrack, but we haven't got to him yet.

Pondisyke! That was it! This character, the Stanningxin chieftain, he was Pondisyke!

Anything else Pip?

Yes, something else I'm confused about is Pandora.

Pandora? Yes, I'm sure you are.

Well over there, sat by the door is Pandora the clown. Yet you talk about Pandora the clown from years ago, but surely they cannot be the same?

Can't they? Said Van.

Well how?

You tell me, you're the academic.

CHAPTER 11

Paranoid

    HMM::IN('DPDC Alert: Update on murker in Hellsborough park')
`hits:: 1226354 //
[this]2001:0db8:85a3:0000:0000:8a2e:037g:7334
[loc::hellsborough//middlewood_road//467]__ // now:: 79.hail
ripperthroat.12.15.21.42.7`

`No admittance to Hellsborough park.`

    HMM::OUT('How do I get back to my digs?')
`ask:: Rippon, Pip // stat:: accept[ok]__ // src::
2001:0db8:85a3:0000:0000:8a2e:037g:7334 [loc::hellsborough//
middlewood_road//467]__ // now:: 79.hail
ripperthroat.12.15.21.42.9`

`HMM::IN('..Middlewood road  go South, Bradfield road, Owlerton Green, Great causeway_ 1056 paces_ \/\ Proceed with caution_')`

`HMM::IN('..Alternative route: Middlewood road  go North, Parkside road, Great causeway_ 1408 paces_ \/\ Proceed with caution_')`

When we got outside, the two female guards whose job it was to watch over Pandora rushed up and tried to take her away from me. Pandora shrank from 'em and I felt her clinging onto me.

I told 'em to leave us be and said that from now on, Fenimoss would attend to her and watch over her -- and I warned Gorsithorn that if I saw any more cruelty from her than she'd have me to answer to.

I found Fenimoss and told to her that I wanted her to guard Pandora as she had guarded me, and for her to find somewhere new where she wouldn't be threatened by Gorsithorn. From now on, I said I'd be living with the men, since that seemed the right thing to do.

Fenimoss glanced at the xin garb that I was carrying.

You are a great chieftain now, Van, she said, and I must do your bidding, though I am glad to do it. The man whose metal you carry was young, but he was a great warrior, and had by his promotions and skill won his way close to the rank of Siltibog, who, as you know, is second only to Pondisyke. You're eleventh, only ten chieftains in this community outrank you.

And what if I defeated Pondisyke? I said.

You would be first, Van Hallam; but you can only win that honour by the will of all the council that Pondisyke meet you in combat, or if he attacks you, you may defeat him in self-defence, and win first place.

I laughed, and changed the subject. I had no particular desire to expel Pondisyke from his own lands, and even less to be the top chieftain of the xin.

We found a cottage near the audience chamber. The pictures on the walls showed many folk like me and Pandora -- some with patterned skin, some not. They were dressed in robes and wore lots of jewellery and other fine stuff. The paintings showed peaceful people at play, and it were a welcome sight, I tell thee Pip -- totally different to the constant nastiness of the xin.

Pandora smiled like a snarling scratcher -- a grin, but almost a grimace -- as she looked at these works of art, the artwork of her ancestors -- or maybe humans -- long gone from The Dark Peak, long forgotten. Fenimoss didn't seem to see 'em at all.

This cottage would be all reyt for Pandora and Fenimoss; there were a room out back for cooking and storing stuff. I sent Fenimoss to get bedding and food from our other shack, telling her I'd guard Pandora 'til she come back.

And where would your prisoner escape should you leave me? Said Pandora.

Tha's right lass, there's no escape unless we go together.

I heard your challenge to the creature you call Siltibog, and I think I understand your position among these people, but what I can't get my head around is your statement that you're not of this place.

Where are you from Van Hallam? You are like me and like my people, yet you are not like us at all. You speak our language, and yet I heard you tell Siltibog that you had learned it recently.

All of us in The Dark Peak speak the same language from north to south and east to west, though our written languages differ -- the xin don't even have one. Only in the valley, where the river Dun flows towards the coast, is there supposed to be a different language spoken, and, except in the legends of my ancestors, there is no record of anyone returning up the river Dun.

Do not tell me that you have thus returned -- they would kill you anywhere in this place if that were true; tell me it's not!

Her eyes were filled with a strange, weird light; her voice was pleading, she came to me and hugged me -- I am not someone who does hugging so well -- but I held her, awkward as it made me feel, I think it helped though.

I don't know tha customs Pandora, but I doant lie, does tha believe me?

She pulled away from me, and whispered: I believe you, Van; I have no idea where Hellsborough is; but in The Dark Peak no man lies; if he does not wish to speak the truth he is silent. Where is this Hellsborough, your country, Van?

Hang on, you're loosing me Van, I said.

Oh, how so?

Well I need to come back to this Pandora -- the one over there in the bar -- and the Pandora you're talking about, and you say that they're the same person?

I didn't say that.

No, you didn't, I agreed. So they are different people then?

Yes clearly. The Pandora I'm talking about is a generation or more removed from the one tha sees over there, but I knows her there, I knows her very well indeed; estranged that we are.

Van paused now, a pensive look coming over him as he toyed with his cribbage hand, considering first one card and then another, but all the time I knew that he wasn't focused on the cards, but on his daughter, or more likely his granddaughter.

Pandora -- the one in the room -- the one that is all skin and bones was now seated with the crosslander again. He was drinking a beer, and had brought her another glass of the same cocktail that she already had on the table.

I made a note to try and find out who the crosslander was, or even whatever clan he was part of. He was a handsome man, no more than a boy really, probably late teens, early twenties maybe.

No xaexs as yet, so not really raising any suspicions for the authorities, but to me another indicator that something is afoot.

Do you know the crosslander Van? I indicated the table where

Pandora sat with my eyes.

Hmm... Said Van, I'm not entirely sure, but tomorrow try asking in the shop on the corner. I'm pretty sure I've seen him buying baccy in there.

Ask them what? I said, how will they know who I'm talking about?

He's a crosslander, we don't get that many of their kind over this way, tha knows the score, they keep to themselves and to their own estates, to their own streets.

This one is a little bit different, he ventures out into Hellsborough, he meets with clowns -- and xaexs, if I recall -- he's a chancer, so they'll remember him, if they've seen him. They might not know his name, but tha never knows until tha asks; old Jarv though, he talks to folk, so tha never knows.

Ok. Thanks. I'll pop in there tomorrow.

Pick me up some baccy while tha's in there. And with that, Van plucked a fly from the heavy air, squashing it with an expertly executed pincer movement of his index finger and thumb -- like chopsticks -- and the fly was gone, whole. May I continue?

Please do.

She -- Pandora, the first one, not this one over there, said Van with an upward nod parodying the one I had given earlier -- gazed at me with troubled eyes. It were difficult to believe what I'd said, and I knew it.

She smiled at me Pip; made me 'eart melt it did. I believe you, though I do not understand. I perceive you are not of The Dark Peak; you are like us, yet you are not like us.

My head struggles with it, but my heart tells me that I should believe you, so that is what I will do. This place is not something to be trusted, but I feel you have a good heart Van Hallam, and you will see me right, so I will have to trust that -- I will have to trust my heart over my head, which doesn't have enough facts to make a decision.

It were good logic, I thought to mesen.

We talked for a bit then, asking and answering each other many questions. Pandora wanted to know about the customs of Hellsborough.

Actually, look, said Van coming back into the present -- there's old Jarv over there now, he's just coming in. I looked over to the door to see an old fella pushing against the door in what seemed like a battle he wasn't about to win, but he did eventually, finally stepping over the threshold, and letting a silo of rain pour in after him; much to the chagrin of the folks by the door, who took a soaking whilst the old fella was struggling (not that any of them helped him with the door, and I just sat on my backside as well, so I can't say that I was any help).

We watched as old Jarv slowly made his way to the bar, passing the table where Pandora sat with the crosslander and nodding at the latter in recognition, but not speaking.

I noted this -- clearly Jarv knew him, or at least recognised him, so I figured I could find out from Jarv who he was, but for now best let Jarv get himself sorted at the bar and settled down, there's no point in rushing about.

Van is here for the evening, and I expect that'll be the same for me. And this ale is just the best thing I have had in a long time.

Before I had chance to talk to old Jarv, Van returned to his story:

Fenimoss came back, asking if we had had a visitor while she was away, and seemed surprised when we said that we hadn't.

As she had approached our cottage, she had seen Gorsithorn heading away from it. She must have been eavesdropping, but as we hadn't said nowt much that seemed important, I didn't think it mattered much. Nosy old crone that Gorsithorn.

Next thing I knew, a messenger had arrived from Pondisyke wanting me back at the audience chamber. I said to Pandora and Fenimoss I'd be back, and told Shad to guard them, and then headed over. Pondisyke and Siltibog were sat on the rostrum.

Back in the bar, Jarv orders a pint and finds himself a seat at a table by himself. He takes a couple of sips and then does something which I don't expect. Without even scanning the room, he gets up again and wanders over to the table where Pandora and the crosslander are sat, and after the briefest of conversations with them, pulls out a chair at their table and sits down again. Van had clocked the old guy's actions too.

Looks like there's your answer, he said, old Jarv clearly knows that crosslander, and Pandora too, by the looks of it.

I nodded my understanding. Who is Jarv then? I asked myself, but Van answered, since he didn't realise that the question wasn't for him.

He's the owner of the news shop on the corner, he sells newspapers and tobacco and spice for kids, stocks psycmask refills.

Yes, I understand that, but what is he doing sitting with the crosslander and Pandora?

Maybe he's lonely.

If he was, why didn't he come and sit with us?

Maybe he didn't clock us, or maybe he saw you and thought that I was on some sort of date or something, I doant know.

I scoffed at Van's idea that this might be a date, sticking my tongue out in a somewhat inappropriate manner, I later thought to my myself, when going over things in my mind, the way you do if you're tripping on crust.

He didn't even look at us, Van. He just sat down by himself and then went and joined their table.

I'm sure there's nowt in it, said Van.

No, you're probably right, I just can't help myself thinking that it's all a bit of a coincidence, that's all.

Why doant tha go over and introduce thasen? Said Van. If tha's that bothered that someat is going on, go and find out.

Really? Do you honestly think that's a good idea!?

I tells you what I think, I think, if tha thinks something is afoot -- which tha does -- tha should go over to that table, tell 'em who tha is, sit down and ask 'em what's bugging you.

No, we need to work on your biography, that's why I'm here.

We'll get to that. But if thee thinks something is afoot, 'ere in Hellsborough, then tha should make a point to figure it out. Writing my biography, is but a minor thing. I mean, if tha's reyt, and there's a threat to Hellsborough, then that must come first, since if I's not about, or someat happens around here, tha'll not be hearing much of me story anyway. So I tell thee what, I'm gonna play out my hands here, and tha's gonna go over there and ask tha questions; get the answers tha needs, and then come back over 'ere and we'll carry on wi'me story. I mean, what's the worst that can 'appen, eh?

CHAPTER 12

Old Jarv

What's the worst that can happen? The phrase went around and around in my mind. I thought that Van was making light of this.

The worst that can happen is that Pandora, or this unknown crosslander would turn around and land me one with a fist -- or worse, a weapon. I wasn't so worried about Jarv, I didn't see him as a violent sort, for one he was old and two, he was a respected business person on the Middlewood road, but the other two, they -- to me at least -- seemed like unpredictability incarnate.

But here's the dilemma I'm in. I have Van's blessing to go and talk to them, but I am really scared that any questions I ask are going to cause some sort of ruckus. So what to do?

Van is playing his cribbage and, intentionally ignoring me, I feel, so I have no refuge with him any more. I am going to have to face the music and make myself ask the questions that I need to ask for my own sanity.

I leave Van to his card playing and approach the table. Pull out the remaining unoccupied chair and sit down, asking if anyone minds. No-one objects; but they are concerned by my presence, you can tell by the looks on their faces, I mean, this isn't everyday activity, is it? But at least no weapons have been drawn, no fists have been clenched and the feeling is more of intrigue than attack.

Hey guys, I said, breaking the table silence. I got murmurs of Hi in response.

I then didn't know what to say, how to start a conversation, which is strange for me, as a researcher, as an anthropologist, it's something that I'm usually confident with -- asking questions and getting answers -- but, well, this is Hellsbrough and I'm kind of nervous, if the truth be told, so I'm flailing about, and I'm pretty thankful when the crosslander, whose name I have yet to gain, pipes up.

And who's dee den? He says.

Hi, yeh, I'm Pip, I say.

Pip?

Pip Rippon.

I've not seen dee around here much, Pip; just moved in?

I'm here visiting -- Van over there.

Aye, Van, we know Van. At least, I know of him.

I know him, says Pandora. I've known him all of my life, although I don't see him very often. Actually, that's not true, I see him all the time, especially here and hereabouts, but we don't talk a lot, or at all, to be honest.

Old Van, does he need any baccy? Asks Jarv.

Yeah, he asked me to ask you to get him some tomorrow, I'll pop in the shop in the morning.

Seems like we're all friends here then, says the crosslander, since we all know Van in some way or another. I'm Scraith, he says proffering his hand for a shake, Scraith Southey. What can we do for thee, Pip?

I have to be honest, I said, it was Van that sent me over here, because I've had a number of questions in my head for the last two nights, spotting you two together, I wavered my head at Pandora and Scraith; and of course, as well last night, with the xaexs, I managed to blurt.

Who Van scored off, said Pandora.

Yes, who Van scored off, I confirmed.

So go ahead Pip, ask you questions, said Scraith, we're all friends here, we've already found that out.

Being put on the spot, I wonder exactly what my questions are. I mean, I've had some vague suspicions, but I don't really have any questions as such, but then I decide that I may as well go all in:

The xaexs, I said, why was she here last night?

To let Van score, I would assume, Pandora slips straight in.

Scraith lets out a full belly chuckle at that one.

I agreed it was pretty funny.

Seriously though, he said, do you think someat odd is going on?

It had crossed my mind.

Me and Pandora have known each other for years, said Scraith, every now and then we meet up for a couple of nights to chew the fat and have a laugh, there's nothing sinister in that. The xaexs, her name is Dirty Leaves, really is a drug dealer, so that's why she was here last night, and old Jarv here, well everyone knows old Jarv, doant they, and he's just enjoying a pint after work, so tha sees, there's nowt odd going on.

And tha knows what, I need to make a move, it were good to meet thee Pip, and I'll see tha all again soon, yeah?

With that Scraith drained what remained in his glass, scorked out his chair and hastily left. I didn't think that particularly unusual, but maybe I had unnerved him, he was certainly quick out of the blocks.

Pandora then too made her escape, as quickly as Scraith had done, leaving me and Jarv sitting in uncomfortable silence.

I suggested I should go back to Van. Jarv nodded and got up with me, following me back to where Van had finished his crib hand and was staring longingly into the bottom of his empty drinking vessel, which I took from him to go and re-fill.

At my insistence, Jarv admitted that he too would like a refill, and so off I went to recharge the glasses at the bar. When I returned, Van was in full spill of storytelling to Jarv. I don't think I missed much though.

As I entered the audience chamber, Pondisyke waved one of his arms at the podium for me to sit on its edge. Nadden, thee has been with us a couple of days, but in that time tha have won a top job among us. But tha's not one of us; you owe us nowt.

Tha's in an odd spot. Tha is a prisoner, but tha can give commands which must be obeyed; tha is an alien and yet tha is a xin chieftain. And now it 'as been reported that tha's plotting to escape with another prisoner of another race; a prisoner who half believes you are returned from the valley of the deed.

If either one of them accusations is true, it would be enough to have tha executed, but we is a just people and tha shall have a trial when we return to the swamp, if Hagibrack so demands it.

Pondisyke continued, in his guttural mucus-filled tones, but if tha dares run off with that clown it is I who shall have to account to Hagibrack; it is I who will have to face Siltibog, and demonstrate me right to command, or the metal from my expelled carcass will go to a better man, for such is the custom of the xin.

I has no quarrel with Siltibog; together we rule the greatest of the lesser communities of the green men; we do not wish to feight between ourselves; and so if you were no longer here, Van Hallam, I'd be reyt glad.

Only under two conditions can I have tha killed though without orders from Hagibrack -- in personal combat in self-defense, if tha attacks one of us, or if we were to catch thee as tha attempted t'escape.

I warn thee that I wait for one of these excuses for ridding us of tha. The safe delivery of the clown to Hagibrack is of reyt importance. Not in a thousand years has the xin made such a capture; she is the daughter of the greatest of the clown rulers. Anyway, I is done, said Pondisyke, tha can go.

This was Gorsithorn's doin' and I knew it. None other than her could have got to the lugs of Pondisyke so damn quick, and now I thought about the bits of mine and Pandora's chat which had touched on escaping and me coming from Hellsborough.

Gorsithorn was Siltibog's oldest and most trusted female. So she were a mighty power behind the throne, cos no warrior had the lugholes of Pondisyke as did his right-hand man Siltibog.

But instead of putting thoughts of escape from my mind, Pondisyke's words only focused me intentions on it more. Now, more than ever, I needed to get out this place and get Pandora away from whatever fate was waiting for her in Hagibrack's swampy kingdom.

Fenimoss had described Hagibrack as a cruel, ferocious, and brutal monster. Cold, cunning, calculating; he were nothing but a deceitful and power crazed demon with power his only desire.

The thought of Pandora falling into the clutches of this mardy dictator put me in a cold sweat

I wandered about the village lost in me own dooming.

Siltibog approached me on his way from the audience chamber. His way with me hadn't changed, and he greeted me warmly.

Where is tha rooms, Van Hallam? he asked.

I hasn't teken one yet. It seems best that I live by mesen or with t'other warriors -- I was waiting to ask tha's advice. As tha knows, I said smiling, I's not yet familiar with all tha xin customs.

Come with me, he said. Together we walked over the village green to a shack which I was glad to see was next to the cottage that Fenimoss and Pandora were in.

My rooms are on the first floor, Siltibog said, the second floor is full, but the third floor is empty; tha choice of the rooms is upto thee. I 'as 'eard tha has given up tha woman to the clown prisoner. As tha's said, tha ways are not our ways, but tha can feight well enough to go about as tha pleases, if tha wishes to give tha woman to a captive, that's upto thee; but as a chieftain tha should have those to serve you. All the females from the households of the chieftains whose metal tha now wears are at tha disposal.

I thanked him, but assured him that I could get along well enough without help, except in preparing food -- something as unknown to me as the xin and their customs. Siltibog promised to send women to me and for the care of my arms and the making of my ammunition, which he said would be needed. I said that they should also bring some of the sleeping silks and furs which belonged to me, for the nights were cold and I had none of my own.

Siltibog promised he would, and left. Alone, I went up the rickety staircase to the upper floors to find somewhere to sleep. I chose the front room on the third floor, it were nearer to Pandora, and I reckoned I could rig up some way of communicating in case she needed protection.

Several young females arrived bearing a load of weapons, silks, furs, cooking stuff, and casks of food and drink -- some of it loot from the downed clown airship. All this, it seemed, had been the property of the two chieftains I had excommunicated, and now, by the customs of the xin, it had become mine.

I told 'em to put the stuff in the back room, and then leave, which they did -- but then they come back with another load, which they said was the last of it. On the second trip, there were ten or fifteen of 'em, young 'n' old, who it seemed were now team Van.

They weren't the families, or the servants of the two warriors I had banished from the tribe -- the relationship is reyt strange, and not like owt we know Pip -- it's hard to describe: All property is owned in common by the community, except your personal effects -- weapons, ornaments, sleeping silks, fur -- that sort of thing. Owt else, anything not needed, goes to t'community.

The women and children of a man's household are like a military unit -- his brigade, if you like -- and this mebe ain't what you're used to in the off-world, I doant know, but 'ere, he is responsible for their manners and their eating. His women are in no sense wives though. The xin 'ave no word that means wife. Their mating is a community thing, that's it, I ain't gonna go into details. Anyway, I just told 'em to do what they did. Some of 'em made food, some of 'em ammunition, others would do what they do, I didn't much care, I just let 'em get on with it.

Da had a reyt time back then, didn't de Van, said old Jarv. Da know, I really wish that I had been born a little sooner, around the time you were, and had taken some of the risks that dee did.

Tha became a respected retailer here, so tha did take risks Jarv -- owning and running a shop is an 'uge risk in a place like this, said Van. I mean, running a business is nothing but a gamble, eh?

You may not be gambling with money as in a game of chance, but there is plenty of chance involved in the running of any shop, however big or small.

Maybe tha's right Van, maybe tha's right, but wearing this psycmask and listening to all that hive chat, tha forget's to think outside t'box, that tha's in a box. *You*, you really explored; me, I just accepted it and got on with it. But hey ho, never mind, in another life, maybe, eh?

The afternoon is getting on and Van now seems to enter some sort of trance, I've no idea what might have triggered it, but he seemed to be on a roll, and who am I to interject when Van is on a roll.

When one reaches an age like ours, tha's considered ripe for the picking. Picking is the pickers asking the pickee to reflect back on the wisdom he's had over his lifetime: Based on the assumption -- falsely -- that it goes up with age. The pickee is then expected to share with the pickers the bits of wisdom he or she may have come across. But, you know what, whatever wisdom I might 'ave collected over time, it has now been spread like muck over t'field and nowt remains.

Aye, I knows what your saying Van lad, said Jarv. Them pickers seem to think that we are somehow wise n'all, that we can foresee the future cos of our age. Whatever I can see about the future, they think I'll take steps to stop it from happening -- but being the owner of a newsagents -- if I saw tomorrow's newspaper today, then tomorrow would never happen, now would it! Jarv guffawed.

I know what you mean me old friend -- and I has no interest in forecasting t'future, only in creating it by acting inappropriately in t'present! And I ain't no interest in making the past how I would liked it. I learned from it cos it wasn't what I expected -- which explains why I don't remember it so well.

Y'ungry pal?

I could do a bite, what's on t'menu tha sun?

Wha'd'y' fancy?

I doant know, whatever comes to 'and.

Van picked from the air -- seemingly at random -- but there was no randomness in his action -- it was calculated and well done, skewering a flabby buzzer between his sharp thumb and index nails, bisecting its brain, which fell floor-ward into Shad's waiting jaws. He pulled off the legs, the barbed sting, and wings, depositing them next to his glass; I leave them to dry down a bit, he said, I likes 'em a bit crunchier like that.

The remaining abdomen and thorax, he presented to Jarv -- a perfect furry striped bodice, which the latter received gratefully.

Bleedin' starvin', not eaten all day, said Jarv, cheers pal.

Anyway, said Van, Pip here cannot learn from my mistakes, tha can only learn from tha's own mistakes. Don't matter how many I tells you about, or what the circumstances, tha can only learn from tha's own failures. And fail and mistakes tha must make -- by the bucket full -- I encourage, not discourage, tha making tha's own mistakes!

Now where do these self-indulgent reflections leave me? In a bar on the Middlewood road, that's where. Which is just where I want to be: Reminiscing, discussing the most important aspects of life, and having a little fun, eh Jarvy boy?

CHAPTER 13

Stripes

We learn little by being taught at, said Jarv, we learn much more by teaching others. Students should be teaching, and teachers should be learning. But now I must get home, so I'll be getting off and bid thee farewell. Thanks for the beer, Pip, I'll get tha one-in next time I'm over.

Except Jarv didn't leave. He half got up and then slouched down again and waited pregnantly to listen to Van's story.

Jarv's pint glass was empty, as was Van's, as was mine. I am thinking that Jarv is in some way thanking me for the next beer. I get up and get refills. Van is back in recite mode when I get back to the table with the recharged tankards:

Following the battle with them gruizers, the community stayed in the village for ages -- several days it were, abandoning the march to t'swamp until they was sure them clown ships didn't come back: To be caught out in the open with a load of carts and kids was not someat even the warlike xin wanted to chance.

While we was sat about, Siltibog showed me riding and guiding the mentiloth. These creatures are as dangerous and vicious as their masters, but when they're taught proper and not abused, they is the best of mounts.

Two of these animals I had inherited from the warriors whose metal I had on, and I found quickly that I could handle them as well as any of them xin warriors. My method weren't complicated -- but then nothing I do is, is it Pip?

With the xin, if the mentiloth didn't respond well to telepathic instruction, their riders thumped 'em hard at the base of their noggin with the butt of a fungun, and if they tried to fight back, they was thumped again until they were either subdued or unseated their rider. If the xin rider was thrown off, it were a life and death struggle between man and beast. If the man were quick enough, and shot the mentiloth, he'd live to ride again; if not, he'd be torn to shreds, and his body mangled.

I chose a different approach Pip; I treated my mentiloth with kindness. They got to know me, and learned who their new master was. Instead of starving them, I fed them well and talked to them, rather than shouting at them, like the xin warriors did. That won me their confidence -- in much the same way as I had with Shad, here. I was always a good hand with animals, I was kind to 'em. In no time, I were able to climb onto their backs and take to the sky.

My mentiloth were the wonder of the community. They would follow me and Shad about like we were the leaders of our little barker pack. They rubbed their great snouts against me in affection. I think the xin warriors thought me some sort of mystic.

You have bewitched them, how so? asked Siltibog one afternoon, after he had seen me run my arm far between the great jaws of one of my mentiloth which had wedged a piece of rock in its teeth when feeding.

Just kindness, I said. Softer social skills have value even to a warrior. In the height of battle I know that my mentiloth will obey my every command, and we'll feight better -- I is a better warrior cos I is also a kind master.

Tha other warriors would do well to learn from me. Only a few days back tha told me that these brutes could be the difference between victory and defeat, since they might unseat their riders. My mentiloth trust me, I'll not be unseated by them in battle.

Show us, said Siltibog -- and then later, he had me show Pondisyke and the rest of the xin warriors. That marked a new start for the mentiloth. It weren't long before they were all behaving like my brace did.

The effect on the precision of military movements went down so well that Pondisyke gave me a big old anklet of gold off his own leg -- get that Pip, a sign of how 'appy he was with me service to the horde.

On the seventh day after the battle with the gruizers, we began the march to the swamp. Pondisyke had decided that the chance of another attack weren't likely.

In the days before we left, I had seen nothing of Pandora, having been kept busy by Siltibog with my lessons in the art of xin warfare, and the training of the mentiloth.

The few times I had tried to visit her, she hadn't been about -- out walking with Fenimoss, or investigating the village and its local surrounds, collecting samples of plant life and the like -- I had warned them about going to far from the village because of the dangers of The Dark Peak -- but since Shad was always with them and Fenimoss was armed, I weren't that bothered.

The night before we set off, I saw them coming back along one of the tracks to the village from the east. I went to meet 'em, telling Fenimoss that I would take responsibility for Pandora's safekeeping, and sending her off on some trivial errand.

I liked and trusted Fenimoss, but I wanted to be alone with Pandora. There were bonds of mutual interest between us as powerful as though we had been born under the same roof rather than in different places, cultures apart.

That she thought the same about this, I was pretty sure, and her smile was plastered all over her face as she saw me; she placed her right hand on my left shoulder, a clown salute, which made me feel like I had done the right thing.

Gorsithorn told Fenimoss that you had become a true xin, she said, and that I would now see no more of you than of any of the other warriors.

Gorsithorn is a liar, albeit in the way of the xin, a truthful one, I replied.

Pandora laughed. I knew that even though you became a member of the community you would not cease to be my friend; 'A warrior may change his metal, but not his heart,' as the saying goes around here.

A stinger doesn't change it's stripes, I added.

True enough Van, it doesn't.

They have been trying to keep us apart, for whenever you have been off duty one of the older women of Siltibog's household has always arranged to get Fenimoss and me out of sight.

They have had me down in the pits below the buildings helping them mix their awful gunpowder, and make those terrible fungets.

You have noticed that their fungets explode when they strike an object? The opaque, outer coating is broken by the impact, exposing a silk cylinder, almost solid, in the forward end of which is a minute particle of the powder. The moment the sunlight, even though diffused, strikes this powder it explodes with a violence which nothing can withstand.

If you ever witness a night battle, you'll not see these

explosions. Then, in the morning there will be detonations of exploding missiles fired the night before, as the sunlight filters precariously through the murk.

Pandora's explanation of xin warfare interested me, but I was more concerned about their treatment of her. That they were keeping us apart weren't surprising, but that they was making her do dangerous work filled me with anger. Has they been cruel to you?

A little, but nothing that hurt anything other than my pride. They know that I am the daughter of a great clown dynasty, and they, who do not even know their own mothers, are jealous of me. At heart they hate their own horrid lives, and so wreak their spite on me. They crave what they can never have. I pity them for even though we die at their hands we can afford them pity, since we are greater than they and they know it.

Day had now given away to night as we wandered along the village's most western track, lit by the watery gloominess of the moon through the murk. The chill of The Dark Peak night was on us, and I threw silks over Pandora's shoulders.

As my arm rested for an instant on her, I felt a thrill pass through me, and it felt like she leaned toward me a bit, but I couldn't be sure of that -- but she didn't move away and neither did she speak. So in silence we walked.

Is this love Van? I said, things starting to unravel. Jarv looked at me with surprise and what felt like a little suspicion, but I wasn't entirely sure why.

Yes, I loved Pandora. The first Pandora. Tha's Pandora, tha Pandora that tha introduced yourself to earlier, is the third Pandora in the line. That one doant like me as much.

So are you related? I asked.

It's a definite possibly, said Van. Somehow, back in The Dark

Peak, back in the day, I likely made some sort of history, I'm still not sure how myself, since it shouldn't have been possible, and maybe it weren't. It's not like I've ever pressed the matter. But I don't really doubt it either. I mean, look at me eyes, I showed you last night, you've seen them before.

Tha eyes Van? said Jarv, trying to follow the conversation.

Tha doant normally see, Jarv, this psycmask keeps 'em covered, but If I takes it off, and at that moment, Van did take off the psycmask, thee'll see.

And Van showed Jarv the dark green around his tattoo'd eyes, that bore a distinct resemblance to those who we might think of as a descendent of clown aristocracy.

```
    HMM::IN('Background music: Uplifting and adventurous
tune.  Aerial video, moorlands, rolling hills of The Dark
Peak')
`hits:: 6612149 //
[this]2001:0db8:85a3:0000:0000:8a2e:037g:7334
[loc::hellsborough//middlewood_road//467]__ // now:: 79.hail
ripperthroat.12.15.22.58.1`

`Escape to a land shrouded in mystery, where rugged beauty and
untamed wilderness collide.`

`Image: Hikers on scenic trail.. waterfall.. wildlife..`

`Welcome to The Dark Peak, for nature lovers and adventure
seekers.`

`Image: Climber on rocky peak.. cyclists..`

`Unwind and indulge   where comfort meets nature.`

`Image: Sunrise over The Dark Peak..`

`The Dark Peak. Discover the magic. Experience the adventure.`

`This was a public utility broadcast by The Dark Peak District
Council.`
```

And the hivemind butted in with another advert and droned on and on, but this was different -- it wasn't just my pscymask that it was broadcasting to, we could all see this -- it was there, in the ether in front of us, projected onto what I don't know, onto nothingness -- it was a welcome distraction, even if it played away to itself.

CHAPTER 14

Half Way

Goo-on then lad, said Jarv, swiping away the DPDC's intrusive disturbance, I wants to 'ere more about this, this is gerrin intresting. Gerrin a bit sordid, init Pip?

Jarv leered, he was a leery type of character -- unsavoury in his own special way, whilst still being a pillar of the community.

I wondered then whether he might be more than a jellyhead -- as Van refers to the inhabitants of Hellsborough -- and instead, a stooge of The DPDC: A Jellyhead.

Rumour has it, well, it's more than rumour if you read the literature of the netherlander resistance, they posit it as fact, that The DPDC -- The Dark Peak District Council -- its elected members -- the politicians, if you like -- and the senior staff, the Chief Executive, the Chief Finance Officer and all those other members of the "C-Suite", are Jellyheads.

I know, that's confusing right? Jellyheads in the context of the netherlander alliance are nascenti stooges -- puppets -- put in place by the nascenti, who are under the full control of the fungal network, the fungai. They may or may not be human. According to the netherlanders, they are replicants -- or mades: Revenant humans resurrected and animated by the fungai.

On second thoughts, I have made my mind up. Jarv is clearly just a regular jellyhead -- using Van's derogatory term. The man has no likeable features at all. Even the fungai wouldn't be that naive. Or would it? No, stop being paranoid, that's the crust talking now.

While my mind has been meandering, Van and his pal Jarv have been tucking into more murk tucker and Van is back in full-flow; orating like the best of them; and he is right, I'm not missing or forgetting a single word as my mind transcribes his story for later regurgitation.

You're quiet, I said, does tha want to go back to Fenimoss and tha quarters?

I am happy here. I am content with you, even though you are a stranger, I feel safe. And, I know you will soon return me to my father's safety and my mother's tears and kisses.

I wanted to tell her of my love, but I realised that would be a daft thing to do. My job now was to protect her as best I could against the thousands of enemies she would face when we arrived at t'swamp.

Yet, I couldn't keep me gob shut, could I?

Couldn't you Van? What did you say next? Said Jarv, his tongue lolling around his puffy lips. Come on spill the beans.

I just went too far, that's what I did me old murker. I asked her a silly question -- Do people kiss, then, in this place?

Parents, brothers, and sisters, and lovers.

And thee, Pandora, does tha have brothers and sisters?

Yes.

And -- a lover?

Jarv guffawed, unable to control his excitement. The man was practically bent over in supposition and self effacement, gagging on his own words -- what did she say, what did she say Van?

She were silent. We both were for a while. The whole world seemed to have stopped spinning, and if the earth had opened up and swallowed me, I doant think I'd have put up much of a struggle.

Finally -- said Van, she answered me.

Scerm behold us! Exclaimed Jarv, in d'divi we trust!

-- the men of The Dark Peak, do not ask personal questions of women, except his mother, and the woman he has fought for and won.

Jarv was enthralled, positively drooling as he stared at Van.

and then if I hadn't been stupid enough, said Van, like a dolt, I started to say:

But I have feight...

and then I wished my tongue had been cut from me gob; she turned, took me silks off her shoulders, and saying nowt else, turned her back on me and walked off -- every bit the princess -- toward her cottage.

Yeah, but tha followed her, right Van, tha must have done, eh Van, said Jarv with a wink, and a circular motion of his excited, yet somehow flaccid, mould and thrush covered tongue.

Nah kid, I left it.

And for the first time, I sensed Van becoming distracted and annoyed by this Jarv character; the man that runs the corner newspaper shop.

I let her go. I watched to see that she'd reached the building safely, and told Shad to follow, but I just went back to me own room, feeling like a proper gimp.

Aww Van, droned Jarv -- until Van silenced him with a piercing look.

Van talked into the silence. I thought then on what a daft berk I was, and how for all the years I had been held captive in Hellsborough and the hills that circled it, and the wisewood; in spite of the beautiful women there -- here -- in spite of a half-desire for love and the constant search, I had to fall for a creature from another place.

A woman whose span of life might cover a thousand years; whose people had strange customs and ideas; a woman whose hopes, whose pleasures, whose standards varied as greatly as did those of me and the xin.

To me, Pandora were all that were perfect. I believed that from the bottom of me 'eart, as I sat all by mesen in me lonely room in Stanningxin.

The morning we left for the swamp was damp and wet, as are many mornings in The Dark Peak.

I looked for Pandora among the carts as they left, but she had turned her back on me and weren't even looking in my direction. I knew I had done wrong, but thought that after a night's sleep she might have forgotten and we could get back to talking -- clearly I were wrong on that. Our cultural differences must have wounded her more than I knew.

It were my duty to see that she were comfortable, and so I got to her cart and rearranged the silks and furs, which meant that I saw that she was chained by her ankle to the side of the vehicle.

What is this? I said, turning to Fenimoss.

Gorsithorn thought it best, her face showing her disgust.

Where is the key, Fenimoss? Let me have it.

Gorsithorn wears it, Van Hallam.

Without further word, I went and found Siltibog, where I made my objections clear -- it were unneeded humiliation and cruelty, and there were no need for it.

Van Hallam, if thou and the clown were to escape the xin, it will be on this journey. We know that tha will not go without her. Tha has shown yourself a mighty feighter, and we do not wish to manacle thee, so we hold tha both in the easiest way. I has spoken -- let that be the end of it.

I knew that it were pointless to argue, his reasoning was sound -- but I asked that the key be taken from Gorsithorn and that she were to leave the prisoner alone.

This much, Siltibog, tha may do for me in return for the friendship that, I must confess, I feel for thee.

Friendship? There is no such thing, said Siltibog, but have your will. Gorsithorn will cease to annoy the girl, and I myself will hold the key.

Unless tha wishes me to 'ave the responsibility, I said, smiling.

He looked at me a long time before he spoke.

If tha gave me your word that neither you nor the clown would attempt to escape until after we have safely reached the court of Hagibrack you might have the key and throw the chains into the river Dun.

It is better you hang onto it then, I said.

He smiled, and said no more, but that night as we were making camp I saw him unfasten Pandora's manacles himself.

Siltibog was known as a cruel and ferocious warrior, but I knew there were things he was fighting against in 'is noggin.

I approached Pandora's cart and passed Gorsithorn, who looked at me like I was nowt -- the look of a venomtooth about to strike.

Moments later she was chatting with a warrior who I weren't familiar with.

He was unnamed -- an 'uge, powerful brute, but one who had never made any impact in the tribe, and so was a bloke with no name; he could only get a name with the metal of another chieftain, which he would need to banish from the community.

As Gorsithorn talked, the warrior looked over at me and I saw her urge him on. I knew what would be coming sometime soon, as Gorsithorn was nothing if not an 'orrible rooter of a woman, who would stop at nowt to run me out of town.

Pandora was still giving me the cold shoulder, not even paying me the time of day. I desperately wanted to get back on her side, I felt miserable, so I collared Fenimoss in another part of camp.

What's the matter with Pandora? I blurted. Why won't she speak to me?

She said you have angered her.

We broke camp the next day early and marched with just one stop until the gloaming was on us. A couple of things happened while we was marching. About murknoon, judging by the position of the paltry sun, we saw far off below some craggy edge what looked like an incubator; Pondisyke told Siltibog to go and investigate it.

Siltibog commanded me and eleven others to follow him, and we skimmed across the heather on our mentiloth to the enclosure.

It was an incubator, as expected -- the eggs were very small compared to them I'd seen hatching back when I arrived in The Dark Peak, they were no bigger than an honker egg back home.

Siltibog dismounted and examined the enclosure closely.

Eventually, he announced that it belonged to the Strinxin and that the cement was scarcely dry where it had been walled up.

They cannot be a day's march ahead of us, the thought of battle lighting up his face.

The other warriors ripped open the entrance and a couple of them crawled in, I took a back seat Pip, I did for it was horrible and senseless, but then I has already told you what the xin are like. They smashed all them eggs 'til they was nothing. We flew back to the wagon train. During the ride I asked Siltibog if these Strinxin were a smaller people than his xin, as the eggs were so much smaller.

They had just been placed there, he said; but, like all xin eggs, they would grow during the five-years of incubation until they became the size of those I had seen before, on that day of my arrival in The Dark Peak.

Not long after the destruction of the Strinxin eggs we rested the animals, and it was then that the thing that I had been expecting happened. I was rubbing down one of my mentiloth -- they sweat like onetoes -- when that warrior with no name came up, and not saying a word come and struck my animal a vicious blow with his whipo'wil, opening up a dirty gash on his snout.

I was reyt angry Pip, it were all I could do to stop mesen from shooting him with me fungun there and then. He stood waiting 'is whipo'wil drawn, making it me choice. But tha know what I did? I pulled out me axe -- a lesser weapon, and maybe a poor choice -- but, I run at him, catching him a good un under his jaw -- and that is for hitting me mount, I hissed at him.

We then fought for a long time, with what seemed like the whole of the community surrounding us, but leaving us good enough space to feight each other fairly.

After me first attack, he rushed at me like a bull demonspawn might charge a ripperthroat, but I were too quick for him, and each time I side-stepped his charges, and he would go lunging past, receiving a nick from my hatchet.

He was soon loosing blood from half a dozen or so wounds, but I couldn't get in a strong enough blow to fell this giant.

We were circling each other for ages, but I realised he were more tired than I was, and it was then that he closed in on me to try and end things in a final blaze of glory for hisself.

He rushed me blindly with his whipo'wil swingin', just as a flash of dull light struck me full in the eyes, so I couldn't see him coming. I leapt to one side to escape his incoming blade -- a stab from him that I could already feel entering me body.

I felt a sharp pain in my left shoulder, but in the sweep of my glance, catching him in the guts with my axe as he passed, I saw what had blinded me as I had taken that blade.

Up on a cart watching were Pandora, Fenimoss and Gorsithorn, and as I looked, Pandora turned on Gorsithorn with the fury of smitten grizzler, striking someat from her hand, which flashed in the murklight as it spun to the ground.

Then I knew what had happened, and how Gorsithorn had tried to kill me without delivering a blow.

Gorsithorn, her face livid at Pandora's swipe, now whipped out her shard and lunged -- only Fenimoss seeing what had happened put herself between that blade and Pandora, taking Gorsithorn's knife full in the breast.

The nameless xin had now recovered from his thrust and charged me again, but I was now distracted Pip, and urgent to get this thing done.

We clashed several times. I felt the sharp point of his whipo'wil at my breast in a thrust there were no way I was gettin' out of the way of.

VAN HALLAM

I launched mesen on his blade and with all the weight of my body, and brought that axe down on 'is 'ead. I felt his steel tear into me chest, and all went black, as me knees gave way, and pain shot through me body.

The look of horror was palpable in my face when Van told me that. I wanted to be sick. Yet I knew he had lived, since the old rogue sat here in front of me, chugging at his ale and puffing his snoughweed stuffed pipe, a wry smile on his face.

```
      HMM::OUT('whipo'wil')
`ask:: Rippon, Pip // stat:: accept[ok]__ // src::
2001:0db8:85a3:0000:0000:8a2e:037g:7334 [loc::hellsborough//
middlewood_road//467]__ // now:: 79.hail
ripperthroat.12.15.23.34.52`

`HMM::IN('..A tentacle like prehensile steel that wraps and
grabs, but at the right angle can be controlled    via wrist
action or button    to slice, hack etc.._')`

      HMM::IN('Y'ungry Murker?!')
`hits:: 42791 // [this]2001:0db8:85a3:0000:0000:8a2e:037g:7334
[loc::hellsborough//middlewood_road//467]__ // now:: 79.hail
ripperthroat.12.15.23.36.9`

`Tapas Farantees Espanyol    We deliver! Wherever you are,
you can get our tantalising tapas    call now: 353 535 333555
555 333`

`Faranteeeeeees!!!`
```

Van could see the look on my face at the distraction from my psycmask, which I had almost begun to forget about.

Yeah, that's the crust wearing off Pip, have a draw on me pipe. He offered it, and I accepted, drawing deeply.

Actually though Van, I am pretty hungry as well, do you fancy a carry in?

Aye, that new tapas place -- I could reyt chomp some venomtooth, eh?! Or maybe they's got skewerwing -- there's a big old skewerwing that stands in the 'ole every now and then, I see him from me window -- your choice though Pip, as I said, I'm blood 'ungry, so owt will do for mesen.

ok Van, after all a ripperwing doesn't feed on flies.

```
      HMM::OUT('Venomtooth')
`ask:: Rippon, Pip // stat:: accept[ok]__ // src::
2001:0db8:85a3:0000:0000:8a2e:037g:7334 [loc::hellsborough//
middlewood_road//467]__ // now:: 79.hail
ripperthroat.12.15.23.35.59`

`HMM::IN('..Colour:   Black_`

`..Diet:   small birds, gnawmards, eggs_`

`..Size:   12" (thumb)_`

`..Defining characteristics:   Venomous, legless_`

`..Class:   Wildlife_`

`..Image:   Incoming_      ')`

      HMM::OUT('Skewerwing')
`ask:: Rippon, Pip // stat:: accept[ok]__ // src::
2001:0db8:85a3:0000:0000:8a2e:037g:7334 [loc::hellsborough//
middlewood_road//467]__ // now:: 79.hail
ripperthroat.12.15.23.36.3`

`HMM::IN('..Colour:   Grey / White`

`..Diet:   Slippers_`

`..Size:   4'" (hands)_`

`..Defining characteristics:   Flyer_`

`..Class:   Wildlife_`

`..Image:   Incoming_      ')`
```

CHAPTER 15

Fenimoss

When I got back from the bar -- I'd wobbled over and had our three glasses recharged -- old Jarv had gone. Maybe realising he had overstayed his welcome, he was heading out of the door and back into that wild evening, letting the detritus blow back inwards again as he egressed.

Jarv's gone, said Van, as I set the pint pots down on the table; but he'll be coming back, worst luck -- he forgot to do something over at the shop, he said. Have you seen this though Pip, he said, holding up a scrap of paper -- The cult of the bitter finger, doesn't say much here -- the scrap literally said what he had just read -- but I remember this snippet Pip, he said, tapping the side of this nose -- can't remember when I heard it, or even if I did first hand, maybe I overheard it somewhere -- could 'ave been a symbiot, or maybe I sensed it, but it was some sort of conversation -- or an echo from somewhere -- could have been static in the hivemind or something I picked up in the scerm, I ain't really sure, but here you goes anyway:

I have no love either for the clowns or the xaexs, they turns me stomach, especially that Pandora flit. I mean, those eyes of hers, and she's all skin and bones, makes me shiver to think about it. Sure, I've met with her a few times, her and the xaexs

-- Dirty Leaves, she's called -- they are very useful contacts in my -- our -- cause, they have their own networks, you can get things done with them, you can use them. Ha ha, we should probably honour them come the day, but we haven't got there yet, Southey.

Sounds like you Van, but what is that? Where did you get it?

As I said I dunno its source; could have been from anywhere, but I reckon it's something to do with that crosslander that was in 'ere earlier, the one you went and talked to -- before he legged it smartish and took the clown with 'im.

Van saw the look on my face.

Right Pip, they didn't leave together, but from where I was sat it seemed pretty close, and straight after you'd started your little chat.

You're right Van, it was a little chat, I found out nothing at all.

Here in the void is silence, no sound at all, like a vacuum and so many stars -- so many I can't see the constellations. There is a sound that I bottle and check like a miscreant child. Everyone is just trying to pull the wool over yours, and everyone else's eyes -- all of the time. That is what life is about -- faking it, ripping people off, pulling the wool over the eyes, said Van. He was rolling with the music in the bar. The blind and the blaggards, snivelling like sick barkers; chaotic and pestering, mildewing about like they have a purpose, but they do -- everything and everyone has a purpose, it's just that sometimes them jellyheads don't know what their purpose is -- it is the preserve of the nascenti to understand such things -- so they mill about, chastise and carol each other, bicker and bitch, poke and stab, wind each other up -- such is the way of things -- which ain't that different to the off-world, is it Pip?

Let's get the story done and then we can talk about this other stuff that has been happening.

Stuff has been happening?
Well maybe, I still don't know.

    HMM::OUT('I need to contact Pip Rippon, danger!')
`ask:: unknown // stat:: accept[ok]__ // src::
2001:0db8:85a3:0000:0000:8a2e:142j:i618 [loc::hellsborough//
unknown__location//000]__ // now:: 79.hail
ripperthroat.12.15.23.54.14`

`HMM::IN('..Request made_')`

    HMM::IN('DM!')
`hits:: 1 // [this]2001:0db8:85a3:0000:0000:8a2e:037g:7334
[loc::hellsborough//middlewood_road//467]__ // now:: 79.hail
ripperthroat.12.15.23.54.15`

`From unknown, hellsborough//unknown__location//000`

`Hi Pip Rippon, this is unknown//unknown__location, you are in danger!`

I've already flagged this as scum, why am I receiving it again?

    HMM::OUT('delete, flag as scum')
`ask:: Rippon, Pip // stat:: accept[decline]__ //
src:: 2001:0db8:85a3:0000:0000:8a2e:037g:7334
[loc::hellsborough//middlewood_road//467]__ // now:: 79.hail
ripperthroat.12.15.23.54.15`

    HMM::IN('Flagged a high priority, are you sure you do not wish to receive?')
`hits:: 1 // [this]2001:0db8:85a3:0000:0000:8a2e:037g:7334
[loc::hellsborough//middlewood_road//467]__ // now:: 79.hail
ripperthroat.12.15.23.54.15`

    HMM::OUT('Ok, allow this message. More detail.')
`ask:: Rippon, Pip // stat:: accept[ok]__ // src::
2001:0db8:85a3:0000:0000:8a2e:037g:7334 [loc::hellsborough//
middlewood_road//467]__ // now:: 79.hail
ripperthroat.12.15.23.54.17`

    HMM::IN('Message accepted. Providing more detail.')
`ask:: unknown // stat:: accept[ok]__ // src::
2001:0db8:85a3:0000:0000:8a2e:142j:i618 [loc::hellsborough//
unknown__location//000]__ // now:: 79.hail
ripperthroat.12.15.23.54.18`

```
    HMM::OUT('We should meet.  You are in danger.  Beware of
the cult of the bitter finger.')
`ask:: unknown // stat:: accept[ok]__ // src::
2001:0db8:85a3:0000:0000:8a2e:142j:i618 [loc::hellsborough//
unknown__location//000]__ // now:: 79.hail
ripperthroat.12.15.23.54.29`

    HMM::OUT('What is that?')
`ask:: Rippon, Pip // stat:: accept[ok]__ // src::
2001:0db8:85a3:0000:0000:8a2e:037g:7334 [loc::hellsborough//
middlewood_road//467]__ // now:: 79.hail
ripperthroat.12.15.23.54.37`

    HMM::OUT('The crosslander    clown    xaexs alliance.')
`ask:: unknown // stat:: accept[ok]__ // src::
2001:0db8:85a3:0000:0000:8a2e:142j:i618 [loc::hellsborough//
unknown__location//000]__ // now:: 79.hail
ripperthroat.12.15.23.55.1`

    HMM::OUT('Who are you?')
`ask:: Rippon, Pip // stat:: accept[ok]__ // src::
2001:0db8:85a3:0000:0000:8a2e:037g:7334 [loc::hellsborough//
middlewood_road//467]__ // now:: 79.hail
ripperthroat.12.15.23.56.19`
```

I could hear the chirring of a beetle's wing through the din of the bar, but Van was way ahead of me -- our carry-in had yet to arrive, and he snagged it deftly.

Refreshed and prompted by my request for him to continue with his story, he came back in where he had left off, seemingly without missing a beat:

When I come to I sprung up, looking for me axe. I found it buried to the shaft in face of that unnamed xin. His blood was starting to congeal around it, and it weren't a pretty sight. His body lay among the brown ferns on the moor where he had attacked me. I hadn't passed out for long though I reckoned, since no-one else had moved from where I had last seen 'em.

Me, mesen, me injuries, I were lucky; his whipo'wil had gone through me left breast, but only through flesh and muscle over me ribs, coming out below me shoulder at the back. As I had fair chucked mesen at 'im, I had turned so that his whipo'wil just passed beneath the muscles, it 'urt, alot, but it weren't a dangerous wound.

I pulled 'is blade out of me, and then pulled me hatchet out his head; then, turning me back on his carcass, I moved, sick, sore, and disgusted, toward the carts which carried me 'ousehold and belongings. There were a few slow claps from the xin, but I weren't thinking about that.

I were bleeding and weak. One of me female xin come and bandaged me up, putting on the 'ealing 'erbs which started to make me feel better straight away, they has an amazing way with their 'erbs the xin, they is reyt good with 'em: Give a xin woman a chance and death must take a back seat. She soon patched me up, and after that, other than feeling weak from loss of blood and a bit of soreness where that whipo'wil went in, I suffered nowt in the way of pain.

What do you reckon to that then Pip?

I know that back here in Hellsborough -- or in the off-world -- you'd have out been of action for days or even weeks.

Aye, I'd have been flat on my back for ages, I reckon -- and you know what was in them healing herbs that I was treated with doant you?

I didn't have to think long before I came up with an answer, and although I phrased it as a question with a knowing look, I didn't need to, that was more for Van's entertainment -- and just to prove that I was listening and learning.

Yep, that's right: Rockcrust it was.

```
     HMM::IN('Tapas Farantees Espanyol    Incoming!!!')
`hits:: 1 // [this]2001:0db8:85a3:0000:0000:8a2e:037g:7334
[loc::hellsborough//middlewood_road//467]__ // now:: 79.hail
ripperthroat.12.16.0.1.3`

`Tapas Farantees Espanyol    Your order will be with you in
```

one moment`

`Your order:
2001:0db8:85a3:0000:0000:8a2e:037g:7334//467//12.15.23.41.7`

   Bucket of original recipe fried venomtooth sections & heads
   Spicy hot Skewerwing wings, 6 pcs
   Curried rooter trotters, 6 pcs
   Crispy waffle fries, 3 servings
   Creamy coleslaw dipping pot, large
   Chocolate drizzled churros, 12 pcs

`  any problems call: 353 535 333555 555 333`

`Faranteeeeeees!!!`

And with that, the food was there, in front of us on the table. No utensils of course, this is finger food, and piping hot. I hungrily ripped open the bags and delved into the steaming containers. Help yourself Van, I said.

He holds back momentarily, but I can see the hunger in his eyes, and after he has done his gentlemanly thing and restrained himself, he too dives in, the man is clearly ravenous.

Aw you got skewerwing n'all, he said, greedily stuffing a bite sized morsel of fried venomtooth into his mouth.

'elp yourself, Jarvy boy, an' si'down, he added, as old Jarv was back and stood drooling as he waited for an invitation to return to our table.

Satiated, Van carried on, I was still polishing off a chunk of rooter trotter, but I didn't mind, things all made sense to me at whatever speed Van wanted to recant his journey:

As soon as I was fixed up, I went straight to the cart where Pandora was, and found Fenimoss, her chest covered in bandages, recovering after being stabbed by Gorsithorn. Fenimoss's metal breast ornaments had deflected Gorsithorn's shard, so it were just a flesh wound really.

Pandora were lying on her silks and furs crying, and she didn't see me there. She didn't hear me speaking to Fenimoss neither.

Is she 'urt? I asked Fenimoss, indicating Pandora by a sideways flick of me 'ead.

No, she answered, she thinks that you're dead. The clowns are a proud race, and they are just, as we all are here. You must have hurt her badly Van Hallam, for as she will not admit your existence living, she mourns you now that you are dead. Tears are a strange thing in The Dark Peak, and it's difficult to interpret them. I have only seen two people weep in all my life, other than Pandora; one wept from sorrow, the other from rage. The first was my mother, years ago before they killed her; the other was Gorsithorn, when they dragged her off me today.

This was something of a revelation, Pip, and I said so, since Fenimoss could not have known her mother -- the xin didn't know these things, living communally, as they do.

But I did, said Fenimoss, and my father as well. If you would like to hear my strange and unusual story come to the cart tonight, and I will tell you something that I haven't ever spoken about before, not in my entire life.

The signal had been given for the march to carry on, so we stopped talking, but I knew I needed to know the rest of her tale.

I promised Fenimoss that I would be back later, and told her to tell Pandora I was alive and well, but that I'd not come unless she asked for me; and be sure to not let her know I'd seen her blubbin'.

Fenimoss climbed into the cart, which was taking its place in line, and I readied my waiting mentiloth and joined Siltibog at the rear.

The caravan was something of a sight to behold, Pip. The line of carts, mounted warriors in front, at the back and flanking the procession, with the 'uge maggoty draught animals, the cryptobite, behind the carts. Many extra mentiloth flew loose within the hollow square formed by the surrounding warriors. The metal of the men and women gleamed through the murk, and the colours of the silks and furs and feathers, made the whole thing look official.

We traversed a trackless waste of moor which rose up again behind us, leaving no sign that we had passed. We might indeed have been the wraiths of the departed dead upon The Dark Peak for all the sound or sign we made in passing, no dust or spoor was raised from t'heather.

We camped that night at the foot of the 'ills we had been approaching for the last day, which marked the western boundary of Hallamshire. After eating, I sought out Fenimoss. She were working by torchlight on some of Siltibog's trappings. She looked up at me and smiled -- reyt unusual for them xin she were.

I am glad you came, she said, Pandora is asleep and I am lonely. My own people do not care for me, Van Hallam; I am too unlike them. It is sad, since I must live my life among them, and I often wish that I were a true xin woman, without love and without hope; but I have known love and so I am lost.

I promised to tell you my story, or rather the story of my parents. From what I have learned of you and the ways of your people I am sure that the tale will not seem strange to you, but among the xin it has no parallel within the memory of the oldest living Stanninxin, nor do our legends hold any similar tales.

And so I settled down on t'ground next to Fenimoss and by torchlight, she quietly told me her unusual tale.

My mother was small, too small to be allowed the responsibilities of maternity, as our chieftains breed principally for size. She was also less cold and cruel than most xin women, and caring little for their society, she often roamed the deserted lanes of Stanningxin alone, or went and sat among the wild flowers on the nearby hills, thinking thoughts and wishing wishes which I believe I alone among xin women today may understand, for am I not the child of my mother?

And there among the hills she met a young warrior, whose duty it was to guard the feeding cryptobite and mentiloth and see that they didn't roam off beyond the hills. They spoke at first only of things of interest in the Stanningxin community, but gradually, as they came to meet more often, and, as was now quite evident to both, no longer by chance, they talked about themselves, their likes, their ambitions and their hopes. She trusted him and told him of the repugnance she felt for the cruelties of their kind, for the hideous, loveless lives they led, and then she waited for the storm of denunciation to break from his cold, hard lips; but instead he took her in his arms and kissed her.

They kept their love a secret for six long years. My mother, was of the household of the great Hagibrack, while her lover was a simple warrior, wearing only his own metal. Had their defection from the traditions of the xin been discovered both would have been thrown into the arena at the great games.

The egg from which I came was hidden beneath a great glass vessel upon the highest and most inaccessible cave on the escarpments of Stanedge. Once each year my mother visited it for the five long years it lay there as it incubated. She dared not come more often, as she feared that her every move would be watched. During this period my father gained great distinction as a warrior and had taken the metal from several chieftains. His love for my mother had never diminished, and his own ambition in life was to reach a point where he might wrest the metal from Hagibrack himself, and thus, as ruler of the xin, be free to claim her as his own, as well as, by the might of his power, protect the child which otherwise would be quickly dispatched should the truth be known.

It was a wild dream, that of wresting the metal from Hagibrack in five short years, but his advance was rapid, and he soon stood high in the council of the Stanningxin. But one day the chance was lost forever: He was ordered away upon a long expedition to the far north of The Dark Peak, to make war upon the natives there and despoil them of their furs, for such is the manner of the xin; we do not work for what we can take in battle from others.

My father was gone for four years, and when he returned all had been over for three; for about a year after his departure, and shortly before the time for the return of an expedition which had gone to fetch the fruits of a community incubator, the egg had hatched. After that, my mother continued to keep me in the cave, visiting me nightly and pouring her love onto me. She hoped, upon the return of the expedition from the incubator, to mix me with the other young, and to escape the fate which would follow any discovery of her sin against the ancient traditions of the xin.

She taught me rapidly the language and customs of my kind, and one night she told me the story I have told to you up to this point. She impressed on me the need for absolute secrecy and the caution I must exercise after she had placed me with the other young xin. I could never allow anyone to guess that I was further advanced in education than they were. And never, in the presence of others, could I show my affection for her, or knowledge of my parents.

Then, pulling me close to her, she whispered the name of my father.

And then a light flashed out in the darkness of the cave, and there stood Gorsithorn. The torrent of hatred and abuse she poured out upon my mother, turned my heart cold in terror. She had known something wrong by my mother's long nightly absences from her quarters, and had now heard the entire story.

One thing she had not heard was the whispered name of my father. She repeatedly demanded my mother to tell her the name of her partner in sin, but no amount of abuse or threats could wring this from my mother, and she lied, telling Gorsithorn that she alone knew and would never tell her child.

Babbling curses, Gorsithorn went off to Hagibrack to report her discovery, and while she was gone my mother, wrapping me in silks and furs, descended to the causeway and ran wildly away toward the outskirts of the village, in the direction which led to the far south, out toward the man whose protection she might not claim, but on whose face she wished to look once more before she died.

As we neared the southern edge of the village, a sound came to us from across the moors. The sounds we heard were the squealing of mentiloth and the grumbling of cryptobite, with the occasional clank of arms. My mother thought it was my father returning from his expedition, but she held back from running to greet him.

We shrank back into the shadows, and from our hiding place saw that the expedition was not that of my father, but the returning caravan bearing the young xin. She knew, what I didn't, that never again after that night would she hold me to her breast, nor was it likely we would ever look upon each other's face again.

In the confusion of the village square she mixed me with the other children, whose guardians during the journey were now free to relinquish their responsibility. We were herded together into a great room, fed by women who had not been with the expedition, and the next day we were parcelled out among the retinues of the chieftains.

I never saw my mother after that night. She was imprisoned by Hagibrack, and every effort, including the most horrible and shameful torture, was brought to bear upon her to wring from her lips the name of my father; but she stayed steadfast and loyal, dying at last amidst the laughter of Hagibrack during some awful torture she was undergoing.

I learned afterwards that she told them that she had killed me to save me from a like fate at their hands, and that she had thrown my body off Stanedge to be pecked clean by the corvids. Gorsithorn alone disbelieved her, and I feel to this day that she suspects my true origin, but does not dare expose me, because she also guesses, I am sure, the identity of my father.

When he returned from his expedition, I was present as Hagibrack told him my mother's fate -- and not by the quiver of a muscle did he betray the slightest emotion -- only he did not laugh as Hagibrack described her death struggles.

From that moment on he was the cruelest of the cruel, and I am waiting for the day when he shall feel the carcass of Hagibrack beneath his foot.

Is tha father with us now? I said.

Yes, but he does not know me for who I am, nor does he know who betrayed my mother to Hagibrack. I alone know my father's name, and only I and Hagibrack and Gorsithorn know that it was she who carried the tale that brought torture and death to the one he loved.

We sat in silence and didn't say nowt for a while, she wrapped in the gloomy thoughts of her terrible past, and I in pity for them poor creatures and their loveless lives of hate.

Eventually Fenimoss spoke up again. I know that I can trust you, and because the knowledge may someday help you or him or Pandora or myself, I am going to tell you the name of my father, and you are free to do with this knowledge what you will. When the time comes, speak the truth if it seems best to you, or lie if a lie would save others from sorrow or suffering.

My father is Siltibog.

Aye, I knows it, I said, I mean, who else could it be, based on what tha's told me?

Jarv just looked confused, but then I wasn't really surprised by that. Things were getting so interesting now, but the trouble was, the night was getting on, and I had to be back at the university tomorrow for teaching -- and of course, to earn some money to keep funding this research, which although not massively expensive, was an expense, and I still had my lodgings here to pay for.

Van was looking longingly at the bottom of his empty vessel, and indeed Jarv -- a bit of a hanger on, this guy -- was doing the same; and hey, you don't get the opportunity to hear stories like this all the time, I thought to myself, so I politely offered to get the drinks in. No one declined. I assume that they thought I was putting them on an expense account.

```
      HMM::IN('Channel left open')
`hits::  1 // [this]2001:0db8:85a3:0000:0000:8a2e:037g:7334
[loc::hellsborough//middlewood_road//467]__ // now:: 79.hail
ripperthroat.12.16.0.9.9`
```

CHAPTER 16

To t'Swamp

Nuthin' much 'appened on the rest t'journey t'swamp, and I were glad of a bit a peace.

We were days on the road, and our progress was slow, such it was moving all them great animals and all them folk -- and the going was never easy, having to get around many cloughs and ridges, and the big bodies of water that stood in our way.

We crossed two great areas of moorland and passed through or around several ruined villages, all smaller than Stanningxin.

Often a warrior would be sent ahead, and if there were no sightings of clown troops we would advance as far as we could without the chance of being seen, and then camp 'til dark.

It required hours to make one of these crossings without stopping, and the other took the whole night, so we were just leaving the moor when the sun tried to break through the murk the next morning.

Crossing in darkness, as we did, I couldn't see owt, except where that tepid moon lit up little patches of landscape, and from time to time showed me walled fields and crumbling buildings -- farms I reckoned, some long abandoned, the odd one still lived in by the hardiest of those still about.

The trees grew raggedly as they do out there; some animals -- demonspawn and wooltard -- watched us with sad eyes from where they was penned up.

Once I saw a man like me, I think he made me jump as much as we did 'im. The fella must have been sleeping rough; as I come near him, he raised himself on his elbows and seeing us lot coming his way, leapt up with a shriek like a squarkwing, vaulted a stile and ran off over the moor.

I saw him scale a wall like a scared scratcher.

The xin weren't interested in him at all; they weren't out on the warpath, and the only sign that I had that they had seen him at all was a picking up of the pace as we got nearer the swamp and Hagibrack's kingdom.

I still hadn't spoken with Pandora, and she'd sent no word that I'd be welcome at her cart, so I didn't bother worrying her; leave her be, I thought, it'll either work itself out in t'end, or it won't.

I cannot have been more than a month in The Dark Peak, when I entered the swamp, the spiritual home of the xin.

The xin horde is about 50,000 strong. Small compared to human standards. They are split into twenty-five communities. Each with its own chieftain and lesser chieftains, but all are under the rule of the imperial xin commander, his holiness, Hagibrack.

Five communities live in and around the swamp; the rest are scattered among the deserted villages of The Dark Peak in the area owned by Hagibrack, and known as Xinlandia.

We entered the great bog -- as it is known -- in the early afternoon. There weren't no friendly greeting, those xin of the swamp that happened to be there spoke the names of warriors or women who they knew, but nowt else until someone must have said that there were a couple of prisoners, and then there were more interest, and Pandora and I become the centre of attention all of a sudden.

We were given quarters and allowed to settle in. I were now living off a track at the south of the settlement, close to the village's main road, where I had a crumbling shack to mesen. Hagibrack, like Pondisyke in Stanngxin, occupied an 'uge public building, the largest of t'village; the next largest was for Pondisyke, and the next for chieftains of a lesser rank.

Warriors slept in the buildings with the chieftains whose household they belonged to; or, if they wanted, found themselves somewhere in one of the empty and ramshackle buildings in the quarter of the village we were assigned to -- each community being given a section of their own.

My shack was put in order by my team, and I set off out to find Fenimoss and Pandora -- we needed to plan our escape. I searched until the gloaming, eventually seeing Shad's great blue eyes staring out of a window on the opposite side of the street.

I headed over, not waiting for an invitation and was greeted by a frenzied Shad, who was so glad to see me that I thought he'd eat me, as his head split from one lug'ole to t'other.

I stopped his dancing with a couple of words of command and a bit of fuss, and then searched about in the gloom for Pandora; not seeing her, I called her and heard a murmur from the corner where I saw her crouching, covered in furs and silks. She stood up and looked straight at me.

I know I's made tha angry me love, I just doant know why. I never wanted to hurt or offend thee, I said, I just wants to protect thee as best a can. Ignore me if that's what tha wants, but if tha want to escape this place then I'll help thee, but we needs to talk. When tha's safe and back home in Hathersage, tha can do with me what tha wants, but from now on until then, we must work together.

She looked at me for a long time, and I thought that she were softening a bit.

I understand your words, Van, she said, but you I do not understand. You are a queer mixture of child and man, of captive and xin chieftain. I only wish that I could read your heart.

Look at tha feet, Pandora; me heart lies there now where it has been since that other night in Stanningxin.

She come toward me -- What do you mean, Van Hallam? she whispered. What are you saying to me?

I is saying, Pandora, that I is yours, body and soul, to serve thee, to fight for thee, and to die for thee; the only thing I ask is that tha let me get on with me job until everything is done and dusted.

I will, Van I understand.

After that brief chat, Fenimoss came in, she seemed mardy and not her usual calm self.

Gorsithorn has been to see Hagibrack, she sobbed, and from what I hear there is little hope for either of you.

What have you 'eard? I said.

That you will be thrown to the dyapnids in the great bog bowl as soon as the hordes have assembled for the yearly games.

```
    HMM::OUT('I have been sent to watch over thee.')
`ask:: unknown // stat:: accept[ok]__ // src::
2001:0db8:85a3:0000:0000:8a2e:142j:i618 [loc::hellsborough//
unknown__location//000]__ // now:: 79.hail
ripperthroat.12.16.0.12.40`
```

Fenimoss, I said, tha is xin, but tha hates the customs of tha people as much as we do. Why don't tha come with us when we escape? I'm sure Pandora can offer tha an 'ome and protection among her people, and it can't be no worse than stayin' around 'ere.

Come with us, Fenimoss, your fate would be terrible if they thought you had connived to help us. I want you with us, I want you to come to our land of happiness, said Pandora.

The Venomtooth Pass passes close to Hathersage and is just a few miles to the south of here, said Fenimoss; a swift mentiloth would make it in three hours. But they would know and follow us. We might hide on the moors for a while, but our chances for escape are small. They would follow us to the gates of Hathersage -- you do not know them like I do.

I thought for a bit: Is there any other way to get to 'athersage? Draw us a map, I said.

Pandora picked up a twig and drew in the dirt -- it were the first proper map of The Dark Peak I'd ever seen.

Her map were criss-crossed with lines and circles. The lines, she said, were rivers and roads; the circles were villages; and one she pointed at, that were Hathersage. There were other villages closer, but she said that they weren't good, they weren't friendly toward Hatheran clowns -- they were closer to the Glossopians.

I looked at that dirt map, and pointed at a road to the northeast -- it went through t'wisewood, and the netherlands, before coming back 'round to Hathersage.

They wouldn't ever think that we'd try that roundabout route, I said, so we should use that. I've travelled through some of t'wisewood, I said, and it holds no fear for me -- and we have Shad 'ere 'n'all.

There were some too-ing and fro-ing until Fenimoss agreed 'n'all.

We would leave t'swamp that neet. I'd saddle me mentiloth. Fenimoss and Pandora would fly on one of 'em and I'd be on t'other. Each of us would carry food and drink to last us for a couple of days, and that would see us through to t'journeys end.

```
    HMM::OUT('Do I need to be watched over?')
`ask:: Rippon, Pip // stat:: accept[ok]__ // src::
2001:0db8:85a3:0000:0000:8a2e:037g:7334 [loc::hellsborough//
middlewood_road//467]__ // now:: 79.hail
ripperthroat.12.16.0.17.2`
```

I told Fenimoss to go with Pandora and go to the south end of the village. I'd meet them there with me mentiloth as soon as I could; then, I left 'em to get food and stuff we might need.

The great herd of mentiloth and cryptobite milled about in the shadows out back of the buildings. As they scented me they got restless and started kicking up a bit of a fuss. This were risky business, entering t'paddock alone, at neet -- first, noise might warn t'other warriors that someat was up, and second, I might be charged by a mentiloth, and then I'd be good for nowt but jellyhead bio-feed.

Moving quiet like, I reached the gates which opened onto the street, and called to my two animals. I thanked my good sense in showing these creatures some kindness, cos I saw two huge bulks forcing their way toward me through the surging mass of the other animals.

They came close to me, rubbing their muzzles against me body and sniffing for the bits of food what I rewarded 'em with. Opening the gates I led me two beasts out.

I walked as quiet as I could toward an empty street where I'd arranged to meet Pandora and Fenimoss. I swear a murk wraith would have made more noise than we did on them deserted lanes, but not until I could see the plain beyond the village did I let out a gasp of relief and start to breathe a bit freer.

I got to the place, but Pandora and Fenimoss weren't there. I thought it best to keep moving, it were unusual for a warrior to be about after murkfall, and I didn't want to attract no attention, so I led the animals to a stable block near by. I thought that maybe one of the other women of the my household might have come in to speak to Fenimoss, and that might have slowed 'em down, so I waited, but after an hour, when I still hadn't seen 'em, I started to worry a bit, I did Pip.

Then I 'eard the sound of others coming, which I knew from t'noise, weren't good news. Soon this party were near me, and from the gloom of the entrance where I was hiding, I saw mounted warriors, whose words put me 'eart into me mouth:

He would have arranged to meet them just outside the village, so...

-- I didn't hear nowt else, they had passed on; but it were enough. Me plan had been found out, and our chances for escape scuppered. Me hope now was to get back to Pandora and find out what'd 'appened, but how to do that? -- with these mentiloth, and knowing that the whole village probably knew that we were trying to escape.

I felt me way through that dark stable, calling to me mentiloth so they followed. We made it to t'other side where the brackish vegetation would provide 'em with food 'til I could get 'em back to their enclosure. I knew they'd be content here and hidden -- the xin wouldn't come to these outlying buildings, they're reyt scared of murkspawn.

Do you know what murkspawn is Jarv? Said Van.

Jarv started to talk and then clamped his jaws back together, no sound seemed likely to be forthcoming.

Tell him Pip.

Murkspawn -- syncarid and morivarid: Revenants of those killed in battle or taken by the Dun river to return as drifters of the ether, swimming through the thick atmosphere with their stinging tails and roving mouths.

Exactly.

Anyway, I made me way back to Pandora's place. I didn't rush in, but listened at the dooer instead -- I needed to make sure that it were Pandora who was there, and that it were safe to go in -- and it were good that I did.

The talking from t'other side of the dooer weren't Pandora at all, but the gruffness of blokes -- a chieftain were giving orders to his warriors:

When he comes back here, when she doant meet him at the village edge, tha four are to grab him and disarm him. When tha has him tied up, bring him to the vaults and chain him where he can be found when Hagibrack wants him. Don't allow him to speak to no-one. There will be no danger of the girl returning, she'll be with Hagibrack by now, and may her ancestors have pity upon her, for Hagibrack will have none; the great Gorsithorn has done a grand night's work toneet. I go, and if tha fails to capture him when he comes, I'll send tha carcasses to the bottom of the Dun mesen.

And with that, said Van, I need to gercher for the neet, and so does thee Pip, it has been a long day for both of us, and if I remember correctly, tha has to be back at t'university tomorrow.

Yes, I said, I do.

```
      HMM::OUT('gercher?')
`ask:: Rippon, Pip // stat:: accept[ok]__ // src::
2001:0db8:85a3:0000:0000:8a2e:037g:7334 [loc::hellsborough//
middlewood_road//467]__ // now:: 79.hail
ripperthroat.12.16.0.29.12`

`HMM::IN('..local dialect, meaning to get off, to go
away.._')`
```

Cheers then Jarv, said Van, it's been a good evening, maybe we can bump into each other again and tha can get me and Pip 'ere a pint, since tha seems to have done well out of our hospitality toneet.

Jarv stuttered some or other excuse which I failed to pick up (which is amazing as I heard everything Van had said as clear as a bell and hadn't forgotten any of it since I'd taken the crust, which is nothing if not an amazing aid in recall and hearing), and then bid us farewell and stumbled out of the bar.

We watched him leave and then Van turned to me: Pip, stay a little longer; stay 'til we're done.

```
     HMM::IN('DPDC Alert: Hellsborough park now re opened')
`hits:: 1226354 //
[this]2001:0db8:85a3:0000:0000:8a2e:037g:7334
[loc::hellsborough//middlewood_road//467]__ // now:: 79.hail
ripperthroat.12.16.0.29.29`
`The park is now passable again, but please remain vigilant.`
```

I'm not sure I can Van, I said, it's true, I do have to be back in the off-world tomorrow to do some teaching, it's expected of me.

Them cracker jacking grizzler smelts in their ivory towers, suck 'em, said Van, what time is it anyway?

Half twelve.

In that case we got many an hour left. I reckon we can probably get reyt through me story by the time the sun tries to peek through t'murk again, so we can 'ave this wrapped up toneet.

But I need to get some sleep Van, this teaching assignment, it's important to me; and it's good money.

Really? Is it more important than preserving the experiences of a dying man for the freedom of every jellyhead in Hellsborough? And anyway, I'll pay thee double, and tha can be me guest until this is all done and dusted, so no more B&B fees to pay.

Well, when you put it like that, maybe not. I'll be staying with you then?

Aye, tha can get tha things in t'mornin', we'll make do until then; ok, that's agreed then! -- let's get them beers in and stoke that pipe up, and now that that chizzler Jarv has cleared off, maybe we can get to some of the better parts. Not sure about 'im anyway, I think he might be a nascenti stooge; what sort of name is Jarvis Fry anyway?

(which is what I had thought, before I dismissed the idea).

```
      HMM::OUT('Tha does.')
`ask:: unknown // stat:: accept[ok]__ // src::
2001:0db8:85a3:0000:0000:8a2e:142j:i618 [loc::hellsborough//
unknown__location//000]__ // now:: 79.hail
ripperthroat.12.16.0.33.56`
```

CHAPTER 17

Hagibrack

So I didn't need to hear any more after that, did I? I tell you what though Pip, a plan had formed in me noggin reyt enough. I crossed that square straight through the murk and into Hagibrack's court.

There was a lot going on over there, and the rooms of the court were filled with folk. I looked up at the floors above, and saw that the third floor were dark. The only problem I had was how I was going to get up there, but being a good clamberer, I soon made it up.

The room I went into were empty, but I could see light in front of me, so 'eaded in that direction. When I got there, I saw that it were an openin' onto the inner chamber of the dome-shaped roof, and I was looking down on Hagibrack's party.

Except this weren't no party like you've ever seen before Pip -- the hall were jammed with chieftains, warriors and women, all of them supping stuff that I ain't seen in Stanningxin and all of 'em looking like they was havin' a reyt good time, it almost brought a smile to me face it did -- until I saw a raised platform, where squatted the most hideous beast I'd ever set eyes on.

Hagibrack. He had all the cold, hard, cruel, terrible features of the green warriors, but he was clearly a debased and diseased individual. Tha could tell that just be looking at 'im.

I made some drawings later, Pip, I'll show 'em to thee when we get back home, cos it don't matter what I say, I can't describe how bad this thing looked. There weren't owt like dignity on his face, and his enormous bulk spread itself out on that platform, like some 'uge black clock, his six limbs squirmin' in an 'orrible way -- like tentacles of The Loxley Kraken.

```
     HMM::OUT('Black Clock')
`ask:: Rippon, Pip // stat:: accept[ok]__ // src::
2001:0db8:85a3:0000:0000:8a2e:037g:7334 [loc::hellsborough//
middlewood_road//467]__ // now:: 79.hail
ripperthroat.12.16.0.36.3`

`HMM::IN('..Black ground beetle_')`

     HMM::OUT('The Loxley Kraken')
`ask:: Rippon, Pip // stat:: accept[ok]__ // src::
2001:0db8:85a3:0000:0000:8a2e:037g:7334 [loc::hellsborough//
middlewood_road//467]__ // now:: 79.hail
ripperthroat.12.16.0.36.5`

`HMM::IN('..Believed to dwell under the bridge in that
most liminal of places    Hellsborough corner   where the
crossroads, the river and the bridge all exist in the same
space, the Loxley Kraken one of the many cryptids of the murk,
is said to grab passersby from the street above, drown them
in the chilly waters of the Loxley river by enveloping them
with its many tentacled arms, and after storing their cadavers
until decomposed, suck the meat from the bones   which then
wash down river to collect at the confluence of the Dun. Some
believe that the bones of those that meet their end in this
way float all the way to the Ripperthroat mountains, where
they are eventually met by Dunlockslyn_')`
```

An' next to this thing, stood Pandora and Fenimoss. Hagibrack leered at 'em both, his 'uge eyes gloating on 'em -- the objects of his torment. Pandora were speaking, but I couldn't hear what she said, or make out what he grumbled in reply. Pandora stood there in front of 'im, 'er 'ead 'eld 'igh! -- and I could see the scorn on her face -- and even though she must have been scared, she didn't show no sign of it.

Hagibrack made a sign for the chamber to empty, and the prisoners be left alone with him. Slowly the chieftains, the warriors and the women left to go to the surrounding chambers, and Pandora and Fenimoss were alone with the imperial xin commander.

One of the chieftains didn't leave as quick as the rest. He stood in the shadows of one of them big columns that held up the roof -- them stingers -- they were architects of mighty buildings, so they were. This chieftain, I knew who it was, of course, it were Siltibog -- his fingers toyed with his whipo'wil and he stared at Hagibrack with hate in his eyes. I could read his thoughts, of course, he was an open book to me: He was thinking of a woman who, forty years before, had stood before this monster -- and if I could have spoken a word into Siltibog's lughole right then, Hagibrack's reign as the imperial xin commander would have been over in a moment. But I didn't speak to Siltibog, and he finally left the room -- not knowing that he left his own daughter at the mercy of the creature that he loathed most.

Hagibrack used his four legs to get himself upright. I could see and read his mind, and knew what he was planning. I ran down the winding staircase of the dome -- no-one was there to stop me, "his holiness" had ordered them all away and so I was by mesen. I hid in the shadows of the column that Siltibog had just left.

Hagibrack were talkin' -- even the sound of his voice was putrid. A princess of Hathersage, he said. I could charge an hefty ransom from tha people for tha return. But I'd rather watch tha pretty face writhing in agony as I torture thee. That will be much better entertainment for me, ha! And a spectacle for the coming games! He laughed and giggled like a, like a child -- no that's not right. How would you put it Pip?

That he laughed raucously? I said.

Yeh, maybe that's it. But it were more sinister, he was having fun at the prospect of torturing Pandora. Hagibrack was an evil murksun -- You can edit it later -- change it to how you think it sounds best.

Anyway, Hagibrack carried on -- tha's torture, he said to Pandora -- will be long and drawn out, that I promise thee; tha'll die ten days after I's started, and the pleasure I get will be too short to show the 'ate that I has for you mithering clowns. The terror of tha death will haunt you clowns through all eternity; they will 'ave nightmares for generations about my vengeance, the vengeance of the green men -- of the power and might and 'ate and cruelty of Hagibrack. But before I torture thee, tha's gonna be mine for this hour -- and word of that will be 'eard by your father, Ptolemy of Hathersage -- and then he will grovel in the agony of 'is sorrow. Tomorrow I'll torture thee; tonight tha's mine, now come!

Hagibrack went to grab Pandora's throat.

He didn't touch her though, as I leapt between 'em. I could have plunged my whipo'wil into his putrid heart -- I've said putrid once already, change that -- before he realised what was 'appening; but right then, I thought of Siltibog, and, with all my rage and hatred of this creature in front of me, I couldn't rob Siltibog of his revenge after all these years, so I swung a fist at his jaw instead.

That lump of flab sank to the floor as if I'd killed him, but I saw his torso heaving for breath, so I knew he weren't dead.

I grabbed Pandora by the hand, and telling Fenimoss to follow, we left the chamber as quietly as we could and went up to the floor above. We reached the rear window, and there, without being noticed, used me trappings to lower Fenimoss -- she were quite a weight, Pip -- and then Pandora, light as a feather in comparison, to the ground. I dropped down after them, and then in the shadows, we went back by the same route that I had used to get there, to the edge of the village.

My mentiloth were in the courtyard where I'd left them, and I put on their saddles. Fenimoss got up on one of 'em, and me the other, pulling Pandora up behind me, and we flew from the swamp to the cover of Bleaklow.

Instead of circling back around the village to the west and making our way to Venomtooth pass, which was reyt close to us, and would have been the fastest way to Hathersage, we turned northeast and headed across the Featherbed moss, an open wasteland of several thousand paces, where we picked up the Woodhead -- the other main artery that would eventually take us through the Netherlands and the Wisewood, and get Pandora back home.

No one said a word until we had left the village a long way back, but I knew Pandora was sobbing as she clung to me with her 'ead resting on me shoulder, I assumed it were the relief of getting out of the swamp and away from his ugliness Hagibrack.

If we make it Hathersage, I will always be in your debt, Van, she whispered to me from behind. And if we don't make it, the debt is no less, for you have saved me from worse than death.

I didn't answer, just reached down and squeezed her fingers where she clung to me, and we continued to speed through the murknight and over the yellow moss. In my 'ead, with Pandora's body pressed close to mine, I were already entering the gates of Hathersage, but I knew we had more dangers to face yet.

Because our plan from earlier had been scuppered, we now had no scran and nowt to sup, and I was the only one with any weapons. We ended up riding all neet we did, until out mentiloth were so knackered we had no choice but to stop and let them -- and us -- rest. We slept for a few hours, then started again before murklight. We flew for the next few hours, but then in the late morning, we found no road -- and the truth become obvious -- we was lost.

Who can say how, but in the murk we must have circled back on ourselves, so we was now almost as near to the swamp as where we started. I wanted to puke my guts up, and I probably would have, if I weren't starving from 'avin' nowt to eat -- we all felt the same -- we were tired and 'ungry -- at least we could sup from the sykes there or thereabouts. Ahead of us we could see some low hills and decided they would be the best bet to head for; murknight was on us before we got there, we lay down and slept.

Good old Shad had managed to track us down and the chuffer woke me up before the murkrise, licking me face, the crazy sun; I know he was just being a barker and that's how barkers are, but I could have done with a bit more kip, reyt enough; I gave him a hug, like you do, you know what I mean, pets is special ain't they. Not long after that, Pandora and Fenimoss woke up, and we made an early start to get to them hills.

```
    HMM::OUT('Heading in tha direction now')
`ask:: unknown // stat:: accept[ok]__ // src::
2001:0db8:85a3:0000:0000:8a2e:142j:i618 [loc::hellsborough//
unknown__location//000]__ // now:: 79.hail
ripperthroat.12.16.0.41.17`

    HMM::OUT('Wait, what?  Who are you?  How will I recognise
you?')
`ask:: Rippon, Pip // stat:: accept[ok]__ // src::
2001:0db8:85a3:0000:0000:8a2e:037g:7334 [loc::hellsborough//
middlewood_road//467]__ // now:: 79.hail
ripperthroat.12.16.0.41.19`
```

We can't have gone more than a thousand paces when me mentiloth started swaying about all over the place, even though she hadn't had to fly since about murknoon the day before. She ditched into the heather and chucked me and Pandora off. We was all reyt, it were a soft landing, but even without us on her back, she were completely shagged out. I took off her saddle and other trappings, but she could do no more than pant on the ground. I kinda thought it would be best to put her out of her misery, but Fenimoss said that I shouldn't do that, and so we left her to her own fate, much as that upset us all.

From then on, Fenimoss and I walked, and Pandora rode on our remaining animal. We got to about another thousand paces from the hills, when Pandora on the back of the mentiloth, said that she saw warriors coming down a pass in them same hills where we was headed. Fenimoss and I both looked where she had said and we could see seventy or so xin -- but they was heading away from us. We breathed a sigh of relief -- for now at least.

I doant think that any of us doubted that they were after us -- fugitives that we were -- but they was heading away from us, so that were good, but to be on safe side, I lifted Pandora down and had the mentiloth lie down. I doant want us to be noticed, I said -- tha can't be too sure can thee?

We watched 'em as they come out of pass and become hidden behind a ridge. As t'last warrior come into view, he stopped and scanned the moors. He were a chieftain, I knew, since he were at the back. As he looked our way, I felt a cold sweat come over me.

I saw him shout to his troops, but he didn't wait for them to join him. He wheeled his mentiloth and came flying in our direction.

I knew I had to act, and I was panicked a bit, Pip, but this guy weren't gonna take no prisoners, I reckoned, so we was all in danger. I raised me fungun, found him in me sights and pressed the trigger; there were an explosion and he flew backards off his mentiloth.

How old is tha young'un, said Van suddenly, catching me off-guard, and making me mentally calculate my own age. They say that the northern vernacular will be dead within a generation, he said, maybe this book can postpone that for a while, ha!

I didn't have time to answer him before he continued with his story.

I got to me feet quick like, and got our mentiloth up 'n'all. I said to Fenimoss to take Pandora with her, and make as best she could to the hills before them xin warriors caught up with us. I knew that in them ravines and gullies they might find some hiding place, and even if they died there of hunger and thirst it would be better than falling into the hands of the xin. I handed them me small funguns and lifted Pandora up beside Fenimoss, who had already mounted.

I wanted to hug her Pip, I did, but I ain't much of a hugger -- I's mentioned it before -- so I just smiled and said that I'd see her in Hathersage yet cos I'd escaped from worse smelt than this.

Pandora started to kick up a bit of a fuss, wanting me to come with them, but I said that I needed to hold 'em off and put some space between us and them, so they needed to get off.

She jumped off the mentiloth then and 'ugged me tightly, and turned to Fenimoss, saying: Fly, Fenimoss! I will stay with Van to die with the man I love.

Those words are engraved upon me heart, Pip.

I pressed my lips to hers for the first time, but then picked her up and tossed her up again behind Fenimoss, then slapped the mentiloth upon its butt, so she bolted with the two of them on-board; Pandora struggling to the last to free herself from Fenimoss's grasp.

```
      HMM::OUT('Thee'll know')
`ask:: unknown // stat:: accept[ok]__ // src::
2001:0db8:85a3:0000:0000:8a2e:142j:i618 [loc::hellsborough//
unknown__location//000]__ // now:: 79.hail
ripperthroat.12.16.0.41.24`
```

I saw the xin warriors coming back over the ridge, looking for their chieftain. They saw him, where I had cut him down and then they saw me; I started firing on 'em straight away, lying flat on me belly in the heather. I had a hundred rounds in me fungun, and another hundred in me belt, and I kept firing until them warriors was running for cover.

But then those warriors were joined by more, and then more come charging into view, all heading toward me. I fired until me fungun were empty and there were nowt left. Then they was upon me. I checked that Pandora and Fenimoss had gone to the 'ills, then got to me feet, threw down me now useless weapon, and ran in the opposite direction to where Fenimoss and Pandora had gone.

The xin horde come after me. Me foot got caught in bramble, and I went sprawling in the heather and bracken. Moments later they was on me; I drew my whipo'wil, but it was over before it had started. They punched and kicked the smelting out of me and I was gone, out of it and unconscious and on me way to the oblivion of Dunlockslyn.

CHAPTER 18

Strinxin

`HMM::OUT('No, stop, don't come here. It's not safe!')`
`` `ask:: Rippon, Pip // stat:: accept[ok]__ // src:: 2001:0db8:85a3:0000:0000:8a2e:037g:7334 [loc::hellsborough//middlewood_road//467]__ // now:: 79.hail ripperthroat.12.16.0.41.29` ``

I thought I was deed Pip, but I weren't, but it must have been several hours before I come to, and I were surprised to come to at all, I has to be honest. I was lying on a pile of silks and furs in the corner of a small room in which were several xin. Bendin' over me an ancient and ugly nurse were treating me wounds.

He will live, chieftain I 'eard her say.

'Tis well, he replied, he will be rare sport for t'great games.

`HMM::OUT('Pfft!')`
`` `ask:: unknown // stat:: accept[ok]__ // src:: 2001:0db8:85a3:0000:0000:8a2e:142j:i618 [loc::hellsborough//unknown__location//000]__ // now:: 79.hail ripperthroat.12.16.0.41.30` ``

I looked over at 'im and saw that he were not Stanningxin -- his ornaments and metal were different. He were huge and reyt scarred about t'face and chest, with a broken tusk 'n' a missing lug. Hangin' from his chest were shrunken skulls and dried hands.

The female xin told him that I was fit to travel, and the chieftain ordered that we mount up 'n' ride. They strapped me to a wild mentiloth, and, with a mounted warrior either side of us, to stop the thing boltin', we rode reyt fast, back toward -- I assumed -- t'swamp. Me wounds gave me little pain -- I has said before that the xin has amazin' powers of 'ealing.

Just before murkneet we reached the rest of the troops just after they had made camp for the neet. I were taken straight to the leader, the chieftain of this horde -- the Strinxin.

Like the chieftain who had brought me, he were badly scarred, and decorated with skulls and dead hands which seemed to be the mark of these Strinxin warriors.

The ruling chieftain was Ridgimoor, young compared to one who had brought be here; his fierce and jealous old lieutenant: Cragimold, the chieftain who had captured me. I could not help notice the efforts he made to try an' better his superior.

I has brought thee a strange creature wearing the metal of the Stanningxin, said Cragimold, who didn't even look at his own chieftain -- he will die feighting wild mentiloth at the great games.

He will die as Ridgimoor, sees fit, if at all, the young ruler said.

```
     HMM::IN(' BackflitPirate: incoming')
`ask:: unknown // stat:: accept[ok]__ // src::
2001:0db8:85a3:0000:0000:ff32:8877:7b45 [loc::hellsborough//
unknown__location//000]__ // now:: 79.hail
ripperthroat.12.16.0.44.1`
```

Interference and static

`Ey up, I got what you're after, it's never too late for a slurp of slime is it murker!  Paste me back  BFP121600. Sound.  Gotta go, call me, you know it's reyt.`

Interference and static

We need more rockcrust, don't we Van? I said, breaking into his oration. I'm kind of getting dry and I've got this nagging thing about someone coming in at the moment, someone I don't know, so I'm a bit on edge, and a delivery of crust is going to take the edge off I reckon'.

Go for it, always up for a bit of crust -- you know me well enough Pip - you know it's reyt, what's the bf's tag this time?

bf?

Come on, Backflit! Our man Delf!

#BFP121600

Van did that trick again and tapped his psycmask without actually doing much else -- that's done then, he said, with a small grin on his face. Anyway, what was I saying? Aye, that's reyt: What's this worry tha has about someon' turning up?

It came in via the hivemind, a Direct Message -- someone says I am in danger.

Danger of what?

The bitter finger -- or maybe you? Whoever it is said I should be aware of the alliance, of crosslander, clown and xaexs.

Me? So you are now afraid of me, because a stranger told you to be on the hivemind? Gi'o'er Pip! Tha knows full well that thou has nowt to fear from mesen!

Do I, I thought to myself: You used to hang out with the netherlanders, and the clowns, and you know Dirty Leaves pretty well it seems to me.

I did, you're right -- a hundred years ago; it's a century since I come back from The Dark Peak! -- this is a stranger you're talking to -- an' this is me, Van! Is tha not on drugs, Pip?

Well no, that's why you just ordered some more.

I doant know nowt about this bitter finger thing, Pip, I swear t'thee.

Ok, let's carry on with your story Van, I'll forget about whatever it is that's going on for now. And with that, Van rolled on again, barely missing a beat:

If at all? Roared Cragimold. By the dead hands at me throat he shall die, Ridgimoor. Your weakness sha'n't save him. Ha! Us Strinxin should be ruled by a real warlord rather than by a water-'earted weaklin', who even old Cragimold could tear the metal from with his bare 'ands!

Ridgimoor stared at his old lieutenant for a short while. I could see the contempt in his eyes. Suddenly, without drawing a weapon or saying a word he hurled himself at the throat of old Cragimold.

I'd not seen two xin warriors feight without weapons before, and it were as scary as owt I'd ever come across. They tore at each others' eyes and lugs with their hands and their tusks slashed and gored until they were both cut to ribbons from head to feet.

Ridgimoor were stronger, quicker and more cleverer, and he went for his final death thrust, but slipped as he tried to break away from Cragimold's clutch. This were the little openin' that Cragimold needed, and he hurled himself at Ridgimoor, burying his single tusk into Ridgimoor's groin, rippin' him wide open the full length of his body, finally wedging his tusk in Ridgimoor's jaw.

Both of them rolled limp and lifeless on the moss, a mass of torn and bloody flesh.

Ridgimoor were dead as a door nail. Cragimold's females saved him though, applying medicines like what had saved me not long before. Three days later he walked to the body of Ridgimoor which hadn't been moved, and placing his foot on the neck of his former ruler took the title Warlord of Strinxin.

Ridgimoor's hands and head were cut off to be dried and added to Cragimold's ornaments, and then his women cremated what remained -- with wild laughter.

After that, in another day or so, we was back at the swamp. There I was thrown in a dungeon and chained to the floor and walls. Food was brought me -- I knew they needed to keep me alive -- I would be someat different for the crowds.

It were proper dark in that dungeon and I doant know whether I was there for days or months. It were bloody awful, Pip -- and me mind were weak then. That place was filled with creeping, crawling things; cold bodies passed over me when I lay down, an' in that darkness I caught glimpses of fiery eyes fixed on me. It were like being back in the wisewood on that first night away from Hellsborough, but more scary like.

Nowt reached me from t'outside, I heard no news at all; me jailer didn't say a word when he brought me food, even though I asked him no end of questions. But I kept me eyes on him -- I noticed he always come with his torch to where he could place the food within me reach and as he stooped to place it upon the floor, his head was about level with me chest.

I think I must 'ave bin bonkers by this time Pip -- throughout me life I has had times when I didn't always think as clearly as maybe a should 'ave.

I know the feeling... I watched the door of the bar slowly swing open, and I hastily chugged what was left of my ale. Van's was already gone and he looked expectantly at me for a refill, indicating with a rub of his adams apple and a tweak of his neck wattle, that his throat was dry. Shalesmoor was back behind the bar serving a number of folk who thronged about, and I got into a half-rise, just waiting for Van to finish this part of his story, since it felt close.

A metallic looking ball rolled lazily across the floor, picking up dust and insect debris in its wake. A small amber light ticked slowly on its tiny "face".

Van swallowed spit and hoarsely continued: I backed into a far corner of me cell, an' when I heard him approaching, I swung me chains above me head and crashed them links on his noggin. Without a sound he were gone, deed as a chuffin' murk wraith.

I were laughing and chattering under me breath, cos I reckon me sanity had gone walkabout then, and me fingers were feeling for his dead throat. I found the small chain and his keys. The touch on these keys brought me back some sense, and I started to come to a bit -- I weren't a gibbering idiot no longer -- but sane, with means of escape in me 'ands.

As I was groping to remove the chain from his neck, I glanced up into the darkness and saw six pairs of amber eyes staring back at me. Slowly they approached and I shrank back from 'em. I went back into me own corner, and crouched holding me 'ands out showing I had nowt, but them eyes weren't interested in me, they just wanted that dead body. They retreated with strange grating sounds, disappearing into the black and distant recesses of their part of the dungeon.

The ball bumped into our table leg and stopped, it's amber lamp ticking like a wink.

```
     HMM::OUT('Murk Wraith')
`ask:: Rippon, Pip // stat:: accept[ok]__ // src::
2001:0db8:85a3:0000:0000:8a2e:037g:7334 [loc::hellsborough//
middlewood_road//467]__ // now:: 79.hail
ripperthroat.12.16.1.1.1`

`HMM::IN('..Colour:  Indistinct`

`..Diet:  Souls of the living_`

`..Size:  Indistinct_`

`..Defining characteristics:  Undead spirits of the pained.
Associated with impending doom_`
```

VAN HALLAM

`..Class:   Undead_ Revenant_`
`..Image:   Error_\/\/\/\/')`

CHAPTER 19

Penny and Sinclair

So what's this then Pip? Said Van, looking down at the blinking steel ball. Looks like a gutterball to me.

What's a Gutterball? I managed to stammer, fair scared out of my whits and barely able to move, the fear keeping me rooted to that chair like Van had been frozen in place on that first night of his in the wisewood -- my brain had been calculating that it was a bomb sent in by my new found "friend" from the hivemind, or maybe by the axis of this bitter finger, whatever that was; Dunlockslyn knows that between a xaexs, a crosslander and a clown spy they'd have enough knowledge and firepower to get their hands on a remotely operated drone bomb -- if such a thing existed.

Van reached down to the ground, lifting it up and rotating it so he looked directly into its "eyes".

No Van! My heart was in my mouth.

No what? But it was too late, it was in his hand, sitting there comfortably -- if a metallic ball could somehow show comfort. He's all reyt, said Van, look he's purring. The amber winking lights had changed colour and were now flashing an intense red.

I just looked on aghast.

Watch this, said Van. He stuck one of his spindly fingers into some sort of socket that had become visible in the cortex of the ball, and the thing appeared to rumble with delight -- look he's laughing, said Van -- nothing to fear from this little chap Pip. Give it up then, said Van, and the ball stuck out its "tongue" to reveal its payload -- the rockcrust that had been ordered from the bf.

Much obliged, my little round friend -- now you tell the bf to keep us topped up regular like, we're going to be needin' fresh crust for as long as this night carries on, you get me? The gutterball's eyes glowed a vivid blue (I took it that meant that it understood in the affirmative) as it purred some more, what's your name little fella?

The gutterball's eyes flashed blue this time as it presumably transmitted it's name to Van via the hivemind, but Van, not possessing a full psycmask seemed to pick it up anyway. Nice name young fella, nice name, Let me know when you're on your way back Sinclair. And then Van set Sinclair back down on the floor and it rolled off towards the door -- a kindly patron seeing it coming and making its passage outwards possible.

I made eye contact with Van then -- What?! He mouthed -- and I started to rise again to go over to the bar and get our now long-dry glasses re-filled.

That was when the explosion happened.

With my back now to the door, I expected the glass frontage of the bar to shatter inwards and threw myself headlong towards the bar, crashing down on top of the empty glasses, which, if they had been anything other than dimple mugs would have shattered on the floor and impaled me upon their shards, instead of just being cushioned by my stomach.

I got up, relatively unscathed and looked back at the window, expecting some horror scenario -- only to see many of the folk in the bar with puzzled looks, smirking at me like the rockhead I had become -- and the frontage of the bar fully intact. I recovered myself and got the glasses to the bar, asking Shalesmoor what the explosion was.

Just that gutterball firing itself up, he said, refilling our glasses with a newly tapped ale that he recommended would calm my nerves.

I thanked him and took the ale back to Van, who had already consumed his portion of rockcrust and offered the rotated straw towards my nostril, which was quickly filled with the gloop.

Echoing Shalesmoor's words, Van said this too would calm my nerves and I needed to forget all about this stranger from the hivemind and any fears I had about this supposed bitter finger alliance. Strangely feeling exhausted all of a sudden, I took the advice of both of them and succumbed to the rockcrust and the potent new ale that Shalesmoor has proffered.

Yeah, you look exhausted Pip, and its been a long evening, but you'll pep up in a bit and we have a little way to go yet, and as I said before, I want to get this done, and you'll not be forgetting anything, so let's crack on shall we?

I nodded my assent, checked in with the hivemind about what a gutterball was -- just to be sure I was on the right (or wrong) side of sane:

```
        HMM::OUT('Gutterball')
`ask:: Rippon, Pip // stat:: accept[ok]__ // src::
2001:0db8:85a3:0000:0000:8a2e:037g:7334 [loc::hellsborough//
middlewood_road//467]__ // now:: 79.hail
ripperthroat.12.16.1.32.56`
`HMM::IN('..Colour: Metallic, steel_`
`..Diet: None_`
`..Size: 6" (circumference)_`
`..Defining characteristics: Messenger, tool_`
```

```
`..Class:   Made_`
`..Image:   Incoming...')`
```

-- and then Van launched into his next episode:

For two days I didn't eat, but then a new jailer turned up and things went on as before, but this time I didn't let the place get the better of me -- I kept mesen focused and ready for me next chance to escape.

Another prisoner were brought in and chained up close. I could see in the dim light of the torch, that she were a clown by her painted features, and I knew I needed to talk to her as soon as I could. I spoke low and soft, by way of greeting -- ayup thee.

Who are you who speaks from the dark? She said.

Van Hallam, a friend of the clowns of Hathersage.

I am Hatheran, she said, but I don't know you.

I told her me story as I have been telling thee here, Pip, only leaving out me love of Pandora.

She were excited by the news of Hathersage's princess and positive that she and Fenimoss could easily have reached safety from where they left me. She said that she knew the gulley through which the Strinxin warriors passed well, it were called Winnats pass, and they only ever used it when on t'way to t'swamp, she reckoned they would easily 'ave got away and would be safe.

Penny worked for the Hatheran navy and had been on the same expedition as when the Stanningxin had captured Pandora. She and what remained of their crew, and a the other vessels, had tried to limp back to Hathersage, but they had drifted way way off course, and they was ambushed by the Glossopian clowns, who destroyed everything. She alone had survived, and found herself on the moors close to the swamp. Her only contact with her species had been faint echoes in the hivemind, but she had heard nothing about the whereabouts of Pandora, only knowing that the Hatheran clowns had looked high and low.

For two days and nights she had been exploring the quarters and dungeons of the swamp searching for her princess only to be caught as she were about to leave, after seeing no sign of Pandora. Penny and me become well acquainted, we did, and formed a warm personal friendship. But after a few days, we was dragged from our dungeon for them great games. Before murkrise, we was taken to an 'uge place -- what does tha call it proply, Pip?

A stadium, I said.

Nah, bigger, more grand, classic like.

I racked my brains and rifled through my mind thesaurus. An amphitheatre?

Aye, yeah, one o'them: It had been built on top o'the ground and below it, were dug out, like this 'uge pit that we were gonna 'ave to feight in. We was surrounded by thousands of them xin, all screaming and laughing an' taunting.

It were huge, but a ruin -- it were uneven and unkempt. It had been piled stone on stone, from some ancient city, to prevent the animals and us captives from escaping into audience, and at each end were cages to hold us until our turns came to meet our death in this arena of 'ate.

Penny and I were kept together in one cage. In the others were the animals: Young bull demonspawn and aggressive rooters, as well as other captured clowns, wild dyapnid, hexikid...

-- Wait, what? Hexikid? The nascenti street cleaner, like we saw last night?

Yeah, similar to them, but not as advanced, these would have been earlier breedings that had got loose or something and found their way into xin territory. Anyway, there were also wild mentiloth, mad cryptobites, and many other strange and ferocious wild beasts of The Dark Peak and the murk which I 'adn't never seen before.

The din of all that roaring, growling and squealing were deafening and the appearance of any one of 'em were enough to make tha legs tremble.

Penny told me that at the end of the day one of the prisoners, whatever survived -- man or beast -- would be released -- the rest would all be deed. The winner of each feight of the day would face each other until just two remained; the victor in the last feight would be set free. The next day at murklight the cages would be filled again, and that would carry on the ten days that the games went on.

Shortly after we had been caged the ampy-fe-atter began to fill and within an hour every seat were teken. Hagibrack, with his chieftains, sat at the middle of one side of the arena on a big raised platform.

At a signal from Hagibrack the doors of two cages were opened and a dozen clown women were driven to the centre of the arena. Each was given a shard and then, at the far end, a pack of twelve wild dyapnids were loosed upon 'em.

As the dyapnids, growling and foaming, rushed on the clown women I turned me head that I might not see the horrid sight. The yells and laughter of the green horde were vile. When I turned back to the arena, as Penny told me it was over, I saw three victorious dyapnids, snarling and growling over the bodies of their prey. The women had given a good account of themselves.

Next a mad cryptobite was loosed among the remaining dyapnids, and so it went on through this long and 'orrible day.

During the day I was pitted against first man, then beast, but I was armed with a whipo'wil and that served me well, as I fought off each and every one of them. I didn't believe it Pip, but I became -- I had to become -- a killin' machine -- just to save me own life. It made me feel 'orrible, it did, but that is what I had to do, and I tells you now, it were with no sense of pleasure. Time and time again I won the applause of the bloodthirsty green horde, and toward t'end there were shouts that I be made a member of their kind.

It took ages, but as the gloaming approached, there were three of us left: A great green warrior from some far northern tribe outside of Hagibrack's realm, Penny, and mesen.

The other two had to feight, and then I had to feight the winner -- one of us would get our freedom.

Penny had had several feights during t'day and like me had always won, sometimes by only the weeniest fluke. I felt sick to me stomach about how she might best this giant xin who had mowed down all before him during the day. That green monster were about eight foot tall, while Penny was more like five. They come to meet each other, and then for the first time, I saw a clown trick that amazed me -- It were a risky thing to do, but Penny bravely chanced her life on the cast o' that die -- when she were about twenty foot from this huge bloke, she dropped her arm far behind her, over her shoulder and with a mighty sweep hurled her whipo'wil point first at that green warrior. It flew true as an arrow and went straight through t'xin man's right eye, killing him instantly.

I wanted to laugh Pip, I wanted to cry, I was in such turmoil that I didn't know what to do or how I felt, but now Penny and me had to feight each other.

As we were let into that arena for the last time, I quietly set a seed in her mind to keep things going until murkfall, so that we might find a way to escape; I hoped that my telepathic message was understood by Penny, and not intercepted by the xin.

As we fought, I knew that she understood me but the xin horde also guessed that our hearts weren't in it, as they howled in rage as neither of us finished each other off. Just as the murking was on us, I started staggering about as if knackered out and I whispered to Penny to thrust her whipo'wil between me left arm and me body. She did, and I collapsed clasping the writhing thing with me arm, falling to the ground with her whipo'wil -- now straight -- looking like it were sticking out of me chest.

What really?! That's the sort of thing I used to do as a kid when play fighting!

Yeah, when I think back now Pip, it weren't the best acting in the world neither, but that murkfall were thick out there in the swamp, so me acting skills were kind of let off a bit.

Penny recognised from the roar of t'crowd that she had won, and quickly placed her foot on me neck, and withdrew her whipo'wil from me body, stabbing me through the neck to sever my jugular vein. Yet her blade -- in the murkling -- just slid into the sand of the arena. In the lukewarm grey light, no xin could tell that she hadn't finished me off proper.

I thought at her to go and claim her freedom and then we would meet on the moors east of the village. She left, her arms held up in triumph, to the cheers of them xin.

I laid still, as if deed, until that ampy-fe-atter had gone quiet. Then I made me escape, 'aving no trouble scaling the rubble -- it would keep xin and beasts at bay, but for me -- it were no barrier and I reached the safety of them moors beyond the village quick as a flash.

```
     HMM::OUT('Cryptobite')
`ask:: Rippon, Pip // stat:: accept[ok]__ // src::
2001:0db8:85a3:0000:0000:8a2e:037g:7334 [loc::hellsborough//
middlewood_road//467]__ // now:: 79.hail
ripperthroat.12.16.2.3.9`

`HMM::IN('..Colour:   White_`
```

`..Diet:    Vegetation_`

`..Size:    6"' (hand, at shoulder), 9' long_`

`..Defining characteristics:   Beast of burden, producer of silk_`

`..Class:   Denizen_`

`..Image:   Incoming...')`

CHAPTER 20

Milting

```
        HMM::OUT('You didn't come.')
`ask:: Rippon, Pip // stat:: accept[ok]__ // src::
2001:0db8:85a3:0000:0000:8a2e:037g:7334 [loc::hellsborough//
middlewood_road//467]__ // now:: 79.hail
ripperthroat.12.16.2.17.4`
```

I waited for Penny in t'hills for ages, but she didn't turn up, and I had no way of finding out why -- the hivemind were silent out there; I didn't know where she had gone, or why.

I started off to the northwest, heading for the same road that I was goin' to take with Pandora and Fenimoss, since that was the only map I had in my noggin of where I should be going, and Hathersage was still where I needed to get to. Me only food was from foraging for shrooms, picking off the odd insect and the like, me water come from the brooks and sikes.

I wandered, stumbling about through the neets guided only by the bare murklight and hiding during the day behind some rock outcrop or in t'hills. I were attacked by wild beasts -- strange, uncouth things that leapt at me from the murk, so that I had to use me whipo'wil and be ready for 'em.

Usually me murksense -- that telepathic power I had gained -- warned me in time, but once I was down with fangs at me throat and an 'airy face pressed close to mine before even I knew what were 'appenin'.

This last beast were large and heavy, and me hands were at its throat before its fangs had a chance to rip out mine, and slowly I forced its 'airy face from me and closed me fingers around its windpipe, trying t'squeeze t'life out t'thing.

You've heard of The Don Bog Beast and ripperthroats, right, I said...

I have me love, and I as seen 'em all... And others so aberrant they'd give thee nightmares.

Abhorrent, I said quietly.

Aye, aberrant, it were: We lay there both breathing 'ard, and this beast givin' every effort to reach me with them big fangs, and I straining to keep me grip and choke the life from it as I kept it from me throat.

Slowly me arms started to give way, and it nudged closer and closer. It were them burning eyes that I remember, Pip, and gradually its hairy face was against mine again, and this time, I was pretty sure that I was a goner.

```
        HMM::OUT('Don Bog Beast')
`ask:: Rippon, Pip // stat:: accept[ok]__ // src::
2001:0db8:85a3:0000:0000:8a2e:037g:7334 [loc::hellsborough//
middlewood_road//467]__ // now:: 79.hail
ripperthroat.12.16.2.19.37`

`HMM::IN('Believed to exist in the upper reaches of
the Dun river, there have been many sightings over the
millennia. .._ .._ Building profile .._`

`..Colour: Black, some reports of orange stripes_`

`..Diet: Carrion_ gnawmards_ scrufftails_ slippers_ .._ .._
other flesh_`

`..Size: 5"' (hand, at shoulder), 8' long_`

`..Defining characteristics: Vicious, bloodthirsty protector
```

of the source of The Dun_`
`..Class: Cryptid_`
`..Image: Incoming...')`

And so you died again, right, I said...

I was breathing me last breath, I was Pip, until that beast was knocked off me by someat else that sprang from the darkness.

Two great forces of nature now tore and ripped into each other, rolling about growling on the moss.

It were soon over, but the beast that had saved me now stood with lowered head above the throat of the dead thing which would have killed me.

The murkmoon cast a turquoise glow on the scene, and showed me that it were none other than Shad -- I love this barker, he is a better friend than any I 'as ever 'ad -- ain't that right you old padfoot, said Van, ruffing up Shad's great mane, with a tear in his eye. This creature had saved me; his great blue eyes was glowing like that murkmoon. Where he had come from, or how he'd found me, I didn't know. But I was reyt glad, I were -- I'll tell thee that for nowt Pip.

Only thing I was worried about was why he weren't with Pandora. I was thinkin' that only her being deed would stop him being by her side.

Shad had no need for food then, as he doant now; but it's a strange thing that an undead barghest should need to eat so voraciously -- I guess it's like muscle memory -- the spirit and soul of the barker.

Interesting, I said, physically and physiologically, he had no need, I patted Shad on the head and tossed him a beer nut, but psychologically, he did.

I was in a raggedy state, said Van, but I couldn't bring mesen to eat that uncooked flesh, even if I could digest it -- which I doubted I could -- and I had no means of cooking it. When Shad had finished eating, we started off again.

I think I was close to the netherlands, but I cannot have been there yet, since I remembered from Pandora's map that the netherlands were near the Wisewood, and I was still on moorland.

I climbed this big hill, and down in t'valley, I saw this big buildin' -- its dirty chimneys looking out o'place in this wilderness. I felt like it would have been more at home in Hellsborough -- and it did look like some of the buildings there, but this place were much bigger and far more, more -- what's the word, Pip?

Imposing?

Yeah, it were imposing. I approached it warily, but I couldn't see no door in them big old walls, despite walking around it a couple of times. Finally I sat down -- shagged out I was -- with me back against them walls. There seemed to be no sign of life -- the place looked deserted.

I didn't know nowt about t'organic network back then, so I nearly jumped out of me skin when the wall -- or at least what felt like the wall -- started talking to me:

You wear the metal of a green warrior and are followed by a barghest, yet you have the shape of a clown man. In colour you are neither green nor patterned. In the name of Dunlockslyn, what manner of creature are you?

I were on me feet and looking warily about, trying to figure out where this voice were comin' from and how I was bein' looked at, but I had no idea -- but that voice saw me panicky behaviour:

I can see you, but you cannot see me. My voice comes from inside this humidity plant. If you explain your presence and what it is you want, then maybe I will see to it that you can gain entry, if not, you can stay where you are.

I said that I had escaped from t'swamp, was lost, exhausted, and hadn't eaten nowt for days. Rightly or wrongly, I added that I were a friend of the clowns of Hathersage.

Can your barghest behave itself?

I swear to thee that he will do as he is told.

Yes, I'm sure he will. But nevertheless, you may enter, but the barghest remains outside.

I agreed with the voice and told Shad that I would be ok and to wait, which seemed good enough for the owner of the voice, and part of the wall slid back. At t'other end were a door. There were no-one about, but as soon as I went through that first door it slid back into place behind me, locking Shad outside.

A second and then third door slid back as I come up and then closed shut behind me, until I reached an inner chamber with food and drink set out on a big stone table.

The voice told me to eat, and I did -- it were just simple bread and biscuits and water, but a great feast for someone who ain't eaten in days -- and me invisible 'ost put me through a bit of a grilling on how I found mesen in this -- what I now found out, were an area of high security.

Your statements are remarkable, said the voice, on finishing its questioning: You seem to be speaking the truth, and it is clear that you are not of The Dark Peak.

Now all that made sense to me Pip, but then this voice without a body says some technical stuff that went a bit like this, and you've got to remember this were a while back, so I might have got some of the words mixed up by now. It said someat like:

I can ascertain this by the conformation of your cerebral structures and the exotic positioning of your internal organs and the shape and size of your heart.

Tha can see through me? I said. If this man or woman, or whatever the voice was could see me heart, then I thought me logic was sound on that.

Yes, I can see all but your thoughts; if you was of The Dark Peak, I would be able to read those too.

A door opened on the far side of the chamber and a strange, dried up little man came in -- at least I think he was a man, I might have been wrong, since his vocal range was not what I was used to, and he -- I'll stick with calling him a he -- had a strange way to him he did.

The way he walked was kind of stilted, if that's the right description Pip, ask me some more questions about him later, but for now, just let me try and describe in the words that come to me what this strange little bloke was like -- he was, like a pecker, his movements were deliberate and full of small pauses, where he seemed to listen and wait and watch, but without any of it taking up much time, if tha knows what I mean, almost like his internal clock was running ten times faster than mine does.

His eyes were steady and staring, but also flitting this way and that so that I felt nothing would pass him without him seeing it.

He wore a heavy hooded robe that shimmered the darkest shades of black, the lightest shades of white and the dullest and murkiest shades of grey all at once interwoven with the pinkishness of murksun and turquoise of murkmoon. There were other colours in there which I can't even begin to explain, the gold of tha sun, the silver of tha moon...

The old man sat and stared, analysing me more, and we talked -- and here's the strange thing Pip, I have no idea what we were talking about for so long, since when I said we talked, what I really meant was, that he talked.

It weren't a monologue, I did ask some questions, and he answered them, but he talked about stuff I didn't understand -- but I know that tha knows something of them already, from your time passing through The Hinge and tha research into t'ancient history of The Dark Peak.

The strangest part of our chat was that I could read his every thought while he could not fathom owt from my mind unless I spoke.

He was milting, I said, from what you have told me.

```
      HMM::OUT('Milting')
`ask:: Rippon, Pip // stat:: accept[ok]__ // src::
2001:0db8:85a3:0000:0000:8a2e:037g:7334 [loc::hellsborough//
middlewood_road//467]__ // now:: 79.hail
ripperthroat.12.16.2.22.29`
`HMM::IN('..Colour:  Pale_`
`..Diet:  Varied, but likely the best food in The Dark Peak_`
`..Size:  4   5' (feet)_`
`..Defining characteristics:  Humanoid_`
`..Class:  Precedent_')`
```

He were Pip, tha's reyt -- and the first milting I ever met. I didn't let him know that I could read his thoughts, course I didn't, and so I learned much stuff that would do me well during me time in The Dark Peak, and if he had known of me ability -- me murksense -- I wouldn't ever have found nowt out.

The building where we was sat contained the machinery which produced the artificial moisture which sustains the murk in The Dark Peak.

Pumped to the five main districts of denizen territory -- North and South Xinlandia, Hatheran, Glossopia and Hellsborough. As it's released, contact with the ether of space transforms it into murk, where the thick and oily atmosphere is maintained to suit all of the denizens.

The only fear, the milting told me, were that some accident might 'appen to The Dark Peak. For eight thousand years, he said, he had watched them pumps every day. He had one assistant and they divided the watch between 'em -- six months each they would work in this huge, isolated plant.

```
      HMM::OUT('Differcultties')
`ask:: unknown // stat:: accept[ok]__ // src::
2001:0db8:85a3:0000:0000:8a2e:142j:i618 [loc::hellsborough//
unknown__location//000]__ // now:: 79.hail
ripperthroat.12.16.2.27.1`
```

Every clown, xin and nascenti, is taught what 'appens in that humidity plant, but only two milting at one time ever hold the secret of getting into the building, which has walls a hundred foot thick -- the place is proper solid, Pip, there ain't no way to get into that place through them walls.

I watched his thoughts, and found out that them outer doors were controlled by the mind -- them doors only open when the reyt thought waves is in tha' noggin. I asked 'im how he 'ad managed to unlock them massive outer doors for me from in 'ere in t'middle of the building. As quick as a flash I saw nine colours -- each one was in the sparkles of that robe of 'is -- but them colours faded quick -- as he said it were a secret he couldn't let on.

After that he changed toward me, I reckon he thought I might know too much, and I might have done.

The milting offered me a bed for the neet, and I took him up on that, course I did -- I hadn't slept proper for many a neet. Before I got mesen off for the neet he said he'd contact a nearby clown outpost, who would help me on my way to Glossop, which he said, were the nearest town.

Glossop? I said, I'm on me way to Hathersage. He said he knew that, but in the murk I must have travelled in the opposite direction to that which I'd wanted to go. I realised that might have been true, it's easy to loose tha way in the murk, and after I had been attacked that murkspawn, I could have wandered in any direction, I supposed. I took up his offer, and he gave me someat else:

```
HMM::OUT('Differcultties? You mean difficulties?')
`ask:: Rippon, Pip // stat:: accept[ok]__ // src::
2001:0db8:85a3:0000:0000:8a2e:037g:7334 [loc::hellsborough//
middlewood_road//467]__ // now:: 79.hail
ripperthroat.12.16.2.27.57`
```

Do not let them know you are bound for Hathersage as they are at war with that village. My assistant and I are of no country, we belong to all The Dark Peak and the way we look protects us in all lands, even among the green men -- though we do not trust ourselves to their hands if we can avoid it.

And so good-night, my friend, he said, may you have a long and restful sleep -- yes, a long sleep.

He smiled pleasantly, but I saw in his thoughts that he were up to no good: I pictured him standing over me, stabbing me in the chest saying: I am sorry, but it is for the good of The Dark Peak.

As he left and closed the door, his thoughts were cut off, I didn't know why that were -- maybe it was someat to do with them thick walls.

I were in a bit of a quandary now Pip, I mean, how could I escape through them big old walls? If I hurt him, that might stop the machinery of the humidity plant -- and that could kill me -- you remember I told you about the sap I ingested in the Wisewood, Pip -- along with everyone else in The Dark Peak, even Pandora if she weren't already dead.

I opened the door of me room. A scheme had come to me; I would attempt to force the great locks by the nine colours I had read in the milting's head.

I was about to step out of me room, when a noise held me back, and I crouched low in the dark.

The old fella passed close then, going into t'chamber where I was about to head. The light weren't reyt good, but I could see a long thin shard in his hand, that he sharpened up and down on a whetstone.

In his mind were the decision to inspect the pumps -- that'd take thirty minutes, he reckoned -- then he'd return to me bed chamber and plunge that shard into me 'eart.

He went through that big hall, then disappeared down to the pump-room. I left me hiding place and went across the hall to the door. Concentrating me mind on the lock I focused on the nine colours, and waited.

After what seemed like ages, the door move toward me and slid to one side. One after t'other them doors opened, and each time I stepped into the darkness -- free, but not a lot better off than I'd been before -- other than I'd tossed a bit of scran in me gob.

```
    HMM::OUT('No, I know what I said, I ain't chuffing stupid
    differ cult ties    the bitter finger, remember?')
`ask:: unknown // stat:: accept[ok]__ // src::
2001:0db8:85a3:0000:0000:8a2e:142j:i618 [loc::hellsborough//
unknown__location//000]__ // now:: 79.hail
ripperthroat.12.16.2.29.31`
```

I scarpered away from the place, but didn't 'ave a clue which direction I was heading in -- not that I knew before.

After running full tilt for a bit with Shad by me side, murklight appeared and I holed up in the first place that I come to.

There were low buildings, all with heavy doors, and no amount of hammering and hollering brought about no response.

I were exhausted from lack of sleep, so just threw mesen on ground, and commanded Shad to stand guard.

I were wocken by Shad's growlings, and opened me eyes to see

VAN HALLAM

three clowns standing not far off.

Each of 'em had a whipo'wil in their 'ands.

I is not armed, I said, and no enemy, I has been a prisoner of the green men and is on me way to Glossop. All I ask is food and rest for mesen and me barghest and t'directions for reaching me destination.

They lowered their whipo'wils then, and come toward me, placing their right hands on me left shoulder. Smiling, they took me to the house of one of 'em which weren't far off.

    HMM::OUT('Yes, you said. I should be beware the bitter finger')
`ask:: Rippon, Pip // stat:: accept[ok]__ // src:: 2001:0db8:85a3:0000:0000:8a2e:037g:7334 [loc::hellsborough//middlewood_road//467]__ // now:: 79.hail ripperthroat.12.16.2.30.14`

Them buildings I had been hammering at in that murklight, were just outbuildings. Their house proper were in a grove of big trees, and, like all them clown homes, they had been raised five foot from the ground on a big old shaft -- to protect 'em from t'boggy ground and t'dangers of murk.

Instead of bothering with bolts and bars -- like we does in Hellsborough -- them clowns just got their homes up out of harm's way during the neet.

These brothers, with their wives and kids, lived on this farm. They did no work themselves. The labour were done by convicts, prisoners of war, them that owed chits and clown folk too poor to pay tax.

I ain't never got me head around tax, Pip. We doant have none in Hellsborough. But from I could make out, it's to make folk fend for 'emselves as much as possible and use their noggins to get on in life.

Yes, and to fund the council, I added. Without tax, they can't pay for community things like health care and the like.

Ain't no health care in Hellsborough, unless that pays for it thasen. Anyway, these clowns, they were reyt good to me and proper 'ospitable -- is that the word Pip, I doant know, look it up later -- an' I spent several hours with them, resting and the like.

After they had 'eard me story -- I left out Pandora and the milting -- they said I should paint me body to look more like them, and then I should try and get a job in Glossop in the navy. That were reyt good of 'em want it? They didn't need to do that, and to this day, I doant really know why they did -- it doant make alot of sense -- but that's what happened, that's what they did, they painted up me pale skin so I looked like a clown mesen.

I looked at mesen in the mirror Pip, and no word of a lie, I didn't recognise mesen. I were staring at this bloke, painted in all sorts o'colours, and I didn't recognise mesen at all -- it were reyt strange, it were Pip...

So like an out of body experience? I said, since Van seemed to be waiting for some sort of response.

Aye, he said, someat like that. Van snagged a flutterby from the ether and pasted it into his gob; quickly followed by a mouthful of ale.

When I were ready to get off, they gave me chits that I could spend in Glossop, and a mentiloth -- a small un, not like the ones the xin uses -- the size of a onetoe and reyt gentle, but in colour and shape, the same as the wild xin ones. I said I couldn't pay 'em back, but they just laughed and slapped me mentiloth -- tha'll have plenty of time to pay us back they said, as me ride bolted down the Venomtooth pass on our way to Glossop.

```
     HMM::OUT('They're here, the clown, the crosslander, the
xaexs.  I am strong, but I ain't that strong.')
`ask:: unknown // stat:: accept[ok]__ // src::
2001:0db8:85a3:0000:0000:8a2e:142j:i618 [loc::hellsborough//
unknown__location//000]__ // now:: 79.hail
```

VAN HALLAM

ripperthroat.12.16.2.31.3`

CHAPTER 21

The Glossopian

```
HMM::OUT('You there?')
`ask:: Rippon, Pip // stat:: accept[ok]__ // src::
2001:0db8:85a3:0000:0000:8a2e:037g:7334 [loc::hellsborough//
middlewood_road//467]__ // now:: 79.hail
ripperthroat.12.16.2.34.11`
```

What's up Pip? Tha seems distracted.

Distracted? I said, no, no carry on, just getting a little tired.

Ah, tha needs more crust, says Van, preparing more for snorting.

Truth is though, I am distracted, I don't know what to think or what's going on, and the crust is doing its job and making me one with the great Dunlockslyn, I am dancing with the scerm and making my way to The Ripperthroats in my own simple way. I am joyous, I don't want to know anything more about Van Hallam or this stranger that is DM-ing me from the hivemind, I just want to float in the murk and do my own thing -- but something keeps dragging me back -- two somethings -- Van here, and the stranger who thinks I need to be protected. I just want to be left alone, I just want to get on with my own thing, to do what it is I do.

But then I take a sip of ale and it jolts me back to where I should be and I know what my job is and what I am here to do. What it is that earns me a little "crust" -- which now has two connotations, that of money and that of recreational drugs. Van is talking again, I zone in with little difficulty:

That journey through t'murk toward Glossop were thick 'n' ugly, and I were always learnin' about new stuff and methods and manners of The Dark Peak. With t'chits I now had, I were able to barter for food 'n' rest at a farm on me route, and 'ave some of the food that they growed for 'emselves. For first time in me life, I ate steaks and chops, and fruit and veg I'd never seen back 'ome. That food in Hellsborough -- fed to us by psycmask -- were pale grey slop, nowt in comparison to this lush fodder.

It still is, I added.

It is, Pip, tha's reyt, said Van with a chuckle, which is why I don't bother with it and stick to hopping and flying meyt, nice and fresh, the ways I likes it. But tha has to say, that we did 'ave a grand dinner toneet, for which I is grateful.

    HMM::IN('DPDC Alert: Disturbance, The Middlewood road')
`hits:: 43792 // [this]2001:0db8:85a3:0000:0000:8a2e:037g:7334 [loc::hellsborough//middlewood_road//467]__ // now:: 79.hail ripperthroat.12.16.2.37.19`

`Hexikid cleanup device 0103018201209 violent activity detected_ Middlewood road_ Avoid area_ Exacids alerted__`

Me next stop was a tiny hamlet, just half a dozen houses and an inn, in which I took a room for t'night; there were some right hoity-toity folk there, apparently some were some sort of clown nobles of the Glossopians.

We -- that is, me and Shad, who no-one seemed to be bothered about, which I found strange, but then you've got to remember you're out on the moors, so they is used to strange stuff happening, and one of the other locals even had a barghest of his own; Shad made acquaintances and everything, bit of a sniff of the backsides, you know, that's all, perfectly civil -- got to chatting about Hathersage over a few ales, and then a few more and then a little bit of crust -- that may have been the first time I dabbled in crust, Pip -- make sure you make a note of that, might be important.

One of the older guys had been a diplomat or missionary of some sort and said what she called "circumstances" which seemed to keep the Glossopian and Hatheran empires always at war.

Hatheran, she said, rightly boasts the most beautiful women in the whole of The Dark Peak, and of all her treasures the daughter Pandora, was the most lovely of all.

The Hatherans, she said, worship Pandora and since her loss on that expedition, all of Hathersage had been in mourning. That our ruler attacked the Hatheran fleet as it was returning to Hathersage was a blunder which will sooner or later make the Glossopian folk replace him with a wiser man.

Even though our armies surround Hathersage, the people of Glossop aren't happy, this war is not popular. Our forces took advantage of the absence of the principal fleet of Hathersage on their search for the princess -- but it is said Hathersage will fall within the next few days.

```
      HMM::OUT('What's happened?   You ok?')
`ask:: Rippon, Pip // stat:: accept[ok]__ // src::
2001:0db8:85a3:0000:0000:8a2e:037g:7334 [loc::hellsborough//
middlewood_road//467]__ // now:: 79.hail
ripperthroat.12.16.2.38.1`
```

What does tha think 'as 'appened to the princess, to Pandora? I said.

She's dead of course, she said. A green warrior was captured by our forces in the south, and that's what he said. Pandora escaped from the swamp with a strange creature not of The Dark Peak, only to fall into the hands of the Strinxin. Her mentiloth was found wandering upon the moorland and there was evidence of a bloody battle nearby.

I wanted to smelt me pants to be honest Pip, this didn't sound good to me at all, but I thought, quick for me, that neither did it mean Pandora were deed. I knew I needed to get to Hathersage as quick as I could.

The next day I set out early -- ale and crust had floored me, and I were a bit worse for wear, but I pushed through it as best I could. I got to Glossop a little after murknoon. Shad drew a lot of attention: Away from t'moors, a barghest ain't seen a lot by clowns -- barghests is a bit of an 'uman thing -- them clowns, they ain't bothered by such supernatural stuff, whether it's real or not.

```
      HMM::OUT('I repeat, you ok?')
`ask:: Rippon, Pip // stat:: accept[ok]__ // src::
2001:0db8:85a3:0000:0000:8a2e:037g:7334 [loc::hellsborough//
middlewood_road//467]__ // now:: 79.hail
ripperthroat.12.16.2.39.7`
```

It brought tears to my eyes to do, it did, but it had to be done Pip. I told Shad to g'oer and begone back to Stanningxin or the Wisewood, or somewhere else other then 'ere, where I was right now, cos he just wouldn't fit in, and he'd stop me doing what I were there to do, and that were reyt enough. Poor old Shad, he had been nothin' but loyal and faithful to me since that time we first met in the Wisewood. We had a big old hug, then, understanding, he were gone.

Tha always understood didn't thee lad!? Van pulled the sturdy beast towards his face and gave him another great hug. Had he wanted to, Shad could have bit Van's head clean off at his slender neck, but of course he didn't, since although a barghest, Shad loved the attention poured on him as regular as a barker would.

I've been playing about with "talking" to Shad for a while via the hivemind, since I have to wear a psycmask when I'm in Hellsborough and Shad being a murkdweller also has access to the hivemind, we share a common communications medium.

Van too, should be able to do this, based on what he's told me so far, but he's never mentioned it outside of his travels in The Dark Peak.

Anyway, Van is ploughing on with his story, so this is just a distraction, but I definitely felt from Shad, as Van has reached this point in the story, that he (Shad), knew that what Van had to do was for the best -- and he held no ill feeling for Van's decision to send him away -- on the contrary, Shad looked forwards to a bit of solo travel, haunting and general nuisance causing.

I got to gates o'Glossop and a few chits were enough to get me in. Them brothers had told me where I had to go to find somewhere to sleep, and their directions were pretty much spot on, I found me bearings reyt easy. I knew I needed to get to the navy recruitment office, and the main street in Glossop were a pretty obvious place to find the recruitment office. It being an official building, it stood out like a sore thumb among all them other posh places, since it were reyt battered looking.

As I crossed t'square toward t'recruitment building, I saw a clown coming reyt at me. She weren't threatening or nowt -- she wasn't paying no interest to me at all, but as she come close I recognised her, I did.

Eyup, Pen! 'ow goes it?! I said.

She wheeled 'round faster than a crickerjack on crust, her whipo'wil pointed reyt at me chest.

Who are you? She growled, but I was like woah pal, it's me Van!

She dropped her whipo'wil to the ground and laughed, there is no one in all The Dark Peak with an accent likes yours, Van Hallan. By the mother of the murkmoon, how did you get here? And what's with the clown getup, how come you look like one of us now? I didn't recognise you my friend!

I told her about me travels since we'd last seen each other in the arena at t'swamp.

After that Penny told me what she'd been up to and why she was 'ere in Glossop town.

```
    HMM::OUT('Send me a sign that you're ok')
`ask:: Rippon, Pip // stat:: accept[ok]__ // src::
2001:0db8:85a3:0000:0000:8a2e:037g:7334 [loc::hellsborough//
middlewood_road//467]__ // now:: 79.hail
ripperthroat.12.16.2.44.13`
```

Were my name and village known to these Glossopian's I would be sitting on the banks of the Ripperthroat mountains right now, with my departed ancestors, Penny said. She kept her voice low, I am here because Ptolemy sent me to discover the whereabouts of Pandora, our princess -- I know she is alive.

I know it too, I said, I has heard rumours that she was gone, but I doant believe it.

Penny carried on quietly: Ocnus, the prince of Glossop, has her hidden in the town and has fallen madly in love with her. His father, Onesimus, the king, has made her marriage to his son the price of peace between Glossop and Hathersage. Ptolemy is having none of it though, and has said that he and his people would rather look on the dead face of their princess than see her wed to any than her own choice, and that personally he would prefer being engulfed in the ashes of a lost and burning Hathersage to joining the metal of his house with that of Onesimus.

Ptolemy has really put the scratcher in the rooterwings as far as Onesimus and the Glossopians are concerned, but his people love him the more for it and his popularity in Hathersage is greater now than ever.

I've been here three days, she carried on, but I've not found where Pandora is being kept. Today I'm joining the Glossopian navy as an air scout to try and gain the confidence of their commander Ocnus. Then, I'll learn the whereabouts of Pandora.

If she's here Pen, we'll find her, you and me, doant worry about that. I remembers saying that Pip, since me heart was beating so hard it were about to burst through me chest.

```
      HMM::IN('DPDC Alert: The Middlewood road closed at
junction')
`hits:: 43792 // [this]2001:0db8:85a3:0000:0000:8a2e:037g:7334
[loc::hellsborough//middlewood_road//467]__ // now:: 79.hail
ripperthroat.12.16.2.47.57`

`Middlewood road shut at junction_  No passage North_  Avoid
area_   Exacids on scene_`
```

How are we going to get back to your place now? I blurted.

My place? Said Van, looking at me with an eyebrow raised above that little psycmask of his.

Middlewood road is shut at the junction, exacids are on the scene.

I wonder what's gone on there then? Said Van, but without any genuine interest. But not to worry, we'll be in 'ere for a while yet, and if it's still closed after that, we'll just go 'round via Taplin and 'ellsborough place; nowt to worry about.

There's been an attack, I said, Pandora might be involved.

Pandora? What's that murker been up to now?

It could be something to do with that bitter finger axis I was talking about earlier.

I don't no nowt about any bitter finger, I said earlier, and you should just forget all about that and get on with the task at hand, which is recording me story.

Ok, ok, I'll try and forget about it.

Good, I were just about to get to the bit where we get into the Glossopian air-scouts -- Penny showed me the headquarters, and introduced me to her boss, asking if I could join n'all. That meant I had to be examined, but Penny said it were nowt to worry about -- it were just a simple case of measuring me height and weight and that sort of thing -- they were at war with Hathersage, so they were cuttin' corners left, right and centre. Later, there would be a more in-depth examination like the milting did at the humidity plant, but by the time they got 'round to that, we'd be done and our mission either be done or we'd be deed.

The next few days Penny taught me all about flying and repairing clown fliers. They're built for a single person, Pip, about sixteen foot long and two foot wide. The pilot sits on top of the plane on a seat over a locomotor muscle engine. These little things sail through the thick murk of The Dark Peak, as graceful as a sycarid -- but you probably haven't met one of them, have you?

I'd only been in Glossop a few hours when I made me first flight, and I were pretty good; good enough to get promoted to the quarters in the palace of Onesimus at least -- looking good eh, Pip?

They sent me out on patrol, and I circled the town a few times, as I had seen Penny do, then revving up my engine, I headed out south for a bit, following the venomtooth pass.

I'd gone maybe half a dozen thousand paces or so when I saw below me three green warriors racing toward a small figure on foot which seemed to be trying to reach a walled field.

I dropped the flier toward 'em, they didn't hear me, the locomotor muscle engine being as quiet as a squeeker, and I circled behind 'em.

They were chasing a clown wearing Glossop metal.

His flier was down and he must have been trying to repair it, when the xin surprised him.

The xin were almost on him; their mentiloth charging down on him fast, their spears angled toward him. Each warrior wanted to be the first to skewer that poor Glossopian, and if I hadn't turned up when I did, I think they probably would have, but I brought my flier down fast and rammed its nose in between the shoulders of the green warrior who was at the front.

The impact knocked his head clean off, over the head of his mentiloth, where it fell into the moss. The mounts of the other two warriors turned squealing in terror, and bolted off in t'opposite direction.

When I landed, that Glossopian couldn't thank me enough Pip -- obviously, I'd saved his life hadn't I?!

He said he was the cousin of Onesimus, and I'd be reyt well rewarded, so that was a result, eh?!

But before much more was said the other two xin were back on our case, and the two of us, side by side, faced the charging mentiloth with their owners sat upon them. I have to be honest, Pip, I thought I was a deed man.

Again.

Yeah, again. They came on us with spears hung low and their whipo'wil raised up, and they were swinging wildly, we had no chance of fighting them off. Out of the corner of my eye I saw the mentiloth that had before been the mount of the warrior I had hit with my flier, and I heard it say to me -- telepathically, of course -- Don't worry Van, it's me -- and with that, she hit both of the incoming warriors full on, destroying herself and them in a bloody carnage that covered the heather the in turquoise blood of xin and mentiloth. Flesh on flesh, bone on bone, crushing, cracking, pain, death.

Her last words were one of thanks for the way I had treated her when I had been her master.

I didn't know Pip, I hadn't recognised her, they all look the same, but I did recognise those eyes, and I will never forget them -- she gave her life for me, I will be forever grateful.

I saw a tears from Van's eyes then, just a couple, but tears all the same.

In shock and exhausted, we finished repairing his plane and he reckoned he felt ok to attempt getting back. He would have to pilot his own craft, but he said that were fine by him, and so we returned to Glossop.

As we got near the town we saw that a big crowd were in the square. The sky was dark with craft, private and military, and they were all trailing banners and flags of bright colours -- I think it was the Glossop flag, Pip.

We slowed down and watched what was going on below, and me new buddy let out his banner, which showed him to be a member of the royal family of Glossop. On doing that, Onesimus himself waved to us, and requested us both to descend to the ground. Once down, I felt a little nervous, as all eyes seemed to be on me.

Van Hallam, air-scout! Was called out.

Tha could have blown me over with a feather, I were so surprised, but I went forward as I had seen the others do. I stopped in front of Onesimus: In recognition, Van Hallam, he said, of your courage and skill in defending my cousin, and vanquishing three green warriors, you will be quartered in my palace from now on.

I thanked him, and joined the members of his staff. After the ceremony I took my machine back to the roof of the squadron's barracks, and reported to the officer in charge of the palace.

Ha, ha what about that then Pip, you can't bullsmelt a bullsmelter, eh?!

HMM::OUT('Locomotor muscle engine')
`ask:: Rippon, Pip // stat:: accept[ok]__ // src::
2001:0db8:85a3:0000:0000:8a2e:037g:7334 [loc::hellsborough//
middlewood_road//467]__ // now:: 79.hail
ripperthroat.12.16.2.53.54`

`HMM::IN('..Bioengineered engine consisting of thick bundles
of locomotor muscle fibres, that when injected with nutrient
solution, expand and contract at different frequencies to
generate power_')`

HMM::OUT('Sycarid')
`ask:: Rippon, Pip // stat:: accept[ok]__ // src::
2001:0db8:85a3:0000:0000:8a2e:037g:7334 [loc::hellsborough//
middlewood_road//467]__ // now:: 79.hail
ripperthroat.12.16.2.53.59`

`HMM::IN('..Colour:  Various_  Pale white to deep black_`

`..Diet:  Unknown_`

`..Size:  1   8' (feet)_`

`..Defining characteristics: Winged fliers of the murk_
Stinging prehensile tails_`

`..Class:  Denizen_')`

CHAPTER 22

Where is this clown?

V an belched, that's better, he said, I reckon a bit o'that venomtooth were lodged somewhere queer, where it shouldn't have been like.

His glass was empty again and he was searching about for some crust, I could tell -- he had that hunger in his eyes.

Where's me pipe? He said, finding nothing else, before he curled a passing green maggot through his fingers and over his tongue. I'm getting bored now Pip, this is tekin' too long, I's getting fidgety. Maybe I's had enough ale -- we should step it up a bit and do some rhum. Aye, let's do that.

Then he was back where we were and he was back in his monologue, I is gonna try and channel this as best I can though Pip, so I doesn't 'ave to ask you about some of them big words that them clowns used back then:

I were part of Onesimus's personal guard, and was shown me apartment which were close to his. I were taken to where t'ruler were talking with his son, Ocnus, and some other folk -- he didn't see me come in. And me job were just to stay out of sight, unless anything 'appened, an' then I were supposed to jump in and save the Glossopian king.

As soon as I was left, four soldiers of t'royal guard entered room, surrounding a female. They went up to Onesimus and when they left, I could see not ten foot from me, that it were Pandora who they had brought to t'king of Glossop.

Ocnus, Prince of Glossop, advanced to meet her, and hand in hand they approached Onesimus, who looked up in surprise, and saluted her.

Aye, I'm getting it now Pip, am channellin' me thoughts from back in the day, they might be a but fuzzy, but this is about the long and short of it:

To what do I owe this visit from the Princess of Hathersage, who, two days ago, with rare consideration for my pride, assured me that she would prefer the xin Hagibrack to my son?

Pandora smiled before she answered. A woman has the right to change her mind, she said, and two days ago I wasn't sure of Ocnus's love for me, but now I am, and so I will wed Ocnus, Prince of Glossop.

I am glad that you have decided to, said Onesimus. I did not want to push war further against the people of Hathersage, and your promise shall be recorded and a proclamation to my people issued forthwith.

It were better, Onesimus, interrupted Pandora, that the proclamation wait the ending of this war. It would look strange indeed to my people and to yours were the Princess of Hathersage to give herself to her country's enemy in the midst of hostilities.

Cannot the war be ended at once? said Ocnus, end it, end this unpopular war.

We shall see, replied Onesimus, how the people of Hathersage take to peace. I shall at least offer it to them.

Pandora, after a few words, turned and left the apartment, still followed by her guards.

I knew what I'd heard Pip, and I couldn't believe me ears, I wondered if maybe I was hallucinating this whole thing, but I knew that I weren't. I decided I needed to find her rooms and get her to repeat to me alone what she had said so I knew it were true. I deserted me post and ran down the passage toward the door by which she had left the chamber. There were many corridors running in all directions, and I went first down one and then another until I became reyt lost -- it was worse than being in t'Wisewood it were. I was stood panting against a wall when I heard voices near me.

They were coming from close by, and I could make out Pandora's voice. I couldn't hear her words but I knew that it were her. A little further along I could see a dooer, and I pushed into the room and found mesen in a small chamber. There were the four guards, and one of 'em got straight up and asked me what I wanted.

I is from Onesimus, I said all official like, and I needs to talk privately with the Princess of Hathersage.

And your order? asked the fella.

I didn't know what he meant, just told him I were a member of the guard, and moved towards the opposite dooer of the chamber, where I could hear Pandora talking.

The guards got between me and the dooer -- no-one comes from Onesimus without carrying an order or the password -- give me one or the other.

I were anxious to get to Pandora, so I might have been a bit daft at this point, Pip, cos I snapped back at him a bit, saying that if he didn't get out of me way, he'd loose an arm.

Of course, he didn't like that and drew his whipo'wil, and

the other three blokes did same, which meant I weren't goin' nowhere without a feight, so I pulled out my whipo'wil n'all.

Put that away, said the guard who were doing all the talkin', you're not going to take us all on are you?

I realised that the odds were stacked against me, and resheathed me whipo'wil.

What's that? Dirty Leaves? Van had begun another conversation with someone other than me -- The xaexs Dirty Leaves presumably -- and was staring straight at me -- but through me; he tapped his nose as if to do something important, and then snapped a passing flutterby from above his head as if it was the most natural thing in the world.

I couldn't really understand what was going on, but Van was happily chewing on the bodice of the creature whilst it audibly squealed.

What are you trying to tell me Dirty Leaves?

I could hear nothing, not even a click.

Van stopped then and did something I didn't expect at all. Spitting what was uningested from his mouth, and flinging the remainder from his fingers towards Shad, he got up and walked over to the bar. He ushered Shalesmoor into a corner and appeared to be in deep conversation, but what was said, I had no idea.

```
     HMM::OUT('what time is it?')
`ask:: Rippon, Pip // stat:: accept[ok]__ // src::
2001:0db8:85a3:0000:0000:8a2e:037g:7334 [loc::hellsborough//
middlewood_road//467]__ // now:: 79.hail
ripperthroat.12.16.2.57.9`

`HMM::IN('..79.hail ripperthroat.12.16.2.57.9_')`
```

Moments later he returned to the table and banged down a brace of glasses and a just opened bottle of dark viscous liquid.

There we go, he said, rhum. Now let's get this story done, I might have work to do anytime soon.

Work, I said, what work? As I uncorked the bottle and began to pour us a couple of fingers worth each of the liquor.

Sshhh... It's not for here, let's take care of the here and now and worry about that when we need to.

And with that, he was back in story mode, albeit chugging on the rhum.

I don't think you're here by the order of Onesimus at all, said that guard, and you're not going anywhere near that door. But what we will do is take you back to Onesimus so you can tell him why are are making this request to speak to the princess.

Now, I know what I was about to do wasn't only daft Pip, it were damn reyt stupid. Probably the most stupid thing I 'as ever done in me life -- and there has been a few, but this were a classic in the all Dunlockly dumb moments in me life.

I took out me whipo'wil and with a swipe I did take off that fella's arm. It fell to the floor with a splatter and the other three gawked at me while the one at the front passed out in the mess that squitted from that open wound.

The other three had me backed against the wall in no time though, fighting for me life I was.

I figured that if I could get mesen into a corner, only one at a time could get at me, so that's what I went for, and we were feighting for twenty minutes, and I was getting tired Pip, I was about ready to drop, but then with a lucky cut I brought down another one, and then, with only two of 'em left, I rushed them down as I had done with many a feight that I had won in the arena at t'swamp. The third fell within ten seconds after the second, and the last lay dead upon the bloody floor moments later.

All that noise had brought Pandora to the door, and there she and Fenimoss peered out at t'carnage.

Pandora's face were in shock, and I could tell that neither of 'em knew it were me.

I sheathed me bloody blade and went over to her, but she started to shut the door on me.

Pandora, I shouted, and she looked back at me.

Who are you, Glossopian? Another enemy to harass me in my misery?

Tha' doant recognise me, I said, but tha knows me well.

No friend of Hathersage's wears that metal, she said, and yet your accent; it is not -- it cannot be -- no, for he is dead.

It is me, Pandora -- I is not deed. I is painted like a clown and I wears the metal of Glossop, but it is me, Van Hallam.

I went to hug her and at first she came towards me, but then backed off into Fenimoss's arms instead. You're too late Van, she said. If you had been an hour earlier, things might have been different, but I thought you was dead. I thought that you lay buried in the pits of the swamp -- now I am promised to another to save my people from the curse of the Glossopian army.

But I is not deed, I said dumbly, my words trailing off to nowt.

It's too late, Van, my promise is given, and here, in The Dark Peak, that is final. The ceremonies which follow later are but meaningless formalities. I am as good as married. No longer may we be together.

You should do some research on the customs of The Dark Peak, Pip, they is complicated, but you like that kinda stuff doant y' -- folklore and that ant-thrapology and all that. Apparently, a while back, I offended Pandora when I should have claimed her in some way, but I must admit that I doant understand it even now, never mind back then, anyway, it seemed like she had given her word to try and protect Hathersage by getting wedded to this Ocnus character.

I wasn't best pleased, as I am sure you can imagine; to be honest, Pip, I was spitting feathers, but I tried not to show it and kept her talkin' for as long as I could -- until she forced it home through me thick skull:

I may never be yours while Ocnus lives, she said.

I reckon she was sad about it, but I was fuming. That's easy then, I said: Ocnus will die.

But you can't do that either, she tells me Pip, which is starting to do my head in, all these customs that they has in The Dark Peak. She says she can't marry me even if I kills this Ocnus character in self defence.

It is useless, she says, we must never see each other again.

I couldn't stand for that Pip, I mean, this was nonsense. It may be their custom, but in Hellsborough, we don't really have customs, it's all about mekin money and the survival of the fittest and capitalism and the like.

Damn right, I said, none of that lefty socialist nonsense -- I mean look at the xin, that doesn't work, does it? Pandora said that herself.

She did, but out there in The Dark Peak, they have these rituals. I weren't gonna stand for it. I may not be from there or nothin' and I maybe different, but tha has to go for what tha wants and tha has to get what tha is lookin' for, that's the whole point of knowing tha's a bit different to everyone else and feighting against the status quo, which is why I was there in the first place.

But for now, I didn't say any of that, I just turned, dejected and with an 'eavy 'eart, left her -- I knew that Pandora were lost to me until this ceremony were over and done with -- so I had planning to do.

I were now lost in the corridors again. I knew full well that I now needed to get out of Glossop, those four deed guards would be discovered any moment, and with me wandering about like a brain-deed wooltard, I'd be suspect number one.

I managed to find some stairs which I went down and then, on seeing a few guards, hid around the corner from them, listenin' to their chatter. They were just talking and larking about, until an officer come in a said that four of them needed to change with the four that were guarding the princess of Hathersage.

I realised that things were about to get tasty, and it were only moments before the bodies of the four I had cut up were found outside Pandora's room.

All of a sudden the palace were alive with folk. Guards, officers, servants, slaves, they all ran about like headless cluckers through the corridors, carrying messages and orders, and searching for the assassin -- for me, they just didn't know it yet.

I grasped me opportunity, Pip: A load of soldiers come runnin' past where I was hiding, so I joined 'em at back and followed 'em through t'maze of palace until, in t'great hall, I saw murklight coming in through t'windows.

The nearest window opened up on a balcony which looked over one of Glossop's streets. The ground were about thirty foot below, which is a big old drop, but I reckoned I could scramble down a drain pipe or some such thing attached to the building, but I didn't want to try it before dark with all the Glossopians milling about down in the street.

I searched for a hiding place and saw this hanging ornament suspended from the ceiling about ten foot from the floor. I jumped over to it and settled in, hiding myself from view, the sap running through my veins like a grasshopper.

The chances of a grasshopper landing within Van's reach at that moment was poetic serendipity, but land that grasshopper did; it was quickly despatched -- I don't need to go into any more details, and it barely stopped Van in his tracks:

It is the work of the Hatherans', said one of the party that had gathered below me.

Yes, but how had they access to the palace? I wouldn't believe that even a single enemy might reach the inner chambers, never mind a force of six or eight soldiers.

Now I heard another chap, and after making formal greetin's to his ruler, he said:

It is a strange tale I read in the dead minds of your faithful guardsmen. They were felled not by a number of fighting men, but by a single opponent. He paused to let the full weight of this announcement impress the rest of the group.

What manner of weird tale are you bringing me, Oulixeus? Shouted Onesimus.

It is the truth, Onesimus, replied the psychologist. The impressions were strong on the brains of each of the four guards. Their attacker was wearing the metal of your own guards, and his fighting ability was little short of incredible -- he fought fair against all four of them and beat them with his superhuman strength and endurance. Though he wore the metal of Glossop, I've never seen or heard of this happening anywhere in The Dark Peak.

I've also read the mind and questioned the Princess of Hathersage, but she was a blank to me. She has perfect control over the emanations that come from her brain. She said that she saw some of the fighting, and confirmed there was just one man fighting the guards, but she didn't know who he was.

Another of the party spoke, and I recognised the voice of

Onesimus's cousin, who I'd rescued from the xin warriors. The description that Oulixeus has given fits him perfectly.

Where is this clown? Cried Onesimus. Have him brought to me at once. What know you of him, cousin? It seemed strange to me now that I think upon it that there should have been such a fighting man in Glossop, of whose name, even, we were ignorant before today. And his name too, Van Hallam, who ever heard of such a name in The Dark Peak?!

Word was soon brought that I were nowhere to be found, either in the palace or at me quarters. Penny, were brought to Onesimus and questioned, but she knew nowt of me whereabouts, or about me past, since we had only met when we were prisoners of the xin in t'swamp.

Keep your eyes on this other one, commanded Onesimus. She is a stranger too, and likely as not they both come from Hathersage, and where one is we shall sooner or later find the other. Let anyone who tries to leave Glossop be subjected to the closest scrutiny.

Another messenger now entered with word that I was still in the palace.

The likeness of every person who has entered or left the palace grounds today has been carefully examined, said the chap, and no-one sounds like this character.

Then we will have him shortly, concluded Onesimus -- in the meantime we will question the Princess of Hathersage again -- she may know more than she cared to tell you, Oulixeus.

They left the hall, and, as it was the gloaming, I slipped from my hiding place, over to the balcony. I couldn't see no-one lookin', and so I made my escape onto the street and out of t'palace grounds.

```
    HMM::OUT('What is the news from the DPDC?')
`ask:: Rippon, Pip // stat:: accept[ok]__ // src::
```

VAN HALLAM

2001:0db8:85a3:0000:0000:8a2e:037g:7334 [loc::hellsborough//
middlewood_road//467]__ // now:: 79.hail
ripperthroat.12.16.3.5.47`

CHAPTER 23

Slim as gnawmard's tail

I got back to near our quarters, where I was pretty sure I'd find Penny. As I got nearer, I got more careful n'all -- I were pretty sure that the place would be reyt guarded -- and I weren't wrong.

There were loads of clowns hanging about, front 'n' back -- it reminded me of nightclubs 'ere in Hellsborough, Pip, back in the day -- there were just this rammy smell o' trouble hanging about all over, but that's to be understood, I 'ad slaughtered them guards -- of which I is not proud, let thee understand me, but I would 'ave been done in mesen had I not done.

To get to our rooms, I knew I needed to get up on roof, so I shimmied up t'drain pipe of a shop down road, and moved along t'ridge of the terrace. I reached the building where Penny ought to be, and slipped in through t'window.

She were alone and said that I must have finished me work a while back, and she'd expected me sooner. It were obvious that even thought she were questioned about me, she knew nowt of what had gone on in the palace, and when I told her, she got all fidgety. I told her that Pandora had promised her 'and to Ocnus.

D'divi, it can't be, she said over and over -- they must have drugged her on rockrust! She must have lost her mind to have done such a thing. You don't know how us Hatherans love our royal family, none of us will ever accept it. What can be done, Van? She said -- you are resourceful, think of some way to save Hathersage from this disgrace.

If I can get near Ocnus I can sort this, I said, but I needs another to strike the final blow -- the one that frees Pandora.

Penny's eyes narrowed. You love her! She said. Does she know it?

Love is a strange thing, Pip, I knows it, and much as I wanted to say to Penny that I loved her with all me 'eart, I knew that someat weren't reyt -- weren't reyt at all. Like the murkmoon rises at neet, I knew someat weren't reyt. But I answered Penny with what she'd asked for: She knows it, Penny, and she repulses me because she is promised to Ocnus.

That grand lass sprung to her feet, and grasping me by me shoulder raising her whipo'wil above her head said:

Come on then Van, if I was given the choice, I could not choose a better mate for the first princess of The Dark Peak. Here is my hand upon your shoulder, and my word that Ocnus shall die at the point of my whipo'wil for the sake of my love for Hathersage, for Pandora, and for you. This very night I shall try to reach his quarters in the palace.

How? I said. We is guarded reyt proper.

She thought a moment -- I only need to pass these guards and I can do it, she said. I know a secret entrance to the palace through the top of the highest tower. I found it as I was passing above the palace on patrol duty. It is required that we investigate unusual stuff we might witness, and a face peering from the top of the high tower of the palace was, to me, unusual. I drew near and discovered it was Ocnus. He was put out at being detected and commanded me to keep the matter to myself, saying that the passage from the tower led directly to his apartments, and was known only to him. If I can reach the roof of the barracks and get my machine I can be in Ocnus's quarters in five minutes; but how am I to escape from this building?

How well are the machine sheds at the barracks guarded?

Usually one man on duty up on the roof at night.

Go to t'roof of machine shed, and wait for me there, I says to her, and without stopping to explain any more, I went back to street by same way I'd come, and then onto to t'machine sheds. I didn't dare to enter the building, as members of t'air-scout squadron, would be there and they'd all be on lookout for me.

I'd have to climb up to the roof. The only way to get up there were to go up t'face of building, there were no other way. Glossop's architecture is reyt fancy, and that made it easier to get up it than I thought it would -- there was lots of ledges and features, which made it a bit like a ladder. Before long I was up in t'building's eaves.

There I met me first real problem -- them eaves stuck out twenty foot from the wall, and much as I tried, I could find no opening through them. I could see that the top floor was full of soldiers, so that were no good, and I reckoned I had one chance -- clinging to the wall with me feet and one hand, I unloosened the straps of me trappings at the end of which was a big old hook that air sailors use to hang to the sides and bottoms of their craft for repair.

I swung this hook to the roof, and after trying loads of times, it lodged and I gently pulled on it. I reckoned it might bear me weight, but I didn't know, so I took a chance -- either me plan would work, or I'd be plastered all over the pavement a thousand foot down.

I swung out on the end of the strap. Below me, I could see the street lamps peering back at me through the murk, but after that, looking down seemed like a bad idea -- I needed to go up -- so I focused on doing that instead. There was a little jerk and a slip, then a nasty grating sound which made me blood go cold; then the hook caught proper and I felt safe again Pip, but me 'eart had gone reyt up into me throat.

I clambered up quick and grasped the edge of the eaves, drawing myself up onto the roof. Soon as I got there, the sentry on duty was at me -- pointing his fungun reyt at me noggin.

Who are you and where did you come from?

I's an air scout pal, and very near a deed one, I nearly fell to t'street below, I said, breathing hard -- it were some fancy acrobatics I had to do to get mesen hoisted up on roof.

That's all well and good, but why are you on the roof at all? I know no-one has landed or come up from the building for an hour. Explain yourself now, or I'll call for the guard.

Look here pal, and tha shall see how I come and how close a shave I had to not coming at all, I said, turning toward the edge of the roof, where, twenty foot below, at the end of my strap, hung me weapons.

The fella, his curiosity getting the better of 'im, stepped to me side and leaned over the edge. I grasped him by his throat and his fungun arm and threw him down. The weapon dropped from his grasp, and my fingers choked off his attempted shout for 'elp. I gagged and bound him and then hung him over the edge of the roof as I myself had hung. I knew it would be morning before he would be found, and I needed all the time I could get.

Pip! You following me still.

Err... Yes, sorry Van. My eyes flustered open, stuck with mucus. I hadn't been asleep, I knew I hadn't, I had heard everything that Van had said, and I had understood and internalised it all, it was just that my eyes had somehow involuntarily shut as well.

Here, have more rhum, said Van, topping up my glass, it'll do you good young'en. We need more crust n'all, where's that gutterball, I told 'im to keep us supplied.

There seems to be a problem with the hivemind Van, I said, shaking myself fully awake with a grimace as I downed the rhum.

Van stared at me. Problem with the hivemind? How can there be a problem with the hivemind, it's the hivemind, there's never a problem with the hivemind, it just is.

Well it isn't answering me, or it wasn't last time I asked it a question.

Ok, hang on, let me message the bf -- actually, you give it a go -- tell the bf to send Sinclair over again.

How do I do that? The last times, you have just taken his timestamp and tapped your little psycmask and that's been that -- what do I say to the hivemind to make the same thing happen?

Ok, don't worry about it, I thought you wanted to learn a bit about this place. I thought you had a bit about you, young'en, but I'm beginning to wonder, said Van with a chuckle and a wink. Hey John, he shouted at the bar, Pip 'ere reckons the hivemind has gone down!

I do want to learn a bit about this place -- help me, show me what to do Van.

```
      HMM::IN('Background music: Uplifting and adventurous
tune.  Aerial video, moorlands, rolling hills of The Dark
Peak')
`hits:: 898944 //
[this]2001:0db8:85a3:0000:0000:8a2e:037g:7334
[loc::hellsborough//middlewood_road//467]__ // now:: 79.hail
ripperthroat.12.16.3.25.2`
```

`Escape to a land shrouded in mystery, where rugged beauty and untamed wilderness collide.`

      HMM::OUT('skip ad')
`ask:: Rippon, Pip // stat:: accept[ok]__ // src:: 2001:0db8:85a3:0000:0000:8a2e:037g:7334 [loc::hellsborough//middlewood_road//467]__ // now:: 79.hail ripperthroat.12.16.3.25.3`

      HMM::IN('Yo, fellas! Are you tired of having a wack hairstyle that's not doing you justice? Say no more!')
`hits:: 371 // [this]2001:0db8:85a3:0000:0000:8a2e:037g:7334 [loc::hellsborough//middlewood_road//467]__ // now:: 79.hail ripperthroat.12.16.3.25.5`

`So, come through to our barber shop and let us show you some love. We gonna hook you up with the perfect cut that's gonna make you`

      HMM::OUT('skip ad')
`ask:: Rippon, Pip // stat:: accept[ok]__ // src:: 2001:0db8:85a3:0000:0000:8a2e:037g:7334 [loc::hellsborough//middlewood_road//467]__ // now:: 79.hail ripperthroat.12.16.3.25.6`

      HMM::IN('Farantees Riiide up!')
`hits:: 81901 // [this]2001:0db8:85a3:0000:0000:8a2e:037g:7334 [loc::hellsborough//middlewood_road//467]__ // now:: 79.hail ripperthroat.12.16.3.25.9`

`Yo..`

      HMM::OUT('skip ad')
`ask:: Rippon, Pip // stat:: accept[ok]__ // src:: 2001:0db8:85a3:0000:0000:8a2e:037g:7334 [loc::hellsborough//middlewood_road//467]__ // now:: 79.hail ripperthroat.12.16.3.25.10`

And with that, the hivemind appeared to have started working again. I'm confused. I need some help. I'm stoned on crust and snough, I'm blathered on rhum and ale, I'm overwhelmed by pretty much everything. I grip the table with both hands and hold on, because I feel like I'm about to fall off. I don't know why I sat on this chair, and all of a sudden I have a tune going around and around and around in my head and I can't get it out -- it's a song from my childhood -- or maybe my parent's childhood:

Well, I don't know why I came here toneet. I got a feeling that something ain't reyt. I'm so scared in case I fall off my chair and I'm wondering how I'll get down those stairs. Clowns to left of me, jokers to the right, here I am stuck in the middle with you...

Around and around and around, I think I'm shaking and my heart feels like it's going like the clappers. I'm still gripping that table in front of me like a ripperwing grips a flufftail with its talons.

Hey, Pip. Focus will ya. Tha's 'ad an overload from the hivemind, that's all. Tha'll be fine, tha just needs a bit of crust to steady tha nerves. Focus and listen and learn.

Ok, ok, I can do that now the hivemind is up, I can contact the bf and get some more crust.

Woah, wait up, I am your guide here, don't thee worry yourself about that: Tell tha psycmask to mock your transid.

Mock my transid? I spluttered. Is Van laughing at me?

Yeah, mask your transmission id, and shell out via someone else.

Wait. What? Why?

Isn't it obvious why?

I just looked at Van dumbfounded.

We need to maintain some sort of secrecy with our dealings, otherwise, the hivemind, the fungai, the nascenti, they know what we're up to, and we're trying to avoid that lot knowing owt about what we're up to, reyt? Taking crust ain't illegal or nowt, pretty much nowt is illegal in Hellsborough, but we needs to keep a low profile at all times, that's tha way things is done. That's why the bf operates in secrecy, we ain't feedin' them overlords nowt if we can 'elp it. That guy over there by the bar. You seen him?

The chap with the suit, yeah, I see him. I thought I might have been shouting, but Van didn't raise an eyebrow, so maybe not.

Yeah, him, now connect to his psycmask.

But he's not wearing one.

He is, tha just can't see it, it's part of his face.

Ok, ok, how do I connect? I think my breathing is returning to normal and my heart seems to be slowing down. Van puts his hands over my fingers and I feel them slacken and release their grip from the edge of the table. Then he picks this translucent thing off my little finger -- a blood lipid -- he says -- eat it. My face tells him that I don't want that thing anywhere near my mouth. But, he says, it will help you recover, help your focus, and he slides the thing onto my bottom lip. I don't gag, I don't chew, it slips into my mouth, past my teeth and tonsils and is gone. And I do feel better. My concentration is back.

How do you connect to another's psycmask?

You hack it.

How do you hack it? Wait, you want me to hack that poor bloke's face? I feel like I'm shouting again, but Van doesn't shhh me.

He's just a jelly, he'll not feel a thing, but tha's back now, so let's just finish off what I were saying and then I'll take thee through it step by step:

I got me weapons, then ran over to the sheds, getting Penny and my machines out and strapped together before I started me engine, and skimming over the edge of the roof I dropped down into the streets of Glossop. In less than a minute I was settled on the roof of our apartment.

I didn't tell her how I'd done it, but told her me plan for what we were going to do now. I were going to Hathersage, while Penny was to get into the palace and see off Ocnus. When she were successful she was then to follow on. She set my compass for me, a clever little thing that remains fixed on any point in The Dark Peak, and saying ta-ra we rose together and went in t'direction of t'palace which were on the route I needed to take to get to Hathersage.

As we neared the high tower a searchlight fell full on me, and a tannoy told me to stop. Penny dropped quickly into the darkness, while I rose fast up in to the sky -- followed by a dozen air-scout craft which were now after me. I twisted and turned me little machine -- like a venomtooth sidewinding across the moors -- I kept out of sight of their search-lights most of the time, but I was losing ground, so I focussed on a straight course and left things to the will of Dunlockslyn and the speed of me flyer.

Penny had shown me a trick that the Hathersage navy used, and that increased me speed, so that I could put some distance between me and them. Their fungets screeched past me, but I raced away at full speed, heading for Hathersage. I left 'em further and further behind, and was just starting to relax, when a lucky funget hit me craft. Me craft spluttered, and I started a downward spiral through the thick murk.

How far I fell before I regained control of me flyer I ain't a clue, but I must have been close to t'ground when I started to pull up, as I 'eard animals squealing below. I scanned the murk for my pursuers, and made out their lights well behind me. They was landing, I reckon they thought I'd crashed into that moorland.

Not until I could no longer see their lights did I flash that little lamp on me compass, and then I found that it had been brock by that stray funget -- as too 'ad me speedometer. All I could do now, Pip, were follow the stars, as best I could through the murk, and me chances of finding Hathersage at the speed I were traveling were about as slim as gnawmard's tail.

Hathersage is many thousands of paces southeast of Glossop,

across the most treacherous mountains of The Dark Peak, and with me compass intact I should have made the trip in few hours. But in the early murklight, I found mesen over moorland that stretched to the horizon.

```
     HMM::OUT('Gnawmard')
`ask:: Rippon, Pip // stat:: accept[ok]__ // src::
2001:0db8:85a3:0000:0000:8a2e:037g:7334 [loc::hellsborough//
middlewood_road//467]__ // now:: 79.hail
ripperthroat.12.16.3.29.37`

`HMM::IN('..Colour:   Grey / mottled brown_`

`..Diet:   Seeds, nuts, eggs, carrion, insects_`

`..Size:   10" (thumb)_`

`..Defining characteristics:   Slim tail, clever_`

`..Class:   Vermin_`

`..Image:   Incoming_    ')`

     HMM::OUT('What is the news from the DPDC?')
`ask:: Rippon, Pip // stat:: accept[ok]__ // src::
2001:0db8:85a3:0000:0000:8a2e:037g:7334 [loc::hellsborough//
middlewood_road//467]__ // now:: 79.hail
ripperthroat.12.16.3.31.4`

     HMM::IN('DPDC News: The Middlewood road closed')
`hits:: 65434 // [this]2001:0db8:85a3:0000:0000:8a2e:037g:7334
[loc::hellsborough//middlewood_road//467]__ // now:: 79.hail
ripperthroat.12.16.3.31.4`
```

`The Middlewood road shut at Hellsborough junction_  No passage North_ Avoid area_  Exacids on scene_ Hexikid cleanup in progress__`

CHAPTER 24

Scerm

So, crust Pip, we need to get ourselves some crust -- or rather you do, and I'm going to show you exactly how to communicate with the bf just like I do. Don't look so frightened, there's nothing to it young'un.

Ok, Van, show me what to do, I'm up for it. I'm going to rip the face of that jellyhead at the bar, right?

The same chap was still sat at the bar. He hadn't moved and was staring into his pint like it had no bottom.

We ain't gonna rip anything off anyone young'un; what we are going to go is hack into his psycmask.

But he isn't wearing one.

He is, I said before. His psycmask was installed when he was born. It's nanotech and you can't see it, that's all, but it does the same job as your chunky old council issued one -- it communicates with the hivemind and means that he is tracked by the fungai, just like you. The reason we want to send a message to our old friend the bf from your new friend at the bar over there, is because we want to be able to go about our business without too much hassle, and keep our anonymity -- is that how you say it Pip?

VAN HALLAM

Yes, anonymity.

Well, that's why we're keeping ourselves as unknown as we can to the hivemind and the organic network and the fungai.

Ok, I get that, so how do I hack this guy's psycmask?

Scerm Pip.

Scerm, I remember scerm. The first time I crossed The Hinge, the murk took me, but you was there Van, surfing the scerm. You saved my life.

Aye, I did.

From that day until this Van, I have never forgotten, I'll be forever grateful.

Ok, enough, it is what it is. What does tha know about scerm?

Not a whole lot, I admitted. From what I do understand, it is accessed by rockcrust and is something to do with the fungal network or maybe the murk, or maybe both?

Yeah, not a bad start. Scerm is ideas, combinations of ideas, thoughts, combinations of thoughts and ideas. Scerm is the prayers and worship of Dunlockslyn. Scerm is the missing ingredient, the embodiment of the murk -- the embodiment of Dunlockslyn, that what's experienced when the slime is slurped. Scerm is a greater power. Scerm is quantum code.

But we've run out of crust Van, we haven't got any more to slurp.

We've done enough toneet for this little task, doant worry about that, it's been in thee all neet, this little hack is trivial, trust me. But tha has to be ready Pip. What I is about to teach thee is the most powerful thing in the universe that I knows of; and once tha knows this there is no unknowing it, tha will 'ave this knowledge for the rest of tha life -- And tha knows that that can make thee very powerful -- tha will know more than anyone about most things -- tha will know what's gooin' on around thee, what is gooin' down here and hereabouts, what folk is thinkin', what folk is doin' -- this is mind bending stuff as well as bein' insightful.

I'm ready Van, let's get this done.

Does tha code -- int'off-world, I mean?

I did an introductory course once, but that's all, I wouldn't say I could code, no.

Ok, no worries, but thee'll understand the basics, I know tha will. Listen careful now, this'll be a crash course in programmin' the scerm. When tha has a psycmask -- could be a device like mine Pip, or a council one like yours, it doant matter, it gives thee access to the hivemind, and 'avin' 'ad crust, tha can access scerm, and use it 'ow one needs, to do what tha likes. It's all about trigonomature, think about a triangle, Pip. Triangles, they got three points, reyt?

Three points, yes.

Well them three points is important. Top o't'triangle that is the liminal point -- that's something we're gonna tap into, but then down bottom left, that is the physical point -- that's important too, since we're all physical - everything is physical, reyt -- it's the material world.

So you have the liminal world and the physical world, yeah, I get that. This place has many liminal points, same as the off-world, but I don't yet get what you're getting at.

Tha needs to use the scerm to tap into the liminality of the physical world, Pip. Listen up. This is where the code comes in, tha needs to program on the fly.

Wait though. What is the other corner of the triangle?

The bottom right? Well that's the social, of course. That

completes the triangle: Liminal-Physical-Social. There ain't nothin' else Pip, that's your lot. That's life. Most folk ignore the liminal bit. Some folk just live on the physical plane -- is that what you call it, a plane?

Yes, you could do, I guess, or maybe the physical aspect, or the physical sphere?

Yeah, well whatever, some folk never get out of the physical world, they just exists and does nowt else, they is hedonists, some of 'em. I know that word cos I was one once; actually for a long time I was, I cared little else about nothin' but the physical world.

The Social world, that is important though Pip, we 'as to be social, we is social animals aren't we Pip, us primates. There is lots of stuff that is important in the social world, and if you ain't part of it, you is a bit of an outcast, you is not normal and not rightfully balanced.

But tha sees Pip, that is most folk -- they is in the physical world and they is in the social world, so they thinks of 'emselves as well balanced folk -- but tha's 'eard that thing about the 'uman brain only using ten percent of it's potential and all that, ain't ya? Well that is all down to the top of that triangle -- it's a pyramid in't it? I just realised that mesen -- but that top of the pyrangle -- that liminal bit -- that's the bit that unlocks everything Pip. That's the bit that let's you bend the murk to your will by writing the scerm.

I'm ready Van, I am -- how do I do this? How do I take over Boggy's invisible psycmask and order crust from the bf -- tell me now, enough of the pseudoscience -- I need to know now!

Boggy?

The suit sat at the bar, his name is Boggy Lomas.

Does tha know him?

No. I've never seen him before in my life.

So how does tha know his name is Boggy? I mean it's not a normal name is it?

I just know.

How does tha know though Pip?

As I said, I just know.

Yeah, tha knows, but 'ow comes tha knows Pip? -- I'll tell thee how tha knows, tha knows because thee is tuned into the liminal plane -- tha ain't just thinkin' about physical and social, tha's tuned into the liminal plane already, that's how tha knows that that suit's name is Boggy Lomas!

Show me how to write the scerm Van, I'm ready. I know you said that you were beginning to wonder about me, but I'm back now, I'm ready for this -- help me, show me what to do!

You see the murk Pip, you see it all around, reyt?

Yes, of course, hard to avoid.

Well you can't avoid it, but tha can control it, watch...

I watched as Van coaxed the murk, curling tiny tendrils this way and that, reaching out here and there, rhizomes shooting out into the ether like tiny meteors, snaking like weeds across the smoky shroud. Van made the murk whirl and circle in tiny spirals, rings in the murk, tiny dark matter holes in the existence of the world.

Tha sees Pip, tha can control the murk; this is me programming the scerm to make the murk do my bidding -- try it.

I had a go, I really did. But nothing happened. I couldn't make the murk do anything that it wasn't doing, it just kept polluting the world like it always does, not a jitter of anything intentional.

Come on, concentrate, said Van, tha can do this, tha has the crust in thee to do this -- sense the scerm, Pip.

I tried again, but nothing; then, slowly, I saw a tiny flicker of activity that I had visualised; a minute twine shot out as if exploring my fingers and pint glass.

There you go Pip, I saw it, that little wisp that touched tha 'and there. Tha made the murk do what tha wanted, that's thee programming the scerm.

Maybe it was a gust from somewhere, I said, I don't think I have done much.

No, said Van, that were intentional murk changing, I saw it, tha bent it to tha will, tha did that, now try it again.

I tried again. And again, nothing.

Try again. Try, try, concentrate, try, said Van.

I concentrated. I tried to bend that murk to my will again, and it did. I sent my own slender tentacles, just like Van had done. I sent them over towards Boggy, the suit at the bar. They kept reaching out. The arrived and touched him. He didn't react, just as Van said he wouldn't. He was smoking a cigarette. My murk made the curl of the cigarette smoke dance about oddly, like a breeze had suddenly encroached from the outside, but the door to the bar hadn't moved.

That's it. Said Van, tha's reached out, tha's programmed the scerm to change the murk. Now, get into his psycmask.

How do I do that?

Tha's there, if not this way, then go that way, if not that way, go this way -- just take that murk into his face, then tha'll see the internals of the thing, then thee'll be able to take over his psycmask.

I did as Van had described. And he was right. As soon as I took the murk up Boggy's nostrils, I saw a schematic of sorts. I was able to tweak things in the psycmask using the murk, I could change settings. But, it wasn't as easy as that -- of course not -- Boggy fought back. The bloke sat at he bar that was Boggy Lomas didn't move, he just kept smoking his cigarette and burying his head in his beer, no reaction at all, but his psycmask was fighting back against my intrusion. They're designed to do that of course, what sort of device would it be that allowed you to just take over? Well, it wouldn't be very good would it, the nascenti have those psycmasks nailed down pretty tightly.

What's happening, said Van, you're into his psycmask now, reyt, and its detected you, reyt, it's fighting back against tha's intrusion -- it knows tha's there. That's normal, that's part of the in-built protection system of a psycmask -- just simple stuff though, tha is a hacker now Pip, so tha needs to be like what tha is and get 'round that.

This reminds me of a computer game from when I was really young, I said. In the off-world, my dad had an old computer from *his* childhood -- battered dirty old thing it was -- a C64 -- we used to load up games using things called cassette tapes. This game, it was something to do with taking over droids on a spaceship -- you had to rewire them -- this is just like that. I can see what I have to do, I have to rewire Boggy's psycmask, just like I had to rewire them droids in that old game, it's the same.

That old game is a parable for you then Pip, what do you see?

I see connections, lines of power, lines of control, circuits. I have to rewire those circuits so that I have control of Boggy's psycmask, but he is more powerful than I am, but I have the upper hand, since I am the one who has initiated the "attack", I have the first move, and that first move is a decisive factor, if I recall from my childhood. I can manipulate the murk Van, I can, I can change those connections, I can make it work, this is fascinating.

It's not just fascinating, young'un, it's power. Even with your basic code knowledge, tha can control the murk with the scerm, if not this then that, and all that sort of thing. Loop this. Do this while tha doant want to do that. For while I am here, keep dooin' that. I doant have much understanding of these things, I aint no scientist is I? But I is able to control the scerm so that the murk does me bidding -- and me psycmask is one heck of a lot more powerful than thees, cos thee is just a beginner with council kit -- that's why Boggy seems stronger than thee.

I have control Van. I've taken control of Boggy's pyscmask.

Boggy Lomas has no idea, he puffs on his cigarette and stares into his pint pot like nothing has happened.

So now then tha needs to dial out to the bf -- just use Boggy's psycmask to place the call. Use the bf's hashtag, that'll do it.

    HMM::OUT(' BackflitPirate send more dope, as promised') `ask:: Lomas, Boggy // stat:: accept[ok]__ // src:: 2001:0db8:85a3:0000:0000:9b3c:14ga:7143 [loc::hellsborough//middlewood_road//467]__ // now:: 79.hail ripperthroat.12.16.3.37.53`

    HMM::IN(' BackflitPirate: incoming') `ask:: unknown // stat:: accept[ok]__ // src:: 2001:0db8:85a3:0000:0000:ff32:8877:7b45 [loc::hellsborough//unknown__location//000]__ // now:: 79.hail ripperthroat.12.16.3.38.0`

    Interference and static

    `Ey up, is tha a new customer, no worries, incoming, chits will be taken from address.`

    Interference and static

Boggy jolted up at this, clearly it was new to him that he was going to receive something from the bf that he hadn't ordered. I took immediate action and replied, encapsulating my response in an encrypted packet that Boggy wouldn't be able to decipher.

```
        HMM::OUT('*** BackflitPirate    Sinclair will recognise
voice pattern, same location, charge to 8a2e:037g:7334***')
`ask:: Lomas, Boggy // stat:: accept[ok]__ // src::
2001:0db8:85a3:0000:0000:9b3c:14ga:7143 [loc::hellsborough//
middlewood_road//467]__ // now:: 79.hail
ripperthroat.12.16.3.38.4`

        HMM::IN(' BackflitPirate: incoming')
`ask:: unknown // stat:: accept[ok]__ // src::
2001:0db8:85a3:0000:0000:ff32:8877:7b45 [loc::hellsborough//
unknown__location//000]__ // now:: 79.hail
ripperthroat.12.16.3.38.9`

    Interference and static

`Jobs a good'un.  Despatched, eta 3m.`

    Interference and static
```

Tha's gettin' the hang of this ain't thee Pip. Three minutes to rock time, come on then, let's get this thing done.

With that, Van launched into a tirade of detail, which I was going to need more crust for, but as I knew it was coming, I had my head in gear, and was on top of it -- my concentration levels were the highest I think they have ever been -- but that crust was beckoning me like a scratcher taunts a barker, and I couldn't wait for it to arrive, but that didn't stop Van, he wanted to get finished as well:

Somewhere around murknoon, I come across hundreds of feighting green warriors. I had only just seen 'em, when fire were directed at me. Me craft was hit, and I come down.

I fell in t'middle of the feighting, but them warriors hadn't seen me coming, so busy they was with their own life and death struggles. The men were feighting on foot with whipo'wil's, while sharpshooters picked off them on the outskirts if they become separated -- much like a ripperthroat will pick off a straggling wooltard, should it get t'chance.

I knew that I had to feight or dee, so my whipo'wil were drawn to defend mesen.

I fell beside a huge guy who was feightin' three blokes at once, I knew it were Siltibog. He didn't see me, as I were a little behind him, and just then the three coming at 'im, who I recognised from their metal as Strinxin, charged at t'same time. The big fella made quick work of the first of 'em, but as he stepped back for another thrust he fell over a dead body behind him and were at their mercy.

Siltibog would have been deed and on his way to t'Ripperthroats had I not jumped before him and clashed with t'other two before they were on him. I took out the first, which gave Siltibog time to get back to his feet and see off t'other.

He gave me a look and I saw smile on them grim lips of 'is. Talking to me in mind talk, he said, I wouldn't have recognised you, Van Hallam, but there is none other in The Dark Peak who'd have done that for me. I thinks I has learned that there is such a thing as friendship.

He said no more, because the Strinxin were closing in on us, and together we fought, side by side, as the murk sometimes light, sometimes volumising heavy, tried to stop our progress and skewed the odds of victory this way and that.

Eventually the battle turned in favour of the Stanningxin, and what was left of the Strinxin horde fell back upon their mentiloth, and fled into t'gathering gloaming.

A thousand men had fought that day, and on the field of battle three hundred lay dead. Neither side took no prisoners, and the dead lay where they were, to be picked over by corvid, slyfluffs and grizzlers in the quiet of murknite.

On our return to the village, we went straight to Siltibog's place, where I was left while he attended the meeting which follows a feight. The smell of the place was just like I remembered -- foetid, and the stench got up tha nose, but I soon got used to it again.

I paced about waiting for Siltibog to come back and heard a noise from next door, and then in a rush Shad was on me, pinning me down on me back and licking me face. If tha had seen him Pip, you'd think he was trying to eat me. He had found his way back to Stanningxin and, Siltibog told me later, had gone straight to me room where he had waited for me to come back.

He's a good boy, ain't thee Shad, said Van, ruffing up Shad's collar fur and feeding him a blackworm, which had magically appeared between his fingertips. Shad took that blackworm gentle as a squeaker nibbling on cheese in a trap.

Hagibrack knows that tha's here Van, Siltibog said when he come back from the meeting; Gorsithorn saw us after the feight. Hagibrack has ordered me to bring you to him toneet. I has ten mentiloth -- tha can take tha choice of 'em, and I will take thee to the road to Hathersage. We should go now.

And what happens then? When you get back, pal? I said.

The wild dyapnids, or worse. Unless I has the chance to feight Hagibrack.

Aye, exactly -- then we'll stay, and go see Hagibrack -- it's what you want int'it? We'll go to t'swamp at first murklight.

Nah, tha doant understand, Hagibrack is 'ere in Stanningxin, said Siltibog -- he had personal business with Pondisyke, and come in last neet under cover of darkness, I only found out mesen a few moments back.

Siltibog didn't want me to face off with Hagibrack of course, Pip, saying that Hagibrack often flew off the 'andle at the memory of that punch I had laid on him. He'd said that if he ever got his hands on me I, would be tortured in horrible ways, but that didn't worry me, I knew I had Hagibrack's number.

Me and Siltibog ate, and I told him Fenimoss's story -- does tha remember the one Pip? The one that she had told me that night out on the moors when we marched over to t'swamp.

He didn't say nowt, just listened, but I knew his brain were working overtime by them pained expressions on his face.

After I'd finished, he didn't talk me out of trying to visit Hagibrack, just sayin' that he were gooin' to speak to Gorsithorn first. I went with him -- and you should have seen her face, Pip, she was sour and snarling at the sight of me -- but what could she do, she were in Siltibog's household and had to stay stum.

Siltibog dished out 'is own rough justice -- forty years ago tha brought about the torture and death of a woman named Lillifern, he said to her. I has just discovered that the warrior who loved that woman now knows of your part in it. He may not kill thee, Gorsithorn, it is not the custom of the xin, but I is sure that there is nowt to stop him tying one end of a strap about tha neck and t'other end to a wild mentiloth, just to test tha fitness to survive.

I heard that he were planning to do this after murkrise and thought it reyt I let tha know: T'river Dun ain't so far from 'ere, and tis all down hill from here.

With that, we left. Next morning Gorsithorn were gone, and she weren't never seen again.

I spotted the double negative, but let it go, and with that, the door of the bar swung open and in rolled Sinclair, with our payload onboard -- I hoped.

Sinclair swung about, clearly disorientated, but picked up Boggy Lomas's psycmask signal and trundled towards the bar where he still sat nursing his pint. In contrast to the last time we saw him, his "eyes" were glowing a strange shade of green and he issued an odd bleeping sound that made him sound irate. There was a ticking too, which was a little unnerving.

Hey Sinclair I said, as he sat ignored at Lomas's feet. He swivelled and rolled towards me, his eyes returning to their warmer glow. The bleeping stopped -- clearly recognising my tone of voice from previously. Arriving at out table, he opened his mouth and Van took the rockcrust from his tongue, immediately preparing it for us to slurp.

Done, Sinclair rolled back over to the stool on which Boggy Lomas sat at the bar. All his lights now extinguished, but the ticking from before continued. The slime slurped by us both, Van started up again, he really was intent on getting things done tonight, and very soon. I put the ticking out of my head as best I could.

We made our way over to Hagibrack's place sayin' nowt. Hagibrack, couldn't wait to see me. We was brought straight in, where he lollopsed on the platform glowering at me.

Strap him to that pillar -- him who dares strike the mighty Hagibrack. Heat them irons there; with me own hands I shall burn the eyes out of his head so he can't pollute me with his vile gaze ever again.

I laughed at him Pip, cos I knew that would go down well with the xin who was hangin' about. Then I spoke up -- he was still ranting -- chieftains of Stanningxin, I said to 'em -- ignoring Hagibrack, I has been a chief among you, and today we have fought together against Stanningxin's worst enemy. Thee all owes me an 'earing, at least?

Silence, roared Hagibrack. Gag the creature and bind him.

I said a while back that Pondisyke was a bit of a bit player in this story, Pip, but maybe he were more than that if me memory now serves me reyt, cos it was he who spoke up now:

Justice -- said Pondisyke -- who is thee to set aside our customs Hagibrack?

Aye, justice! I heard a dozen or more voices say, and so, while Hagibrack fumed and frothed, I carried on.

I is not a speaker as you know Pip, I's a do-er, but it were my time to speak and I didn't want to mess it up, me life depended on it, so I gave it me best shot:

Eyup lads, tha lot is brave and tha loves bravery, but where was tha imperial emperor when we was feighting today, eh? I did not see him in the thick of battle -- cos he weren't there that's why. He beats defenceless women and children in 'ere, his lair, but when did one of thee see him feight with men, eh? Even me, a midget beside his great bulk, knocked him down with one punch to his noggin. Is that the man tha want ruling over thee? This bloke 'ere, beside me now, is a mighty warrior -- I put my hand on Siltibog's shoulder then, Pip -- chieftains, how about 'aving Siltibog as emperor of Stanningxin?

At that, Hagibrack glowed a deep shade of red.

Vermillion?

If you say so, and I reckon he probably 'ad steam coming out of is lugholes 'n'all, said Van with a snigger.

Them xin, they roared their approval, and I must admit, me sweetmeats, which had been up somewhere near my throat, had now dropped, and I carried on:

Hagibrack must prove his fitness to rule. Were he a brave man he would invite Siltibog to combat, for he does not love him, but Hagibrack is afraid; Hagibrack, tha emperor, is a coward. With me bare hands I could kill him, and he knows it.

After I stopped it were silent, and all eyes were on Hagibrack. He did not speak or move, but the blotchy green of his face turned a more livid red -- if that were possible -- and froth and spittle spattered from his lips.

Hagibrack, said Pondisyke in a cold, hard voice -- never in me long life has I seen a xin emperor so humiliated. I take it tha accepts this challenge? Tha has no choice. Chieftains, Pondisyke carried on, shall Hagibrack, prove his fitness to rule over Siltibog?

There were twenty chieftains in the room, and all signalled their agreement with whipo'wil's held high and straight.

There were no going back now, Hagibrack pulled out his whipo'wil and shumbled towards Siltibog.

The fight didn't last long. It ain't even worth describing Pip, and with his foot upon the neck of the dead monster, Siltibog became emperor and imperial ruler of all the xin.

His first act was to make me a full-fledged chieftain with the rank I had won by my combats the first few weeks of my captivity among them.

The warriors would follow Siltibog, I could see that, so I used the opportunity to sign them up in my cause against Glossop. I told Siltibog the story of what had happened since the last time we'd seen each other, and let him know the thoughts I had in me 'ead.

He went straight to t'others in the room with what I'd said -- Van Hallam has made a proposal, which you'll find interesting and profitable: Pandora, the Princess of Hathersage, who was our prisoner once, is now held by the Glossopians, and betrothed to the son of the ruler, who she must wed to save her country from the hands of Glossop's army. Van suggests that we rescue her and return her to Hathersage. In return, the loot of Glossop is ours, and we'll get a peaceful alliance with Hathersage. That means we could build our hatchings bigger and use 'em more, this would allow us to become stronger than all the xin of The Dark Peak.

Is tha with me brothers?!

It were a chance to feight and loot, and they rose to the bait as a rainbow slid jumps for a chunkfly. For xin they were reyt 'appy, and before another half hour passed, twenty mounted messengers were flying across the moors and marshes to call the hordes together for the expedition.

Three days later we was on t'march to Glossop, more than a thousand strong, as Siltibog had enlisted three smaller hordes on his promise of the sacking of Glossop.

I rode at t'head of column beside the new lord of the xin, while at the heels of me mentiloth were Shad -- and I swear, he were licking his lips in anticipation of t'carnage.

We travelled by murknight, camping in the murklight in deserted villages, all of us, even the animals hidden during the daytime. On the march, Siltibog the statesman, enlisted five thousand more warriors from various scattered hordes, so that, six days after we set out we halted at midmurk outside the great walls of the town of Glossop, fifteen thousand strong.

The feighting strength and efficiency of this horde of ferocious green monsters were equivalent to ten times their number of clowns, and Glossop was nowhere near that big. Never in the history of The Dark Peak, Siltibog told me, had such a force of green warriors gone into battle together. It was a reyt task to keep even a bit of harmony among 'em, and it was only down to the will of Dunlockslyn that he got 'em to the town without a mighty battle among 'emselves at all.

The nearer we got to the town the lesser their personal quarrels become, as they were submerged in their hatred for the rainbowsun -- as the xin called the clowns. The Glossopians, who had been ruthless in the extermination of the green men for millenia, destroying their incubators, they hated with a vengeance.

As we arrived about a thousand paces from the town's gates, I realised that getting in weren't something that had occurred to me -- But I weren't fazed Pip, I just made it up on the spot, since making things up on the spur of the moment, had often, if not always, been a reyt good strategy for me. We stopped and I spoke to Siltibog, telling him to split his forces into two. Both were to be positioned out of sight of the town's two main gates.

I took half a dozen dismounted warriors and approached one of the smaller gates, that were set into the walls every three hundred foot or so. There was no guard on these gates, they were just covered by sentries who patrolled the streets within the city walls.

Glossop's walls were maybe fifty foot high and thirty foot thick, built from huge blocks of gritstone, and the task of gettin' in seemed to my small band an impossible task. But I told 'em not to worry 'emselves, as this is where some of me rudimentary learning in the art of warfare come in. I got three of them to face wall and lock their arms together. The next two I said to get on their shoulders, and the next one to climb up on the shoulders of them two. That made me little tower someat like forty foot high, and only a leap to the top and over the wall, ok it was quite a big leap, but I were confident I could do it.

And I did it 'n'all, Pip, the sap in me veins burning strong. I bounced from one step to the next until I clutched the top of the wall and drew myself onto it. After that I dragged six lengths of leather one from each of me warriors, which we had already fastened together. Having the top warrior grab one end, I lowered myself down to t'street below. No one was about, and I opened that small gate. After that, six green men stood with me in the town of Glossop.

As luck would have it, we had ended up in the back of the palace grounds. I decided that I would go straight for the palace with four of my guys, and I sent one to each of the main gates to unlock them from the inside and let the hordes in, the one I sent

Siltibog's way, I asked for fifty men to head to the palace where they would find me.

No shots were to be fired and no further advance made until I had reached the palace with my fifty more xin.

Our plans worked reyt good. The two sentries we met were dispatched to the Ripperthroat Mountains, and the guards at both gates followed them in silence -- none of them a match for a fevered xin.

CHAPTER 25

Ticking...

I is dry Pip, said Van signalling to Shalesmoor for refills, all this talkin', it's making me parched it is, and this is an important turning point in the story before we get to the end, so let's recharge while we still can.

Shalesmoor had acknowledged Van's request and was filling two huge tankards with fresh ale. I had a feeling that we were getting close to the end now and Van was running out of steam. The evening was late, but I still felt ready for whatever Van was about to dish out, so I waited whilst the new beer arrived.

And I needs a comfort break Pip, so I'll be back in a moment, said Van disappearing in the direction of the gents, tapping his tiny pscymask and muttering as he did so.

As I waited, I wondered what was going on. I had still heard nothing from my mysterious benefactor -- if that's what he (or she?) was, a benefactor? Van had been talking to Dirty Leaves earlier, and said that he might have to get off, but then he'd carried on with his tale, and nothing more had happened. And what of Pandora (this one) and the crosslander? Or old Jarv for that matter?

I see Van coming back, and Shalesmoor is heading over with

those huge tankards. I refill our shot glasses with a few fingers of rhum and as Van lands back in his chair, so the ale arrives and he has a choice of that or the rhum. He opts to quench his thirst on the ale, quaffing longly, then knocks back a rhum for good measure as well.

Relieved? I say.

Rightly so, now let's bang this thing out before anything else happens.

Anything else? I managed to get in, but he is already back in full flow:

This charge should not have caught the rainbowsun by surprise, Siltibog telepathically roared, as he met me at the doors of the palace with the fifty men I'd asked for.

It shouldn't have done Pip, but we soon realised why we had managed to get this far so quick -- looking through the windows of the palace, we could see Onesimus's throne room. That massive hall was full of nobles -- and someat important was going on. There weren't a guard insight, cos I reckon they thought them palace walls were impregnantable.

Impregnable?

Aye that, but it didn't matter to us -- we peered in; had anyone in the room seen our staring, they'd have been scared witless.

At one end of the room, sat on big old golden thrones, was Onesimus and his queen. They were surrounded by 'angers-on -- officers and dignitaries and the like. In front them a red carpet were lined with soldiers, and then a procession began to come up that red carpet towards them thrones.

Our timing had clearly been proper good, Pip. And there were a reason for that -- we had crashed the wedding of Ocnus, Prince of Glossop and Pandora, Princess of Hathersage.

At the front were four officers of the royal guard carrying a big plate, with a red silk cushion on it, and on top of that there was this 'uge gold chain with a collar and padlock at each end. Seemed a bit kinky to me, Pip, but as we 'as already established, I is no expert on the ways of The Dark Peak. Behind the royal guards there were four more carrying another plate, the same as the first, but this one had crowns on it.

I was a little jealous, Pip, and this galled me a bit, since I didn't want to see Pandora even near to being married, after what she had told me 'n'all that, but I knew we'd stop this thing before it even got started, so I kept me composure and we watched for a little longer, doing a bit more reconnaissance as it were.

As they got to the throne the two groups split apart and stopped, facing each other either side of that red carpet. After them came more hoity-toity types and more royal guards. Lastly two figures followed, entirely covered in reddish silk -- what's that colour you said earlier?

Vermillion?

Yeah, that, and they were so covered that I couldn't see who it was, of course I knew, but apart from the difference in height, they were both completely covered. The two of 'em stopped at the throne and faced Onesimus, and then I could see through the window the king speaking at them -- I couldn't hear his words, but not long after his mouth had finished moving two of the royal guards took off them red robes from one of the figures, and it was then that I saw that Penny had failed in her mission, cos it was Ocnus, Prince of Glossop.

But then you knew that Van, you must have done?

Yeah, I guess I did, but it still come as a surprise, but then I'm not sure who I expected to see.

Onesimus put one of the collars of gold around his son's neck and clamped the padlock shut. After a few more words to Ocnus he turned to the other figure, and the guards removed Pandora's silks.

It wouldn't be long and Pandora would be joined forever to the Prince of Glossop; it were an impressive ceremony, but I'd seen enough and as Onesimus was about to put the collar on Pandora, I crashed through t'window and without thinking hurled myself through the startled crowds and brought my whipo'wil down on that gold chain.

That right put the scratcher among the rooterwings it did, Pip, said Van with a chortle and mirthful grin. And of course, confusion abounded Pip. It felt like a thousand whipo'wil's were pointed at me, and Ocnus came at me with a shard that was part of his ceremonial get up. I could have killed him as easy as I'd kill a fly in this bar, but 'cos of the customs of The Dark Peak I couldn't use me whipo'wil, so a grasped his wrist and pointed to t'far end of hall, where the xin were now coming in.

Glossop has fallen! I shouted.

What's tha doin' there? Said Boggy Lomas to Sinclair the gutterball, toeing him away from the legs of his bar stool, where he had been sat ticking for the last ten moments. The gutterball's eyes flared an intense neon blue and the ticking got louder.

Sinclair then rolled in our direction, still ticking, but his eyes now flashing green. He came to rest at the base of our table, and spoke:

I am in the custody of Dirty Leaves, he said -- yet I knew these weren't his words. These were the words of my mystery benefactor.

Who are you? I said.

Who I is, is irrelevant. Boggy Lomas is a Jellyhead. Capital J. The gutterball Sinclair has been sent to destroy it. You need to get out of there now.

For the love of D'divi! Will I ever get to finish this story! Scolded Van, and picked Sinclair up off the floor, looking directly into his eyes.

Listen thee, if tha is with Dirty Leaves, then all well and good, cos Dirty Leaves an' mesen is thick, and I knows tha ain't gonna be gooin far for a while -- so Sinclair 'ere, he's going sit with me until I say he's not, and tha is gonna shut up with tha rubbage.

Sinclair's lights dimmed and for all intents and purposes, that was the end of the conversation as far as Van was concerned.

You know all about this, don't you Van? I said, maybe a little unprofessionally, since I wasn't sure it was my place to ask Van a question like that.

Let's get this story done, young'un, said Van. He wasn't angry with me, I'm not sure he had the capacity for outright anger any more, he seemed too tired for that.

There'll be enough time for chatter and fireworks after we're done, and I'll explain all then, but for now, tha job is to listen and get down the meyt and spuds o'this, an' I ain't stoppin' until I's done:

Everyone looked to where I pointed to see Siltibog and his fifty warriors barge into the room, and then all 'ell broke loose, as the soldiers and nobles of Glossop were feighting the oncoming xin.

I threw Ocnus into t'crowd, and moved Pandora behind mesen. Behind the throne were a narrow doorway and that's where Onesimus had plonked 'imself -- and with whipo'wil outstretched, we clashed. Ocnus come back to help his father, but his father feared for 'is son, and lost eye contact with me so that I caught 'im a fatal blow. Ocnus was joined by four guards, and with me back against them gold thrones, I were hard pressed to defend myself 'n'not strike down Ocnus -- which I moan't do, if I ever wanted to 'ave t'hand of Pandora.

Me blade were swinging fast and I parried the thrusts that would see me deed. Two of 'em I disarmed, and one was down, when a load more rushed to the aid of their new ruler, and to avenge the death of their old un.

With Pandora still behind me, we worked our way towards t'doorway at back of throne, but they knew what I was trying to do and three of 'em got behind me, blocking our escape.

The xin had their hands full in t'centre of room, and I began to realise that nowt short of a miracle could save Pandora and mesen, when I saw Siltibog surging through the crowd like a bull demonspawn. With one swing of his whipo'wil he laid a dozen corpses at his feet, and he were soon at my side dealing death and destruction right and left. Ocnus were his first victim.

The bravery of them Glossopians was someat to behold and not one of 'em attempted to escape, and when the feighting stopped it were because only xin remained alive in the great hall, other than Pandora and mesen.

After the battle were over, my only thought were for Penny. I left Pandora with Siltibog and took a dozen warriors to the dungeons underneath the palace. The jailers had all left to join the feight in the throne room, so we could search the prison without no bother.

I called Penny's name, and finally heard a faint response, then found her chained up. She were reyt pleased to see me, and t'know meaning of feight, which she had 'eard from her prison cell. She told me that the air patrol had captured her before she reached the high tower of the palace, so she hadn't even seen Ocnus.

I sent the xin to find keys, and soon we had Penny with us in t'throne room.

The sound of firing, and shouts and cries, came to us from t'town streets outside, so Siltibog went off to deal with that. Penny went with him as she could be his guide, and the rest of the xin started a search for surviving Glossopians to take prisoner, and to loot the place -- like they had been promised.

Pandora and I were finally alone. She sat on one of the thrones, and smiled as I turned to her.

Alone. A stranger, hunted, threatened, persecuted. You have done more in a few short months in The Dark Peak, than any man has ever done. You have joined together the wild hordes of the marshes and brought them to fight as allies of a clown people.

I have done many stupid things in me life, many things that wiser men would not have dared. I took her in my arms and kissed her. And that was when I asked my princess to be mine, which was the reyt way to do it in The Dark Peak. I got it reyt this time Pip -- Van was grinning like, as he would say, a reyt fooil.

And there you 'ave it Pip -- in the midst of all that wild feightin', all that death and destruction -- Pandora, Princess of Hathersage, daughter of The Dark Peak, promised herself in marriage to Van Hallam, bastard son of Hellsborough.

CHAPTER 26

Fear and loathing on the Middlewood road

A while later Siltibog and Penny come back and told us that Glossop had been sacked. All of the Glossopian forces were entirely destroyed or captured, and no more resistance were expected. Several gruizers had escaped, but there were hundreds of war and merchant vessels now in xin control.

The lesser hordes had commenced looting and quarrelling among 'emselves, so it were decided that we collect what warriors we could, man as many vessels as possible with Glossopian prisoners and make for Hathersage.

Five hours later we sailed from the roofs of the dock buildings with a fleet of twenty five gruizers, carrying nearly a thousand green warriors, followed by a fleet of transport with their mentiloth.

Behind us we left the town of Glossop to four thousand fierce and brutal green warriors. They had torched hundreds of buildings, and columns of dense smoke rose to mingle with the murk.

Not long after murknoon we sighted Hathersage, and a short

time later, the Glossopian battleships that had been besieging the village come up from their camps to meet us.

The banners of Hathersage had been strung from stern to stern of each of our craft, but the Glossopians did not need this sign to realise we were the enemy, cos our xin warriors had opened fire on them almost as soon as they left the ground. With their uncanny marksmanship they raked the on-coming fleet with volley after volley.

The village of Hathersage, realising that we were friends, sent out hundreds of vessels to 'elp out, and then began the first real air battle I had ever seen.

The vessels carrying our green warriors were kept circling above the feighting fleets of Hathersage and Glossop, since their big funguns were useless in the hands of the xin who, having no navy, had no skill in naval gunnery. Their small-arm fire though, was most handy, and the final outcome were helped no end by them being there.

A great hole was torn in the hull of one of the Glossopian gruizers, and with a lurch she turned completely over, her crew plunging toward the ground a thousand foot below. The gruizer come down after them, burying itself in the soft loam of the ancient moorland.

Two of the vessels of Hathersage then went above the Glossopians, and poured a load of exploding bombs on 'em.

The Glossopians were routed. Several tried to escape, but they were surrounded by hundreds of tiny fliers, and above each hung a Hatheran gruizer ready to drop boarding parties onto their decks. In less than an hour the battle was over, and what was left of the conquered Glossopians fleet was headed toward the village of Hathersage under guard.

We now signalled the flagship of Hathersage's navy to approach, and when close enough, I called out that we had the Princess

Pandora on board, and that we wanted to transfer her so she could be taken home.

Once they had understood me accent and what it was I had said, a great cheer went up, and a moment later the colours of the Princess of Hathersage were flying from every mast.

The flagship docked with our ship, and a dozen officers come on our deck. They stopped in their tracks when they saw the hundreds of green warriors on board, but Penny was there too, and she went to meet them and told them that they were now the allies of Hathersage.

Pandora and I then went towards 'em, and they had no eyes for other than her. She received them gracefully, calling each by name, for they were men of high rank in the service of her grandfather, and she knew them well.

Lay your hands upon the shoulder of Van Hallam, she said to them, turning toward me, the man to whom Hathersage owes her princess as well as her victory today.

They were reyt kind to me, but what seemed to impress them most was that I had won the aid of the xin in me campaign for the liberation of Pandora, and in saving Hathersage.

Tha owes tha thanks more to another man, I said, and here he is; meet one of The Dark Peak's greatest soldiers and statesmen, Siltibog emperor of the Stanningxin.

With the same polished courtesy that had marked their manner toward me they extended their greetings to the great xin, nor, to my surprise, was he much behind them in the way he held himself. Though not a wordy race, the xin are very formal, and their ways lend themselves to dignified and courtly manners.

Pandora went aboard the flagship, and was much put out that I would not follow, but, as I said to her, the battle was not over; we still had the land forces of the besieging Glossopians to defeat, and I would not leave Siltibog until that were done.

The commander of the naval forces of Hathersage promised to arrange to have the armies of Hathersage attack from the village at the same time as our land attack, and so the vessels separated and Pandora was taken back to the court of her father, Ptolemy.

As soon as the last mentiloth was released from the transporter, Siltibog gave the command to advance, and in three parties we crept upon the Glossopian camp from the north, the south and the east.

About a thousand paces from the main camp we encountered their outposts and charged. With wild cries and the nasty squealing of battle-enraged mentiloth we bore down on them Glossopians. We did not catch them napping, but found a well-entrenched battle line confronting us. Time after time we were repulsed until, toward murknoon, I began to fear for the result of the battle.

The Glossopians numbered ten thousand fighting men, while pitted against them were less than a thousand green warriors. The forces from Hathersage had not arrived, and we hadn't had no word from 'em neither.

Siltibog ordered the charge again, and once more the mighty mentiloth bore their terrible riders against the ramparts of the enemy. At the same moment the battle line of Hathersage surged in from the west, and the Glossopians were crushed between two millstones. Nobly they fought, but in vain.

The plain before the village became a shambles until the last Glossopian surrendered, and the carnage ceased. The prisoners were marched back to Hathersage, and we entered the village gates, a triumphant procession of conquering heroes.

We was greeted with endless clapping, and the village went mad with joy. Never before had an armed body of green warriors entered the gates of Hathersage, and as they came as friends and allies, that made the clowns happy as Larry.

My services to Pandora had become known to the Hatherans and my name was shouted out, and loads of ornaments were fastened on me and me mentiloth as we passed up the avenues to the palace -- even with Shad close to my side, the Hatherans pressed close to me.

At the top of the great steps leading up to the palace stood the royal party, and as we reached the lower steps one of them come down to meet us.

He were tall and straight and strong, and looked every bit a ruler of men -- I did not need to be told that he was Ptolemy, lord of the Hathersage clowns.

The first member of our party he met was Siltibog and his first words sealed forever the new friendship between the races.

Get this Pip: That Ptolemy may meet the greatest living warrior of The Dark Peak is a priceless honour, but that he may lay his hand on the shoulder of a friend and ally is a far greater one than that.

It has remained for a man of another place to teach the green warriors of The Dark Peak the meaning of friendship said Siltibog; to him we owe the fact that us hordes of Stanningxin can understand thee.

Ptolemy then greeted each of the other xin in turn and to each spoke to 'em kind and friendly words. Then he laid both hands upon me shoulders. My son, he said; you are gladly granted the most precious jewel in all of The Dark Peak.

I kept my concentration on what Van had been saying -- he is paying me for this after all, and I didn't have any difficulty with the concentration, as has been said before, rockcrust is nothing if not an amazing aid to concentration; and that meant that I could also keep an eye on Boggy Lomas.

Boggy seemingly sank further and further into his own stupor. Like us, he had progressed from ales to rhum, but unlike us, he seemed incapable of even basic communication with Shalesmoor, who was trying his best to elicit some sort of response from him. Or maybe he just wasn't in a talking mood, it was difficult to tell from where I was sitting.

I wondered too what a Jellyhead with a capital J meant. That was a curious thing that my "benefactor" had said, he -- I am now assuming he is a he, I don't really know that to be true -- had said "The gutterball Sinclair has been sent to destroy it" -- "it" -- what does that mean. This Boggy Lomas, whoever he is, doesn't look like an "it". He looks like a rather sad and drab individual who has had too much to drink, not some super-criminal to be anonymously assassinated.

My mind spun like a junkyard speedball. I spotted another blood lipid on the pinky of my left hand and wiped it off on my bottom teeth, letting it do its stuff and calm my buzzing brain. Van quaffed back some more ale in preparation for what I felt likely would be his final chapter, since I wasn't sure what else was to come, but didn't feel like there could be much left.

It occurred to me that I could drop in on Boggy's psycmask and see if I could figure anything out there, but when I tried to connect again, although my proficiency with the scerm had definitely improved and I had no trouble reaching out this time, when I got to his psycmask, its defences were impenetrable. Solid. Whatever I tried, I was repelled every time, so I gave up.

```
    HMM::OUT('Latest DPDC news')
`ask:: Rippon, Pip // stat:: accept[ok]__ // src::
2001:0db8:85a3:0000:0000:8a2e:037g:7334 [loc::hellsborough//
middlewood_road//467]__ // now:: 79.hail
ripperthroat.12.16.4.1.2`

    HMM::IN('DPDC Alert: Continuing disturbances around The
```

Middlewood road area')
`hits:: 9734 // [this]2001:0db8:85a3:0000:0000:8a2e:037g:7334 [loc::hellsborough//middlewood_road//467]__ // now:: 79.hail ripperthroat.12.16.4.1.4`

`The Middlewood road remains shut at Hellsborough junction_ Taplin road shut before Hellsbrough place_ House fire_ Avoid area_ Exacids on scene__`

    HMM::IN('DPDC Alert: Further destruction to Hellsborough Park')
`hits:: 9965 // [this]2001:0db8:85a3:0000:0000:8a2e:037g:7334 [loc::hellsborough//middlewood_road//467]__ // now:: 79.hail ripperthroat.12.16.4.2.17`

`Bin fire reported at the Middlewood road / Hawksley avenue exit of Hellsborough park_ Avoid area_ Exacids alerted__`

They, whoever they are, are hemming us in: Me, Van, Sinclair the gutterball, Shalesmoor, Boggy Lomas, or any one of the other twenty or so revellers that are still in the bar at this D'divi forsaken hour.

And Van knows more about this than he's letting on. Dunlockslyn protect us all, I'm scared.

CHAPTER 27

The last dooer

For ten days the hordes of Stanningxin and their allies were feasted and entertained, and then, loaded with gifts and escorted by a thousand soldiers of Hathersage, they began the journey back to their own lands. Clown nobles accompanied them to Stanningxin to cement more closely the new bonds of peace and friendship.

Fenimoss was with her father, who before all his chieftains had acknowledged her as his daughter.

Three weeks later, Siltibog and Fenimoss, returned upon a gruizer that had been sent to Stanningxin to fetch them in time for the ceremony which joined Pandora and me. Our marriage.

For six years I served in the councils and fought in the armies of Hathersage as a prince of the house of Ptolemy. The people seemed never to tire of heaping honours on me, and no day passed that did not bring some new proof of their love for princess Pandora.

In an incubator on the roof of our palace lay a snow-white egg. For nearly a year ten soldiers of Ptolemy's Guard had constantly stood over it, and not a day passed when I was in the city that Pandora and I did not stand hand in hand before our little shrine planning for the future, when that delicate shell should break.

In my memory is the picture of the last night as we sat there talking in low tones of the strange romance which had woven our lives together and of this wonder which was coming our way.

Aww Van, you old softie.

I is at 'eart Pip, I is.

In the distance we saw the bright-white light of an approaching gruizer, it were a common sight. We didn't think much about it, but it raced toward Hathersage, it's speed making it unusual.

It flashed signals saying that it had an urgent message for the ruler, and it circled waiting for the tardy patrol boat to escort it to the palace docks.

Ten moments after it touched down at the palace, a message called me to the council chamber, which was filled with members of t'council.

Ptolemy were pacing backards and forwards, his face looking reyt tense. When everyone had arrived he turned towards us and spoke:

This morning, word reached the several councils of The Dark Peak that the keeper of the humidity plant had made no wireless report for two days.

The ambassadors of the other nations asked us to take the matter in hand and hasten the assistant keeper to the plant. All day a hundred gruizers have been searching for him until just now one of them returned bearing his dead body, which was found in the pits beneath his house horribly mutilated.

I do not need to tell you what this means for The Dark Peak. It could take months to penetrate those mighty walls, in fact the work has already commenced, and there would be little to fear were the engine of the pumping plant to run as it should and as they all have for hundreds of years; but the worst, we fear, has happened. The instruments show a rapidly decreasing humidity in all parts of The Dark Peak -- the engine has stopped -- the murk is thinning.

I fear, said Ptolemy, we have at best three days to live.

There was silence for several minutes, then a young clown got up, and with his whipo'wil held above his head addressed his king:

The men of Hathersage have prided themselves that they have ever shown The Dark Peak how a nation of clowns should live, now is our opportunity to show them how they should die. Let us go about our duties as though a thousand useful years still lay before us.

The chamber rang with applause and as there was nothing better to do than to calm the fears of the people by our example, we went away with smiles on our faces and sorrow in our hearts.

When I got back to my palace I found that the rumour had already reached Pandora, so I told her all that I had heard.

We have been very happy, Van, she said, and I thank whatever fate overtakes us that it permits us to die together.

The next two days brought no noticeable change in the supply of humidity, but on the morning of the third day breathing become difficult. The streets of Hathersage were filled with people. All business had stopped. For the most part the folk looked bravely into t'face of doom.

Around murknoon many of the weakest started to wither, and within an hour the people of The Dark Peak were dropping like flies into unconsciousness, and death.

Pandora and I, with the other members of the royal family had collected in an inner courtyard of the palace. We spoke in low tones, when we spoke at all, as the shadow of death crept over us. Even Shad seemed to feel the weight of this impending doom, for he pressed close to Pandora and to me, whining like a pup.

It weren't pleasant were it mate, said Van.

Pandora had asked that the little incubator be brought down from t'roof of our palace, and she sat gazing at the young life that we would never now know.

As it become 'arder and 'arder to breathe Ptolemy got up, and said:

The days of the greatness of The Dark Peak are over. Tomorrow's sun will burn through the murk onto a dead world. It is the end. Let us say our goodbyes now.

He stooped and kissed the women of his family, and laid his strong hands on the shoulders of the men.

As I turned from him my eyes fell on Pandora. Her head was drooping and she looked lifeless. With a cry I went and raised her in my arms.

Her eyes opened and looked into mine.

Kiss me, Van, she murmured. I love you! It is cruel that we shall be torn apart when we are just starting out on a life of happiness.

As I pressed her lips close to mine, the old feeling of power rose in me, it were like that sap were rising in me veins again. The feighting blood of Hellsborough sprang me to life.

It shall not be, my princess. There must be some way, and I, who has fought my way through a strange world for your love, will find it.

And then, into my brain, dulled by the lack of humidity, I heard the nine tones that would open the door of the humidity plant.

Turning toward Ptolemy, as I still clasped Pandora, I cried: A flier, Ptolemy! Quick! Order your swiftest flier to the palace top. I can save The Dark Peak yet.

He did not question me, and in an instant a guard were racing to the nearest dock and though the air was thin and almost gone at the rooftop they managed to launch the fastest one-man air-scout machine that the artisans of The Dark Peak had ever made.

Kissing Pandora a dozen times and commanding Shad, who would have followed me, to remain and guard her, and with all my remaining strength I made it to the high ramparts of the palace, and in another moment I were headed toward t'humidity plant.

I had to fly low to get sufficient air to breathe, but I took a straight course across moors flying only a few feet above the ground.

After an hour as the gloaming were upon us, the great walls of the humidity plant loomed up before me, and I plunged into the ground before the small door -- a door which was withholding life from the inhabitants of the whole of The Dark Peak.

Beside the door a crew of men had been labouring to pierce the wall, but they had scarcely scratched the flint-like surface, and now most of them lay in the last sleep from which not even air would awaken them.

Conditions seemed much worse here than Hathersage, and it was with difficulty that I breathed at all. There were a few men still conscious. If I can open these doors, I said to one of them, is there a man who can get them engines started?

I can, if you open it quickly. I can last but a few moments more. But it is useless, for three days we have tried, but the keepers are both dead and no one else in The Dark Peak knows the secret of these locks.

I had no time to talk, I was becoming reyt weak and it were with difficulty that I controlled me mind at all.

But as I sank weakly to my knees I hurled the nine thought waves at that wall before me. The Hatheran had crawled to my side and with staring eyes fixed on the single panel before us we waited in the silence of death.

Slowly the mighty door opened before us. I attempted to rise and follow it but I was too weak. But my companion crawled forwards -- if tha reaches the pump room, turn loose all the pumps, I choked out -- it is the only chance The Dark Peak has to exist tomorrow...

From where I lay I opened second dooer, and then t'third, and as I saw the hope of The Dark Peak crawling on his hands and knees through that last dooer... I passed out.

CHAPTER 28

Thinge

So, what just happened there, I said, you died, right?

Clearly, said Van

I stopped thinking for a moment, and took a hefty heave of ale; that wasn't enough, so I downed a shot of rhum and then requisitioned Van's pipe and had a long drag on that.

My head is whirling, spinning -- I'm a murk wraith, fading in and out of consciousness, ingesting the murk, breathing it in, breathing it out. I compose myself, readying myself for the torrent of questions that dance upon the tip of my tongue -- the anthropologist in me coming out.

A question slammed into my brain, and erupted involuntarily from my mouth -- I get that why the humidity plant would be important to Pandora, and any other denizen of The Dark Peak -- they're dependent upon the moisture in the air because of their hereditary evolution, but you, you're a native of Hellsborough Van, how come you were as dependent upon the the humidity plant as the denizens?

Ah, good question young'un, I was 'oping tha'd ask me that. Tha remembers back when I first went into that Wisewood and met Shad 'ere, reyt?

I nodded.

Well I told thee that I bit down on a sapling to stop mesen from screaming when I thought we were about to be attacked by them damn demonspawn, does tha remember?

I nodded again.

Turns out that sapling -- I only found this out quite a while later -- only grows in the Wisewood, nowhere else can you find this plant, and the moment I took that bite on that willowy branch, biting down hard I was, some of it's genetic material -- is that reyt Pip, genetic material, I's not that familiar with this sort of thing -- but anyway, it's sap, went in me mouth and I swallowed it away. That sap was what I found out later was responsible for someat of a transformation in me. It made me stronger and faster, turned me into a bit of a super'uman, it did. It turned me muscles into something like a tree, not static like, but bendy and lithe and able to stand a lot more force than I could as just a regular bloke. The downside of that...

There has to be a downside, Van, there always is.

Yeah, well, the downside of that, is that it made me into a being of the murk, dependent on the humidity, like anyone else who lives out there, but it also gave me the telepathic power that I have told you about -- that way that I can read folks minds and tap into the hivemind, even without a psycmask, like you have to wear to be able to do it. It made me this hybrid jellyhead-denizen-murker thing that I is today.

So, you said a while back that you could see dead people, but really it was the sap of that plant that gave you the ability to communicate so well with Shad when he became a barghest?

Well, I always did see deed folk as a kid, but yeah, tha's reyt I think, that Gozava tree -- that's what it's called -- that's what gave me the gift as an adult I reckon. Thing is, that tree, it just kept on breathing in me, kept on making me more like it.

How so? Now I was confused again, as if I wasn't utterly mesmerised by the whole thing anyway.

Even now Pip, even now, it grows within me, and that was like, a hundred years ago that I bit down on that sapling. But it still grows and takes me over.

One day, I will turn into a Gozava tree and then I'll be no more, but until then, it grows and grows and paints me in its vivid colours and special patterns -- I showed you my eyes before, and that pillock old Jarv, I showed him earlier -- that's all the Gozava tree comin' owt, showing itself in me body like.

An' it needs feedin', that's one reason why I is always munchin' on these creatures of the murk -- insects and the like. I mean, I enjoys 'em mesen, but me Gozava tree blood craves its prey as well.

That's how it survives out in the Wisewood, on a diet of passing meyt -- that's why it bound me and Shad to the forest floor in the first place, to eat us, but it didn't bank on me getting that strength from its own sap to allow me to break free of the cage that it had 'cased me in.

Back then at the start, after you had bit down on the sapling and you were bound to the floor, by the Gozava tree as you now know, there was a strange sound. I rifled back through my notes to find Van's words: You talked about a distinct moaning sound, a subsonic moan, and a shadow beast -- what was that all about, what was that creature -- do you know?

Hmm... It could have been any one of the murk dwellers that I know exist in there now -- a murk wraith, the dun bog beast, a syncarid, or something else entirely -- but I think I stand by me original assessment with that one, it was nowt more than t'wind in t'trees and my own imagination playin' tricks on me, nowt more than that.

So what happened next, Van. You didn't die, you're still here, and the clowns and the rest survived, I've been witness to that these past few nights.

Well we can come to that now if you like. After I had passed out...

The table we was sat at had four chairs, but we only used two. Van and I sat opposite each other, with Sinclair between us in the middle of the table, and Shad -- now resting -- at Van's feet. Taking us both by surprise, one of the unused chairs was scraped across the flagstones and sat in.

We both watched as a decidedly non-sober, but in-control, Boggy Lomas pulled the chair closer to the table with a scork.

Is it true, Boggy -- what the bitter finger says -- that tha's a Jellyhead?

Aye, it's true Van. I works for t'nascenti. I has for many a year my old friend. Ever since that first uprising, that's when they made me. But that is ancient history Van, and this is now. You *do* know what is happening?

By what is 'appening, tha means this supposed leakage?

Supposed leakage, Van -- there is nothing supposed about it -- but what else would I be talking about? This whole problem is entirely tha fault -- it's tha fault because of these damn memoirs of tha's -- tha has threatened the entire safety of our world!

No one cares about tha bloody memoirs Van, that was a hundred years ago. Things has changed -- let it go, but tha can't can thee -- and tha has let Pip here come and go across thinge in t'full knowledge that thinge will be weakened!

Pfft. Ain't no leakage Boggy, that's just tha propaganda, anything tha can do t'keep the folk in-tow tha will do, so don't gimme no nonsense about leakage.

Dark matter is leaving this place Van, t'nascenti scientists have proved it. Thinge is weak, they say it is on the verge of collapse.

Collapse! Don't talk rubbage Boggy boy -- show us tha evidence. Tha ain't got none, I ain't to blame 'ere, and neither is Pip, this is just tha usual rooter licking barker smelt.

I has evidence Van. It is your fault that dark matter is leaving this place. The destruction of this world and the parallel universe of Hillsborough, S6 are on your shoulders. Tha don't care Van, tha never has; tha is old, why should thee. I is old too, but I *do* care about this place, *and* our neighbours on the other side. I is sorry Pip, tha is caught in t'middle of things tha probably doant understand, but that's no excuse.

The door of the bar opened then, with an inward gush of murk, and a couple of official looking types stroad in.

Shush, said Van, uniforms -- the exacid.

I shushed. Boggy didn't, scorking his chair backwards, and standing to attention.

Who in 'ere is Pip Rippon?! Said the first exacid, her raspy voice cutting through the din of the bar like a klaxon.

Van put his left hand around my right wrist, his fingers overlapping and clutching like a vice. He squeezed.

```
      HMM::OUT('Van Hallam')
`ask:: Rippon, Pip // stat:: accept[ok]__ // src::
2001:0db8:85a3:0000:0000:8a2e:037g:7334 [loc::hellsborough//
middlewood_road//467]__ // now:: 79.hail
ripperthroat.12.16.4.22.59`

`HMM::IN('..Colour:  Pale,  grey_`

`..Diet:  Anything_`

`..Size:  5' 7"_`

`..Defining characteristics:  Humanoid_`
```

VAN HALLAM

`..Class: Denizen_ Human_ Murkspawn_ Undead_ Revenant_\/\/\/\/\/`

`..Image: Incoming_   ')`

ABOUT THE AUTHOR

Van Hallam

Van Hallam was believed to born sometime in the year 77.mizzle.venomtooth in Hellsborough, Sheffield, S6 to an unknown father, and mother who died during his birth. After the first uprising, he escaped the confinement of Hellsborough to adventure in The Dark Peak, becoming a decorated xin warrior and clown statesman. He loves his barghest Shad.

Pip Rippon was born in 1992 in Lincolnshire, England. Finding a home in Oxford, and studying anthropology, before going on to work on a PhD in folklore at The University of Hallamshire.

FURTHER READING

If you enjoyed this, please feel free to explore more of the world of Hellsborough and The Dark Peak.

Sign up for "Postcards from The Dark Peak" to stay in touch https://hellsborough.com/subscribe

To understand more, kindle, epub ebooks and online versions of Pip Rippon's Curated Guide to The Dark Peak can be found by visiting: https://hellsborough.com/library

If you'd like to contact Pip, please https://hellsborough.com/subscribe and reply to a postcard from The Dark Peak

Printed in Great Britain
by Amazon